A
DEEP
DIVIDE

Books by Kimberley Woodhouse

SECRETS OF THE CANYON

A Deep Divide

Books by Tracie Peterson and Kimberley Woodhouse

All Things Hidden
Beyond the Silence

THE HEART OF ALASKA

In the Shadow of Denali
Out of the Ashes
Under the Midnight Sun

THE TREASURES OF NOME

Forever Hidden
Endless Mercy
Ever Constant

SECRETS of the CANYON
—BOOK ONE—

A
DEEP
DIVIDE

Kimberley
WOODHOUSE

BETHANYHOUSE
a division of Baker Publishing Group
Minneapolis, Minnesota

© 2021 by Kimberley R. Woodhouse

Published by Bethany House Publishers
11400 Hampshire Avenue South
Bloomington, Minnesota 55438
www.bethanyhouse.com

Bethany House Publishers is a division of
Baker Publishing Group, Grand Rapids, Michigan

Printed in the United States of America

Library of Congress Cataloging-in-Publication Data
Names: Woodhouse, Kimberley, author.
Title: A deep divide / Kimberley Woodhouse.
Description: Minneapolis, Minnesota : Bethany House, a division of Baker
    Publishing Group, [2021] | Series: Secrets of the canyon
Identifiers: LCCN 2021031571 | ISBN 9780764238000 (paperback) | ISBN
    9780764239441 (casebound)
Subjects: GSAFD: Suspense fiction. | Mystery fiction.
Classification: LCC PS3623.O665 D44 2021 | DDC 813/.6—dc23
LC record available at https://lccn.loc.gov/2021031571

Scripture quotations are from the King James Version of the Bible.

This is a work of historical reconstruction; the appearances of certain historical figures are therefore inevitable. All other characters, however, are products of the author's imagination, and any resemblance to actual persons, living or dead, is coincidental.

Cover design by Create Design Publish, LLC, Minneapolis, Minnesota/Jon Godfredson

Author is represented by The Steve Laube Agency.

Baker Publishing Group publications use paper produced from sustainable forestry practices and post-consumer waste whenever possible.

21 22 23 24 25 26 27   7 6 5 4 3 2 1

Soli Deo Gloria
Glory to God alone.
Without Him, I am nothing.

This book is lovingly dedicated to my big brother, Ray Hogan.

My childhood memories would be so dull without you. From tossing me around in your football equipment in Arkansas, to tackling me across the floor vents, to stomping through the icy ditches in Michigan, to trying to kill Fred the Snowman, to hiding under the bed to scare our older sister, Mary—you were always there in the midst of the mayhem. And then you grew into the most caring, self-sacrificing, loving, teddy-bear-of-a-big-brother a girl could ever want.

No matter how much time or space separates us, I know you are there for me. You are the best. I love you.

Dear Reader

Wanted: Young women 18 to 30 years of age, of good moral character, attractive and intelligent . . .

This series started in my heart and mind over twelve years ago. Some stories are like that; they sit and simmer in an author's mind until the time is right. When Bethany House contracted it, I couldn't even begin to imagine the beauty they would bring to it. I'm so grateful for this amazing publisher and the wonderful opportunities they have given me. What a privilege to bring this series set at El Tovar to you now.

The first time I saw the Grand Canyon with my own eyes, I couldn't say anything other than "Wow." Everywhere I peered into its majesty, the view was magnificent. The more pictures I took, the more viewpoints I visited, the more that one-syllable word came to my mouth. And what blew my mind even more was the fact that visiting the South Rim of the Grand Canyon and driving the thirty-plus miles back and forth to take in all the vistas still meant we saw only a small percentage of the vast canyon that is actually more than 270 miles in length.

My dear friend and fellow author Becca Whitham went

back with me to the canyon to do research for this series last spring before I started writing this story. No matter how many trips I take, I'm always amazed and in awe. On this particular trip, I FaceTimed my parents at the different viewpoints since my dad had just had surgery and they had never seen the Grand Canyon themselves. One of my favorite memories is when Becca and I were at the Watchtower. My mom said, "Don't fall in!" It gave everyone around us a chuckle and reminded us that we never stop being parents, no matter how old our kids get.

I owe Becca a deep well of gratitude for all her help, wonderful questions, insight, and just plain ol' friendship. And now we're family. This past year, her son married my daughter. Talk about fun. We are having a blast with this. To keep up with all our escapades, check out TheAuthorMoms.com.

My research into the fascinating history of the Harvey Empire and the Harvey Girls was quite extensive. Even so, I did take a few artistic liberties when details weren't known. To find out more about the research and historical facts behind *A Deep Divide*, make sure you check out the Note from the Author at the end of this book and sign up for my blog/newsletter at kimberleywoodhouse.com.

I'm so excited to share this story with you.

Enjoy the Journey,
Kimberley
James 1:2–4

Prologue

1891
BOSTON, MASSACHUSETTS

The sugary-sweet cherry flavor burst on Emma Grace Mc-Murray's tongue and made her mouth water. Pulling the striped candy stick from her mouth, she sucked at it so she wouldn't dribble any of the yumminess down her chin.

"I take it you like it?" Mr. Cooper raised his eyebrows.

"Oh yes." She spun around in a circle. "I think cherry is my new favorite."

"We'll take a few extra for a treat later." He nodded at the man behind the counter and then looked back to her. "I have to say, Miss McMurray, that's quite a pretty dress you're wearing today. If I had to guess, I'd say pink is your favorite color." Mr. Cooper leaned up against the tall oak counter at the mercantile, his smile warm and his eyes twinkling, then he winked. The man always bought her a penny stick of candy whenever he saw her. Now that he worked for her father, she got to see him more often. And she liked that.

Not just because he continued to buy her candy but because he was nice.

Eight-year-old Emma Grace glanced down at the layers of gingham and swished the skirt back and forth. "Thank you. It *is* my favorite color."

"Well, it's perfect for you." He tapped the end of her nose. "Did you pick out a present for your friend's birthday party?"

She nodded, and a little thrill of excitement ran through her. Most of the time, Papa never allowed her to go to parties, but this was for her best friend in the whole world. And Papa liked Mary's father, so he'd said yes.

"Ah, I see it. It's on the counter. Looks like a very nice choice." Mr. Cooper straightened and looked at the clerk. "Wrap this for a party. With ribbon." He tapped his chin and put on a puzzled face as he looked at her. "Pink?"

"Oh yes." She giggled.

"Please put this on the McMurray account as well."

"Of course, sir." The skinny man in the apron must be new because Emma Grace didn't recognize him. His mustache had big loops in the ends of it. She'd never seen one like that. It was funny-looking, but she couldn't say that out loud. That wouldn't be very good manners. He wrapped the fancy china doll with a pink dress and matching bonnet in tissue paper and then gently placed it in a large box. Then he tied it with a wide pink ribbon before offering it back.

Mr. Cooper tucked the package under his arm and held out his hand to her. "Are you about ready to head to the party?"

"Yes, please." She took his hand and swung their arms back and forth as they walked to the carriage. "Thank you for the candy."

"You're welcome. It's not every day that I get the privilege of accompanying such a pretty young lady about town."

His words made the laughter she'd been holding back

bubble up to the surface. "You're silly, Mr. Cooper. It *is* every day that you drive me."

"Really? Are you certain?" He scrunched up his forehead like he was thinking quite hard.

It made her giggle even more, and she covered her mouth.

He winked again. "You are correct, of course. But what fun that I get to do this every day."

"May I sit up front with you again?"

"Most certainly."

She climbed up into the open two-seat carriage.

"You're a lot more fun than Nanny Louise." She made a face. Nanny Louise never left the house. She'd never take Emma Grace to the park or to parties. Since Papa hired Mr. Cooper, he'd assigned the nice man to drive her around. He and Mother were so busy all the time.

She liked Mr. Cooper. He was fun. And he gave her candy. As she leaned back in the seat, she let out a long sigh that turned into a yawn. Last night she couldn't sleep a wink since she was so excited for Mary's party.

"What's this? Are you tired already?" He climbed up and took the seat next to her, then took the reins.

"Just a little." She couldn't tell a grown-up why she didn't sleep. He'd think it was silly.

He pulled a blanket out from under the leather seat. "Here, why don't you lay your head down for the ride? That way you'll be nice and refreshed when we get there."

With a nod, she pulled her legs onto the seat and curled up. She wasn't little anymore and didn't need afternoon naps like Nanny Louise insisted upon, but she was oh-so-tired. Maybe if she just closed her eyes for a few minutes.

A smelly hand clamped over Emma Grace's mouth and woke her up. What was happening? Her breaths came faster and faster as a big scratchy arm picked her up off the carriage seat. *No!* She wriggled and kicked, screaming against the fleshy palm, but she couldn't force out a sound loud enough to do any good. The world tilted as she was tossed about until all she could see were the branches of an oak tree waving against the blue sky, a frayed rope hanging all alone from a branch. She didn't recognize the tree. Where was Mr. Cooper?

Kicking and squirming for all she was worth, she tried to move her mouth enough to be able to bite her attacker, but it was no use.

"Stop it." His chest rumbled. Tighter and tighter he squeezed. Fear clawed at her throat. She couldn't breathe!

The blue sky above dimmed as they came under the shade of another tree, and she gasped for air. What would happen if she couldn't get enough air? Would she die? The grip on her released a bit just as spots danced before her eyes. She felt her arms and legs go limp. No! She needed to fight. But the darkness was winning, and she couldn't move.

He put her over his shoulder. With every step he took, her head pounded. Lifting it, she forced her eyes to focus. Darkness remained at the edges of her vision as pain stabbed her eyes. She took a long breath. Anything to clear her head. Tried to squeak out something, but she couldn't. What was wrong?

The scent of horses and leather made her want to wiggle to see what was going on, but the pressure built in her head and made her dizzy. Her arms and legs felt like they weighed more than her father's prized stallion. Hanging upside down had never been something she liked. Not like their butler's son, who would drape his knees over the ladder in the barn and swing back and forth for what seemed like hours. For a moment she was transported home . . . in the barn. She could see him. They were hanging upside down together. Swinging, laughing. Maybe she was dreaming.

Wake up. Wake up!

But then the man stopped for a second and as the motion stopped, her vision cleared.

It wasn't a bad dream. She wasn't in the barn. This was real. She took another large breath and put all her effort into screaming. "*Help!*"

He shifted her to the ground, and his hand tightened over her mouth. Hot breath hit her face. "Don't make another sound and don't fight me anymore."

The smell of tobacco assaulted her nose, and her stomach turned. It was bad enough she'd been hanging upside down over his shoulder and her head didn't like the sudden shifts. Now the smell. *Ew.*

"Did you hear me?" The voice was low and sounded full of grit. She couldn't get away from his breath.

She moved her chin up and down and tried to turn her head as far away from him as possible.

"Now, I'm not aiming to hurt you . . . *unless* you don't cooperate. In fact, I'm going to treat you like a princess. So, there's no need to panic. You'll be home with your family before you know it. Got it?"

Emma Grace nodded. But his breath kept washing over her.

"What's wrong?" The man narrowed his eyes and got closer, making it impossible to not breathe in the scent.

She shook her head and closed her eyes. Maybe if she didn't think about it. Or if she held her breath. If he would just move away. She didn't want to make him even madder. But her stomach turned.

When she was only four, she'd tripped over a spittoon in the railroad office and spilled it all over her shoes and stockings. The smell had made her lose her lunch in the middle of the floor. She'd forgotten that rotten stench until now.

"Don't go gettin' sick on me. I said I wasn't gonna hurt ya."

But it was no use. As her stomach revolted and she started to heave, the man eased up his hold and moved his hand from her mouth . . . just in time.

After several moments of her losing her breakfast, the man patted her back. "You done?"

She slumped, hoping to get out of his grip, but his hands held fast to the bow and sash on the back of her dress. The one that *had* been her favorite.

Wiping her mouth on her crinoline, she straightened. He said he'd treat her well if she cooperated. Mother always told her God made her stubborn for a reason. Stubbornness could be negative, she'd said, but it could also be good. Like tenacious and determined. Emma Grace liked those words. Maybe she could be stubborn and get through this.

She refused to admit defeat. "I'm quite finished. Just keep your foul tobacco breath away from my face, and maybe I won't have to empty my stomach again, mister." She cringed. Another trait—she often spoke without thinking about the consequences.

A loud guffaw eased her worries. The man leaned back and slapped his knee. "You're quite the character. Your vocabulary isn't too shabby either for such a young'un."

She dared to look at him directly. He might smell bad, but he was dressed like a businessman. Like one of Papa's railroad partners. She tucked the little nuggets about his appearance into the back of her mind and looked away. Wouldn't do her any good to be caught staring at him. Not that he even seemed to be worried.

She glanced around. There wasn't a house, person, or

horse in sight. Where were they? Putting her hands on her hips, she frowned up at him.

"Like I said, I'm gonna treat you like a princess, but if you don't behave yourself, you're gonna have trouble." His voice was gruff, but his face had softened.

Even though she knew she should be really scared, she kicked at him with her right foot.

He didn't even flinch. "Now, Emma Grace. What did I just tell you?"

The way he said her name made her shiver. Wait. What did he just say? "How do you know my name?"

With one swift move, he tucked one arm under her knees, while the other hand went back around her mouth. "That's enough talkin' for now." Lifting her up against his chest, as if she was sitting in a chair against him, he started to whistle and walked up the hill in front of them.

Where was he taking her? Who was he? And where did Mr. Cooper go? This man had grabbed her out of the carriage. Did he hurt Mr. Cooper?

The more her mind swirled through everything that had happened, the more questions she had. And the more scared she became. Closing her eyes, she counted to one hundred. Maybe it really was a bad dream and she just had to relax so she could wake up. Turning her mind back to the barn at home, she pictured Jimmy swinging like a circus artist from the ladder. She was dreaming. That was all. *Wake up. Wake. Up!*

But the smell of her own vomit made it all too real. When she opened her eyes, they were almost to the door of a little white house.

The man opened the door and set her down, grabbing onto the back of her dress again. "Now, don't do anything stupid. There's no one for miles. No one can hear you, and there's nowhere to run." He pushed her forward and down a hallway. The door at the end was open. "In you go."

Taking slow steps, she made it to the doorway and looked around the room. A small bed with a pink coverlet. A little table with a tea set. A bookshelf lined with books, dolls, and toys. It wasn't a scary dungeon. But what was it?

He let go of her and blocked the door behind them. "I'll be right back with some food." He left the room, closed the door, and then there was a loud click.

As she looked down at her dress, she started to cry. It was covered in the remnants of her breakfast. And the stench of that awful man. The dress that once made her smile made her sick to her stomach. She hated it. She hated pink. She hated this room. This place. That awful man. And tobacco. She hated that too. She stomped her feet and marched around the room, her sorrow turning into anger. Why would he kidnap a little girl?

She walked over to the door and tried the knob, but it held fast. Locked tight. She went to the window and tried to open it, but it wouldn't budge. Maybe she could break the glass! But as her gaze focused beyond the panes, she saw barbed wire crisscrossing its way across the frame. There was no way she could fit through without hurting herself.

She turned back to the door and stared at it. It was the only way of escape. But how could she do it? Footsteps sounded in the hallway. Then the door opened with a squeak of hinges and the man entered.

"There's no use tryin' to get out, Miss McMurray. But like I said, I will treat you well as long as you behave yourself." He set down the tray he'd been carrying. "Here's some food and a pitcher of water. You may wash yourself up over there. You'll notice a water closet is attached to this room. Help yourself to clean clothing, and there's plenty of books on the shelves. I'm sure it won't be too long before you're back home again." He turned on his heel, shut the door, and then she heard the lock click again.

Emma Grace ran to the door and squinted so she could see through the keyhole. Nothing. Just a wall on the other side of the hallway.

"Let me out, mister! Let. Me. Out!" She pounded on the door with her hands and kicked it with her feet. "My papa is gonna be so mad at you! I hope he comes and shoots you!" She slumped down at the door. But then her stomach rumbled. That achy, raw, awful kind of rumble. The kind that could only be satisfied with food. But she didn't want to eat. She wanted to go home.

But how long would that take? Wouldn't Papa do anything to get her back from this bad man?

Mother's words kept coming back. *I pity the man who ever crosses you, Emma Grace. That fierce independence of yours will either protect you or push everyone away.*

But she didn't want to be independent right now. She wanted Mother. And Papa. Tears slipped down her cheeks. What was the man going to do with her? He said he wasn't going to hurt her, but he'd taken her and locked her up. Bad men did bad things. So how could she believe him?

Sobs shook her shoulders, and she hugged her knees to her chest. What was she supposed to do?

Sucking in her bottom lip, she tried to stop the tears and swiped at her face with the back of her hand. She wasn't in a horrible dungeon. She wasn't tied up. But no matter how clean and neat the room might be, no matter that there were plenty of toys and books, it was still a locked room. Her prison.

Standing up, she worked at the wrinkles in her dress and straightened her shoulders. Walking over to the small table where the tray of food sat, she then picked up a napkin and a biscuit and positioned herself in a chair to eat. But the smell on her dress overwhelmed her. She'd have to change her clothes first. But she didn't like the idea of wearing clothes that weren't hers.

Glancing around the room, she fisted her hands at her sides. New determination filled her. She'd wear the clothes and sleep in the dumb bed. She'd read every book on those stupid shelves if she had to—anything to pass the time. She'd survive and find a way to escape if her family didn't rescue her. Then she'd come back with the sheriff and make sure that man could never hurt anyone ever again.

Emma Grace counted the scratches on the doorpost and then made another. Eighteen slashes. Eighteen days.

The first few days had been full of tears. But after that, she fell into an odd routine. The man that took her came to see her several times a day. Sometimes it was with her food. Sometimes with a new toy or book. Sometimes he even stayed and played checkers with her. He never put his hand over her mouth again or grabbed the back of her dress. In fact, he hadn't touched her. He really wasn't all that bad. He never yelled at her or hurt her. He even smiled once in a while when she beat him at checkers.

And every day, he brought some sort of a treat. Candy, cookies, cakes. She'd read every book on the shelf. *The Swiss Family Robinson*, *20,000 Leagues Under the Sea*, *Treasure Island*. Every day she wished that she could escape into one of the adventures. For real.

But then the man would come back. And she'd realize she was still locked up.

Flopping back onto the bed, she stared at the wooden planks in the ceiling. How much longer would she have to stay in this room?

Thumps sounded outside the door. A lot of thumps. More than usual. It was more than just one man's footsteps . . . wasn't it? It made her heart jump in her chest.

She held her breath. Was she imagining things? Or was today the day she could go home?

She sat up straight on the bed and then jumped off. Closing her eyes, she listened as the thumps got closer. How many other times had she gotten her hopes up? It was best to just think it was food coming.

The familiar sound of the key in the lock made her open her eyes, then the knob turned.

The door swung open, and Mr. Cooper stood there with a smile.

She ran to him and hugged him. "Mr. Cooper! You're here to take me home?"

"I sure am, Miss McMurray."

"Oh, thank you, thank you, thank you!" She clapped her hands together and then grabbed onto his hand.

But as they exited the room, the man who had kidnapped her stood in the hallway with his arms crossed. Why was he still here? Shouldn't he be in trouble? Where was the sheriff?

"I told ya it wouldn't be long before you went home. See?" The man smiled at her. In all this time, she never knew his name. Every time she'd ask, he'd leave. He leaned down and looked at her. "You know, I sure will miss seeing all those pretty pink dresses."

Looking down at her clothes, she frowned. Pink. Everything had been pink for the past eighteen days. And she was sick of it. Had he picked it all out?

Mr. Cooper tugged on her arm and led her down the hallway as he spoke over his shoulder to the man. "Thanks for your assistance."

Assistance? "But—"

Mr. Cooper squeezed her hand and put his other hand over her mouth. Just like the man who kidnapped her had done. "No questions, now. Let's go find your father." His smile didn't seem as nice as it always had. He escorted her out of the small house.

Emma Grace wanted to kick Mr. Cooper. She put on her best scowl and pulled her hand out of his.

Then she looked ahead and saw her father standing by the carriage. The same carriage she'd been taken out of. As soon as he spotted her, he held out his arms. "Emma Grace!"

She ran toward him. She was finally going home!

Papa scooped her up and swung her around in a circle. "It's so good to see you. Oh, how I missed you." After several more twirls, he placed her up in the back seat of the carriage.

Relief poured through her, and her anger melted away. Then the tears started. She was safe with her father. No longer a captive and locked up in that little room.

Papa handed her his handkerchief. "I'm so sorry. I know this hasn't been easy for you. You just let it all out. I'll be right back."

The tears turned into great big sobs. She'd been so scared. Never knowing if she would ever see her family again. She covered her face with the handkerchief and cried until there weren't any tears left. It was hard being brave.

Wiping at her face, she had to blink several times to be able to see, and when she looked up, Papa was slapping her kidnapper on the back and smiling.

Wait . . . what was he doing? She looked between the men. Mr. Cooper and Papa were both smiling and talking to the man like they were old friends. Shouldn't Papa be furious with the kidnapper? In the last eighteen days, she'd often imagined that he came to rescue her and had to fight the bad man.

She squeezed her eyes shut. Was she really seeing this?

Opening her eyes back up, she took a deep breath. She *was* really seeing this. It was real.

Her father shook hands with the bad man.

Then the man shook hands with Mr. Cooper too. And Mr. Cooper handed him a small bag.

The kidnapper went back inside the house. Like he hadn't just kidnapped her and held her in a room for almost three weeks.

Papa and Mr. Cooper walked toward the carriage. "It worked. . . . There's a sucker born every minute." Her father's words floated to her. But she couldn't hear the rest. Why was he whispering?

What worked? Why weren't they mad at that man?

Mr. Cooper climbed up into the front seat and so did her father. Neither one even looked at her. They just started talking business, like she wasn't even there. Something about a new spur for the railroad.

"Papa?" Her voice squeaked.

He turned back to her. "Yes?"

"Why were you shaking that man's hand? Why didn't the sheriff come arrest him? I was kidnapped." Her eyes throbbed from crying, which made her head pound, but she crossed her arms over her chest and ignored the pain.

"Oh, it was just business, sweetheart. Don't you worry about it." Papa reached back and patted her knee.

But she *would* worry about it. Nothing made sense so she pressed. "What worked?"

He turned back around with a long sigh, his eyebrows raised. "What do you mean?"

"I heard you say 'it worked.' So, what was *it*?" As much as she was glad to be out of that room and with her father, it upset her that they didn't do anything to the bad man.

In fact, she was madder than she'd ever been in her whole life.

"It's nothing for you to worry your pretty little head about, Emma Grace. It was just business, trust me." He smiled. The kind of smile she'd seen him give at the railroad office a hundred times. "Now, why don't you lie down? You must be exhausted, and we have a long drive home." Without waiting for another response, he turned back around and started talking to Mr. Cooper again.

"It was just business, trust me." The words ran over and over in her mind as she watched them. Back and forth they chatted.

The whole thing played through in her mind. Mr. Cooper putting his hand over her mouth and thanking the man. Papa shaking the man's hand. Then he and Mr. Cooper acting all happy that something worked. . . . It didn't make sense. She'd been *kidnapped*. Locked up. Why weren't they mad at the man?

"Trust me." As Papa's words repeated in her mind again, she looked down at her dress. He knew her favorite color was pink. He always brought her gifts that were pink. Always. And every dress in that room the last few weeks had been pink. Even the coverlet and pillows on the bed had been pink.

How did the man who took her know her name and her favorite color?

Well, it wasn't her favorite anymore. She hated it. She'd never wear pink again.

She laid down on the carriage seat and tucked her knees up close to her chest. Letting her anger grow in her belly, she watched the back of Papa's and Mr. Cooper's heads and gave them the meanest look she could. Neither one of them should have been nice to her captor.

Mr. Cooper turned around and dropped a small brown

bag in front of her. "This should make you feel better." Striped candy sticks stuck out of the top.

No. It wouldn't make her feel better.

She wouldn't trust Papa. Or Mr. Cooper.

Wrapping her arms around her knees, she whispered to the backs of the men in front of her, "As soon as I'm old enough, I'll get away. Forever." She could have her own adventure like in the books she'd been reading. "*Forever.*"

"What was that, Emma Grace?" Papa peered over his shoulder at her.

"Nothing." She practically spat the word.

"Mind your manners, young lady. And don't interrupt us when we're talking."

As soon as he turned forward, she mimicked his words with her lips. But her little-girl heart was broken.

NINE YEARS LATER
1900
BOSTON

Emma Grace slid the sheer lace curtain an inch to the right to take a closer look at the happenings below her second-story window.

Just as she expected, her father stood in the circular drive, talking to yet another one of his business friends. With a sweep of his arm—a gesture all too familiar to her—her father invited the man inside. And if Emma Grace knew her father at all, the guest had also been invited to dinner.

Her father was up to his matchmaking yet again.

Before she could arrange the curtain back, her father's guest looked up and caught her eye. He nodded with a smile that showcased his crooked teeth.

Well! Never let it be said she let a man know when he'd

surprised her. Emma Grace opened the curtain fully and tied it back with the satin sash. She graced him with her own nod and a raise of her eyebrows, but she refused him a smile. She knew why he was there. And she didn't like it a bit.

If only her mother were still alive . . .

With a sigh, Emma Grace turned from the window, sat at the vanity, and stared at her reflection. Only a quarter of an hour before she was expected to dinner. Maybe she could pretend to be sick? A headache?

No, Papa—Father as he liked to be called now—would know. Emma Grace had the constitution of the strongest stallion.

She might as well face the dreaded meal with her best foot forward. Father would be more inclined to hear her out if she were a gracious hostess at dinner. She'd give him one last chance. Not that he would change.

She fully expected to put her plan into play. At seventeen years of age, she was ready. She'd planned for this since she was a little girl. Only a few more months until she could leave.

Sliding her fingers over the top of the intricately carved box that had been her grandmother's, Emma Grace thought of the contents locked inside. Underneath a few family trinkets, jewels, and treasured daguerreotypes of her grandparents lay the family birth record she would change and letters she'd prepared. Everything she needed to start over.

With one last check in the mirror, she tucked a strand of hair behind her ear and pasted on what she hoped was a sweet smile.

Two hours later, the man left. A Mr. Brogan. A man she hoped to never see again. Dinner was over, and she was tired of waiting to speak to her father alone. But after seeing the man out, Father walked to his office without a word.

Marching after him, Emma Grace rehearsed what she wanted to say as she stood in the doorway. "I need to speak with you."

"I'm expecting another visitor, Emma Grace. This isn't a good time." He didn't even look up from his desk.

"You need to make time, Father. I'm tired of your match-making."

This time, he looked up over the rim of the reading spectacles perched on his nose. "It doesn't concern me if you're tired of it. You're getting married, daughter. That's the end of it."

She rushed forward. "Oh really? To whom? That Hawkins man from New York you swooned over last week? Or is it that slimy man from St. Louis? Oh wait. I forgot Mr. Sweeney from Detroit." Her temper continued to build.

Father removed his spectacles and threw them down onto the desk. "You impertinent girl. I won't allow you to speak to me in this manner. What has gotten into you?"

For years, she'd wanted to lash out at him—to let him know that she knew exactly what he'd done. She bit her tongue, but the words spilled out anyway. "No need to keep the charade going any longer. I know you were behind my kidnapping when I was a child. Now you're arranging *my* life without any thought to my wishes, but I'm sure it will greatly benefit *you*."

His eyes widened for a moment. Then they narrowed and he looked back down at the papers spread out before him. "So you know." He shrugged. "You weren't hurt in any way. You were treated well. It was simply business. That spur was worth a great deal of money."

The words took all the bluster out of her. Her breath caught in her throat, and the room began to spin. No apology. No feelings whatsoever. Just. Business.

Emma Grace moved to a chair and sat. Closing her eyes, she forced herself to breathe naturally. She couldn't let him know how his words affected her. If that's how things were going to be, then fine. Steeling herself, she fisted her hands. She had a plan. It would work. And maybe one day she'd be able to forget all of this.

Father looked up at her. "This is also business. But it's for your own good. For your future."

"I'm not going to marry a man because you order me to."

"Oh yes, you are." He leaned over his desk, his palms flat, his eyes narrow. "I can do whatever I want. And if that means banishing you to a tiny hovel, locking you up, taking away your clothes, jewels, money, and making you destitute, then I most certainly will."

Was he serious? Who would even think of doing that to their own daughter? Not that she even cared about any of those things anymore.

He picked up a pile of papers. "You know what these are?"

She shook her head.

"Contracts. Legal and binding to whomever marries you." He rattled the papers as he walked around his desk. A slight smile lifted his lips. "These men paid handsomely to have the chance for your hand . . . and to eventually inherit my empire."

If she hadn't already been sitting, she would have plummeted to the floor. So that's what it was all about.

Once again.

Money.

The railroad.

His empire.

Not his cherished little girl.

She held his gaze, determined to not let him see her true feelings. "I see." Every bit of anger she'd been ready to heap upon his head had been destroyed. Just like her heart. There were no more words. No chances for him to change. This was her fate.

Unless she followed through with leaving. Did she have a choice?

Not anymore.

Her stomach dropped. Her eighteenth birthday seemed too far away. The plan wouldn't work until then. What could she do?

"Mr. Wellington is first in line. He will be here in thirty minutes, so you need to excuse yourself before then. We can talk again in the morning. I don't care which one of them you marry, because I will benefit no matter what. But rest assured, you will be married before your eighteenth birthday."

She didn't cover her gasp.

Which only made him smirk. Obviously his intention had been fulfilled. To put her in her place. To show his power. To leave her no way out. He went back to his chair behind the desk and sat. "Good night, Emma Grace."

Dismissed. Just like that.

She stared at him for several seconds, swallowed the bile threatening to clog her throat, and then stood up. "Good night." Turning toward the door, she determined this would be her last time to ever be in this room. No matter what she had to do. Papa had always been a shrewd businessman. But he'd once been softer. Doted on her. But then her baby brother died and everything changed. It hadn't been long after that she'd been kidnapped. And then a few months later, Mother died.

Papa was no longer the man she couldn't wait to see at the end of each day. The man who shared picnics in the park with his family and stories under tents made out of blankets.

That man must have died with his son and wife.

If she thought about it that way, then there really was no

guilt to feel about leaving. She'd endured years of his coldness. Given him chance after chance.

This was what she had to do.

When she reached her wing of the house, Louise was waiting for her. "Would you like anything, miss? Perhaps some hot chocolate?"

Louise was always there. Ready to serve. But now, Emma Grace needed her to go. "Hot chocolate sounds lovely, but I'm also in a bit of a mood for something more substantial. I'm afraid I was too nervous to eat much earlier."

"Would you like me to warm up some of the beef from dinner for you? Or something else?"

"Yes. That would be nice." She waved a hand. "You can choose. You know what I like."

"Of course." Louise smiled and exited. The poor woman likely felt sorry for Emma Grace.

She had a few minutes before her former nanny came back. With a drop to her knees, she reached under her bed and pulled out the bag she'd packed and tucked away. Grabbing a few more things from around the room, she tamped down her fear. She would simply find a way. A new life awaited. A life without all of this.

And she was fine with that.

After she shoved the last items into her bag, she looked at the list she'd tucked into it. A list she'd added to for the past year. Yes. She had everything.

She fetched a coat and hat from the closet and picked up her bag. Without another look back, she padded her way down the hallway. Every step on the plush carpet was taken with care as she listened for any noise. When she reached the landing where she had a view of the massive foyer, voices floated up to her. She slid back and hid behind the wall, hoping they hadn't seen her.

Peeking around the corner, she saw a gentleman shaking hands with her father. They were both all smiles. Father with his smooth-talking voice sounding ever-so-gracious and welcoming. The other man nodding his agreement. His gray hair and beard making him look old. And boring.

They disappeared into his office, and Emma Grace let out her breath.

Time to go.

A jerk brought her awake. The hotel room was small and stuffy. Three days she'd traveled. Back and forth, north, south, east, west—hoping against hope that if anyone saw her, they'd never be able to say where she was headed. It was a risky plan, but one she hoped would keep any investigators off her trail. Because Father would no doubt send the cavalry out after her.

At first, she'd taken the new open subway cars, zigzagging her way around the city as if it were any other day. Then she'd taken a train that took her several hundred miles away. Then a streetcar in another town. Then another train. And another. This last city still had horse-drawn carriages, and she'd taken one to the hotel so she could sleep in an actual bed after two days of attempting to sleep while traveling. She'd registered under a different name and finally fallen asleep after her mind had spun through every possible scenario of how her father would try to track her down.

But today, she would head farther west. A new adventure awaited.

Dressing as quickly as she could, she put on the outfit she'd purchased yesterday. All black. Then the hat with the netting over the front. Also black.

If the mourning attire didn't deter onlookers, certainly the cut of the dress would. These were not the clothes of Emma

Grace McMurray, daughter of one of the richest men in the country. They were a *normal* person's clothes.

After breakfast, she hurried to the train depot and bought her ticket. Keeping her head down, she hoped that she looked the part of a grieving woman.

But a newsboy's words on the platform caught her attention. "Railroad magnate murdered! Read all about it!"

A horrible sensation started in her stomach. Her breath caught in her throat. Her legs wouldn't move.

Then the boy moved down the platform, shouting his news.

It spurred her into action. She had to know. With quick steps, she caught up with the newsboy, paid him his five cents, and took the paper.

But nothing could prepare her for the front page. A picture of her father. Then a picture of *her*. And the headline in big, bold print:

Railroad Baron McMurray Found Murdered, Daughter/Heiress Missing

All the sound around her muffled as her vision blurred. Papa was dead? No. It couldn't be. She tried to scan the article and make sense of it all, but the words wouldn't come into focus. She blinked several times and looked up. But everything around her spun like the world had turned into a carousel.

Someone bumped into her, and she crushed the paper to her chest. She scanned the crowd, but her mind refused to process anything. There was no sound. Just the roar in her ears.

She closed her eyes against the overwhelming sense that she was going to faint. No. She couldn't let that happen.

"Ma'am?" A deep voice broke through the roar. "Let me help you."

Without her permission, someone took her arm and guided her to a bench. She put her bag on the ground at her feet and realized she felt better with her head down. So, she laid her arms on her lap and kept her face buried there in the fabric.

Her dress. It was supposed to be a disguise. And yet it now told the truth of who she was.

Her father was dead? How could that be? She'd left without saying good-bye. Her heart pinched under the weight of living with that fact. Their last words to each other played through her mind. Angry, ugly . . . harsh words. Would they haunt her for the rest of her life?

What did this mean for her? Oh no. The men with the contracts... she swallowed against the thought. Her age made her more vulnerable than ever.

A few minutes passed, and her ears opened up to the world again. Steps shuffled around her. Voices chatted back and forth. Trains hissed.

Lifting her head, she glanced around. No one seemed to care about the grieving woman on the bench. She saw the crumpled paper in her lap and smoothed it out. As much as she wanted to read it, she couldn't. Not yet. Not until she was on her way. The urgency to flee grew inside her. No matter what, she had to run.

She stood up on shaky legs. She needed to get as far away as possible.

Panic built inside her as the conductor called, "All aboard!"

Keeping her head low, she picked up her bag and headed for the train. Tomorrow, she'd read the paper. Then she'd make a phone call. Just the one. Then she'd know the gravity of her situation. But it couldn't be good.

Right now, the only hope she had was her plan.

1

Something touched Emma Grace's shoulder. But she was so tired, her eyelids too heavy.

"Next stop, Grand Canyon and El Tovar!" The shout jolted her fully awake. Clutching her bag to her chest, she blinked away the last vestiges of dreams in her mind. The three-hour ride from Williams, Arizona, had passed in the blink of an eye. At least it seemed that way . . . probably because she fell asleep. Not something she was prone to do, but not sleeping for three days straight as she traveled across the country had obviously taken its toll.

With a deep breath, she sat up straighter and swallowed down every emotion that tried to climb up her throat. Working for the Fred Harvey Company the past five years had brought her to the top ranks. When she heard the El Tovar would be opening, she put in her request that very day. It was Harvey's crown jewel, after all. But why was she doubting? She was good. All her managers even wrote *the best* on her recommendation letters. She deserved this, didn't she?

The job would be great—this was something she could do almost with her eyes closed now. But the jitters in her stomach persisted. It was starting all over again that intimidated her. Five years she'd done it, at seven different Harvey Houses along the rail line. Each time it seemed to get more difficult. But her circumstances demanded it. She needed to increase the distance between her and Boston. A new place was necessary.

This was the farthest west she'd ever been. And it was remote.

But was she far enough away that *he* couldn't find—

"Miss Edwards?" The conductor held out a slip for her. "This is for your luggage. But not to worry about it, they will take it directly to your room."

She pasted on a smile. "Thank you."

"I know Miss Anniston is looking forward to your arrival." The man gave a small nod.

Emma Grace put a hand to her throat. "I'm looking forward to it as well." The fact that the conductor on the train, in addition to some of the railroad personnel in Williams, had spoken of Miss Anniston and her anticipation of Emma Grace's arrival made her throat a bit dry. How lovely that the woman had spoken so highly of her, but would she be gracious and kind? Or would she be a tyrant?

That remained to be seen.

A couple of the head waitresses Emma Grace had worked under were hard—almost to the point of being callous and mean. No two ways about it. But it had made her a better waitress, and if she were honest with herself . . . a better person as well. The training had been difficult, but she had the upper hand of knowing what customers expected in fine dining establishments. She'd lived that life. Been that customer. It gave her a bit of an edge, but she realized quickly how much she truly had to learn about humanity.

Even though she loved being a part of the working class, there were times she had to remind herself about her position in society. She couldn't speak to people the same way she could as Emma Grace McMurray. Not that she had ever been a snob—oh, she prayed she hadn't been—but speaking her mind had been her norm. As a socialite, she could do that. As Emma Grace Edwards, she could not.

Was she doing the right thing? The same question haunted her everywhere she went. She lifted her reticule to her lap and opened it. The aged newspaper article's edges peeked out of the side. But she shoved it deeper inside the bag. Now was not the time. She practically had it memorized, anyway.

This was what new situations did to her. They brought up the past and everything that went with it. All she wanted to do was move forward. Live a simple life. But after all this time, she doubted it was possible.

Still, it didn't keep her from hoping.

The whistle blew, and the train slowed. As it chugged its way into the depot, she took a moment to straighten her hair and pin her hat back into place. It was nice to not have to deal with the wigs anymore, nor push glasses up her nose. It had been five years since she'd let her blond hair be seen. Five years of disguises, different at each place she'd lived.

But it was time to let her natural look be her new disguise. No one had recognized her in all this time. And it wasn't like she hadn't matured over the years. For too long she'd been thin and scrawny—too thin. But she found out the hard way that not eating wasn't a good way to be able to withstand the rigors of her job and its twelve-hour shifts. After a bath one evening, she'd even passed out. When she finally allowed herself to eat and fill out, she found she liked her sturdy frame and curves. She didn't look at all like the young girl who'd run away from . . . everything.

She shook her head of the thoughts and gripped her reticule. That was the past. And it needed to stay there. No man would control her. No one would ever fool her again. No chance that money would dictate her choices. She loved her job and her life. And she had the opportunity for a completely fresh start here, one that hopefully would include new friends and a warm atmosphere. Like family. Something she'd craved for far too long.

As long as it wasn't anything like what *her* family had become.

The brakes hissed, and the train stopped moving. Out the window, the snow-covered, rocky landscape appeared dry and dusty and was dotted with scrubby-looking trees—some tall, some short. It certainly didn't look like much. Could one of the most glorious wonders of the world really be here? She'd seen photographs of the Grand Canyon. It was hard to imagine that such a place even existed.

Passengers scooted out into the aisles of the train. It was time.

Time to face this new world and tackle her job.

The past didn't matter. All that mattered was here and now.

With rhythmic steps, they all shuffled down the aisle toward the door. Emma Grace took a peek around the man's shoulder in front of her. Only a few more steps and she'd have some fresh air and room to breathe.

She closed her eyes for a moment and then stepped forward again. It was almost her turn to disembark. What she wouldn't give to be able to stretch all of her muscles—touch her toes and reach for the sky—but that wouldn't be very proper. She'd have to wait until she was in the privacy of her room. Whenever that would be.

Another step.

Oh, it made her antsy. Only one more person, then she could get off this train.

The conductor nodded at her as he tipped his cap. "Enjoy the most amazing wonder you'll ever see." His smile was genuine as his eyes twinkled. "I look forward to seeing you in the dining room."

"Thank you. I look forward to it as well." Emma Grace turned toward the steps and ventured down.

As she exited the train, the chill of the air took her breath away for a moment, and the wind threatened to take her hat with it.

A lovely dark-haired woman approached. Probably a good ten years her senior, she was still young and beautiful and seemed nothing like the harsh spinster barking out orders that Emma Grace had dramatically conjured up in her mind.

Several inches shorter than Emma Grace, the woman had a soft, warm appearance and moved with confidence and grace. Her hands tucked into the pockets of her long black coat. One eyebrow quirked upward. "Miss Edwards?"

"Yes." She stepped forward as butterflies filled her stomach. Why was she so nervous? She'd done this many times and had years of experience to rely upon. "I'm Emma Grace Edwards."

"Welcome to El Tovar. I'm Ruth Anniston, head waitress." She tilted her head toward what appeared to be the hotel. "Let's get you out of the cold and settled. The rest of the girls don't arrive for another two days." While the greeting wasn't at all unamiable, there was only so much to ascertain in the brisk breeze and bitter temperature.

"Oh? How many are you expecting?"

"Twenty-five in all. We've hired the best of the best. And while they've all been Harvey Girls for at least a few months, there will be training for the El Tovar in particular, as it is expected to attract the most elite of clientele. You—along with the other senior waitresses—will be assigned a trainee."

That made Emma Grace's nerves jitter even more. Would Miss Anniston approve of her? It was so important for her to make a good impression. She wanted this job to last for a long time. Hopefully for the rest of her life.

Following the woman from the rail tracks to a set of stone steps that would take them up the hill, she gazed at the massive structure. As she made her way up the steep incline, the large building loomed in front of her. This side of it was a half-hexagon shape. From where she stepped, she could see that it stretched in length for a substantial distance before her. The large stones at the foundation were topped with giant logs and then more dark wood siding as the building rose for several stories above her. Basement . . . one, two, three stories. Was there even a fourth up there? As they walked around and up the hill, she noticed a turret at the top that seemed to almost touch the sky from this angle. Was that in the center of the hotel? She got dizzy with her neck craned back.

While its height was not much compared to the tall buildings in the cities back east, this one stretched out in breadth even more than its height. The closer she got, the larger it loomed. Its unique design drew her in. "It's a lovely hotel."

"Mr. Whittlesey—the architect of El Tovar—envisions it as a mix of Swiss chalet and Norwegian villa. Would you agree?" Miss Anniston stopped and gazed up with her.

Emma Grace did indeed agree, but she didn't dare say that out loud. The real Emma Grace had seen Swiss chalets and Norwegian villas, but Emma Grace the waitress most certainly wouldn't have had the privilege of vacationing in Europe. So, she shrugged. "I can't say that I have an opinion one way or the other." She let out a light laugh, hoping to convey the innocence of a poor young waitress. "It's a beautiful building though to be sure."

Miss Anniston started walking again before her abrupt stop outside a basement door almost made Emma Grace collide with her. "You'll find your way around quick enough. Are you terribly cold?"

What did her question imply? Was this some sort of test for her ability to work here? She shook her head slightly to rid herself of her anxious thoughts. Everything put her on edge when she was in a new place. "It's chilly, but I'm all right."

A secretive smile spread across the woman's face. "Good. Because I think there's something you need to see before we go inside." With her hands still stuffed into her coat pockets, she tilted her head again—this time away from the hotel—beckoning Emma Grace toward the west side of the building. "Follow me. Just be prepared—it will get even colder at the rim."

CHICAGO, ILLINOIS

A centimeter to the left should do. Ray Watkins straightened the pencil jar on his desk. There. Perfect.

Before he could get to the stack of reports waiting for him, he'd have to deal with the chaos that was his workspace. While blowing at a piece of lint on the blotter, he caught something out of the corner of his eye. One of the files on top of the cabinet was askew. He'd have to ask his secretary one more time to make sure he stacked the files appropriately. He walked over to the mahogany cabinet and straightened them. Might as well put them in alphabetical order while he was at it. The satisfaction of the simple task steadied his breathing. As he shuffled them back into a neat position, his mind cleared.

Much better.

With a tug on his pinstripe vest, he went back to his chair.

The tedious reports where he checked the work of the accounting department weren't his favorite task, but alas, it fell to him. His father had poured his whole life into Watkins Enterprises, and one day Ray hoped to be able to add to it. He'd have to earn his way, that's for sure. Dad hadn't created it overnight—a fact Ray was reminded of often. It was a privilege to be able to follow in his father's footsteps.

A few years ago, that hadn't been his opinion, but God had changed him. Each day was a gift now. A chance to live out his favorite verse in Colossians. The words tumbled through his mind, *"And whatsoever ye do in word or deed, do all in the name of the Lord Jesus, giving thanks to God and the Father by him."*

So, even the mundane reports needed to be done well and with a good attitude—something else he needed to be reminded of on a daily basis. His hope was that one day all of the empire his father had built and hoarded could be used to help the poor or used for missions . . . however God directed him.

Two hours into the afternoon, he stretched his arms and back as a sense of accomplishment filled him. He dipped his pen and signed the last page, conveying that he'd checked and double-checked the work. Another task complete.

Shifting his gaze to the window, he took in the sunshine and perfect white clouds dotting a blue sky. It would make for a great picture. Made him imagine what it would look like through the lens of his new camera. The clock chimed the hour. Perhaps he'd be able to get away in time to drive by Lake Michigan. His favorite view.

"Ray!" Dad's booming voice pulled his attention away from the window. Looming in the doorway, with a catlike smile on his features, his dad stroked his beard. "I've got exciting news." Even if it wasn't exciting for anyone but him, Dad would expect anyone and everyone to listen and nod their agreement. His father's presence dominated no matter where he went. "I'm sending you out to the new Harvey House at the Grand Canyon. I've been in discussions with the Harvey boys about the investment opportunities in the West. They've agreed to advertise for us, and we will do the same for them here."

Ray leaned back in his chair. Dad was always looking for new ways to expand and get his name out there. "What exactly will they advertise for us? It's not like we have the same attraction as the Grand Canyon."

"I asked them to start with our art galleries and jewelry stores. Since the wealthy will most likely be the ones to make that trip, it will give them something to look forward to when they come home. Or perhaps those who aren't from Chicago or New York will want to take a trip so they can visit one of our fine establishments. I'm even thinking of building out west myself. Oh, make sure you pack that box-camera-photograph thing of yours." He waved a hand, as if that would make the right word appear.

Ray's eyebrows shot up. "Oh?" He couldn't trust himself to say much more. All he could do was attempt to mask his shock. When had Dad ever expressed *any* interest in his photography?

Dad sat in the chair across from him and leaned back with his hands folded across his chest. "It's supposed to be a grand affair—the El Tovar I believe is what it's called. My investors are eager to hear how we can capitalize on the Atchison, Topeka, and Santa Fe rail line. Everyone is fascinated with the West and wants their piece of it. Harvey has a good corner of it now, so we need to find our own niche."

Ray's heart sank a bit. It was just another errand for the investors. What would he have to do this time? Make a list of all the Harvey Houses along the way? Journal the food that people could purchase along the line? His initial shock about being asked to bring his camera faded fast. Another waste of money for Dad and a waste of time for him. He let out a sigh. Not exactly the good attitude he'd been aiming for.

"The brand-new hotel is a charming, Swiss-chalet-looking lodge. Supposedly it has every amenity the social elite will enjoy." He leaned forward and lifted his chin, that telltale sparkle in his eye. "But next door—or across the court-yard—is the Hopi House, designed by a Miss Mary Colter. She's been a decorator for Harvey and a designer. But she knows the Indians. It's a lovely Pueblo structure that repre-sents the magnificent people of the West and houses their art. Apparently, they've got real Indians from nearby villages who create the art right there in front of people. This is Har-vey's new plan, to have Indian art and souvenir shops next to their hotels. But at this location, they've put an exhibit of rare and costly specimens. It's the priceless Harvey col-lection that won the grand prize at the Louisiana Purchase Exposition."

That actually *was* interesting to Ray. "So, you'd like me to visit and detail what El Tovar offers its visitors?"

"Yes, but I also need you to think bigger. Our class is fascinated with the West, didn't you hear me? *Fascinated*. Primitive as it may be."

Next would come the lecture on how to charm the rich into spending money. Again. Investing in something new and interesting. Building the company into something big-ger than Rockefeller or Vanderbilt dared to dream. Ray had heard the spiel before, but he nodded at all the appropriate places and listened.

His father had been criticized often for his unfocused way of doing business. Rather than investing in oil, steel, coal, the railroads, or even creating or making something, Ray Watkins Senior was all about trying his hand at everything: investing in real estate, jewelry, art, restaurants, hotels . . . it was all over the map. And he'd made quite a fortune, but their investors were always looking for more. Lots more.

"What I'm saying is that I'm giving you an incredible opportunity. You need to ponder the tough questions. What could we—our investors—capitalize upon? What else could we build there that could attract our social crowd? What would people want to spend money on? I've heard that more and more people are willing to venture down into the canyon. The stories good ol' Ralph Cameron has sent state that he's getting a hefty profit from his toll on the Bright Angel Trail. You need to find out if we can get in on something like that too." Dad stood and began pacing. A sure indicator that he was winding up for even more ideas.

Not one to usually interrupt his father when he was on a roll, Ray couldn't let one thing pass. "Why did you want me to bring my camera?"

Dad's face turned very serious. "To send me pictures, of course. I need to see what's there: the canyon, the hotel, the opportunities, the art." Dad pointed a finger at him. "Don't forget the art. Perhaps we could even acquire some of it for the galleries here." He went back to stroking his beard. "I know this is a larger task than I've given you before, and it will be quite time consuming, but I need you to be my eyes and ears. It may be some time before I can get away myself. So be thorough."

He clasped his hands behind his back and lifted his chin.

"I'm counting on you. This could be huge for us. Expansion into the West is our future." With a dramatic flair, Dad sat back down in the chair and leaned forward. "I'll send at least two or three men with you to help. Put them to work for whatever you need, but keep in mind I've got several other errands for each of them to run."

Of course he did. Dad always had an agenda other than just the errands he'd send Ray to pursue. But one day, through hard work and perseverance, he was determined to have his father trust him with the entirety of the business. But Dad wasn't one to let things go easily. He liked being in complete control. "How long do you want me to stay?"

"It will probably take several weeks. Or even perhaps a couple months, I would imagine. I'll let you know when you've accomplished all that needs to be done. Once I've had time to look over everything you send, I'll need to meet with the investors here and possibly bring some of them out to see it for themselves. That's why it's crucial for you to send me detailed reports—something I know you are outstanding at producing."

"Thank you, Dad." He'd take the compliment, seeing as his father didn't hand them out very often. "When would you like me to leave?"

"Within the week, if possible."

Ray stood, straightened the papers he'd been working on, and placed his pen back in the holder. He offered Dad a smile. "I guess I better start packing then. I wonder what the weather is like in the Arizona Territory this time of year?" He shrugged. "I guess I need to prepare for multiple seasons if I'm to be away for a couple months."

His father stood as well, gripped Ray's upper arm with his left hand, and shook his right hand vigorously. "I'm excited for this next stage for you, son. One day, I know you'll make a fine head for this company—my legacy—and bring even more pride to the Watkins name."

Still shaking Dad's hand, Ray smiled. "I hope to make you proud."

"You have." With a brief nod, he turned on his heel and left.

Ray sat back behind his desk and pulled a small notebook out of a drawer. Best to start a list of all he needed to bring with him, especially if he was to be away for months. Which really wasn't a problem. It wasn't like there was anyone or anything that truly tied him to Chicago. The senior Watkins had sent him on many trips since he'd come home as a college graduate hoping to take on the business. At least this one didn't seem to be as tedious or even as frivolous as so many of the others had been. Perhaps Dad was ready to start handing him some more responsibility. It was an encouraging thought.

The patience he'd learned the past few years after he'd turned his life around had begun to feel like it would never bear fruit. Today was proof that Reverend James had been correct. The pages of the notebook in front of him blurred as his thoughts rushed back to their last conversation.

"You've been given a second chance. Don't waste it by complaining about what you wish you could do. Instead focus on what you can *do. Be grateful to Almighty God. It's time to show your family that you've changed. You've given your life over to the Lord and are allowing Him to work in you. Perhaps you will have an impact on them as well. The wild Ray Watkins of your youth is gone."*

"But there's still so much guilt inside," Ray had replied. *"How do I get past the horrible things I've done? Is it even* fair *for me to have a fresh start?"*

"Thankfully, the good Lord doesn't give us what we de-

serve. *Your sins were covered on the cross. They're paid for in full. Now, go and live for Him.*" Reverend James squeezed his shoulder and then headed for the door. Hat in his hands, he turned back toward him. "*You didn't kill that young boy, Ray. Remember that.*"

2

Thankful that she only had her small reticule to carry, Emma Grace couldn't help but latch on to the excitement in the head waitress's voice. Was Miss Anniston going to take her to see the canyon? It was unheard of to take a staff member out for sightseeing before giving them their new assignment and duties. It definitely went against everything she'd learned of life as a Harvey Girl.

Miss Anniston must have seen the confused look on Emma Grace's face when the head waitress turned toward her. "Don't worry, we have plenty of time to talk about the job. I know you are well versed in Harvey House rules, but this is an exception. A prerequisite of sorts before you start working."

As they walked the steep path up and around the hotel, Emma Grace's breath caught in her throat. The sun's rays from the west lit up the snowy landscape as she glimpsed her first view. "Oh my."

Miss Anniston reached out a hand and tugged on her elbow. "It gets even better." The smile that lit up her face made her eyes sparkle with merriment. She tucked her hands back into the pockets of her coat and set an even faster pace.

Emma Grace could hardly wait to get to the rim in front

of her. Every step closer brought more into view. The deep rusts, oranges, and reds of the canyon shone in the winter light. Her breaths came in gasps as they stopped and stood at the rim. She let her reticule drop into her left hand and put her right over her chest. Never in her life could she have imagined anything so beautiful.

"Take a moment to catch your breath. We're a lot higher here. I know it seemed like it was flat coming in on the train, but we are at an elevation that is close to matching some mountains. I believe it's over seven thousand feet here, so that's why it's a lot easier to get out of breath. The house doctor spoke to me about preparing all of the girls for this, especially since there's a lot of stairs in the hotel. You'll want to drink plenty of water." The woman's lighthearted chatter made her feel even more at ease. "It's amazing, isn't it?"

"I'd seen a photograph in a newspaper before I came. But it couldn't capture this. I had no idea." Emma Grace couldn't take it all in. As she let her gaze roam the horizon in front of her, the sheer vastness of the canyon overwhelmed her. Words were inadequate. It was almost as if her eyes were incapable of taking in such glorious wonder. "It's so much larger than I imagined. I would have never guessed . . . my goodness."

It wasn't just a canyon cut by the river. It was as if she stood atop a mountain looking into the valley below, and it was all sheer cliffs, ripples of rocks in varying colors as far as the eye could see. She couldn't even fathom the height where they stood compared to the tiny ribbon of river she could see far, far below. For a moment, it took her breath away and made her dizzy.

"You'd have to traverse more than five hundred miles if you wanted to circumvent the entire canyon. God is quite the artist. There's nothing quite like seeing it in person to be in awe of the Creator."

Miss Anniston's casual references to God made her cringe. Growing up, she'd gone to church with her parents, before her mother died. The boring reverend touted the wrath of God, especially for those who were willful and stubborn—two things Mother called her often. God definitely hadn't helped her as a child. And there'd been no sign of Him once she was grown either. If He was all powerful and concerned about her, why would He take her mother? Why had He allowed her to be kidnapped? And then why would He let her father try to sell her off to the highest bidder?

She blinked away the thoughts and focused on the beauty before her. None of that mattered anymore. Not her father. Not the past. Not God. She was here and ready to start over again. Hopefully for the last time.

The vivid colors and distinctions of the layers of the canyon contrasted with the deep blue of the sky in the afternoon sun. Nothing like the shades of gray from the photograph in the paper. The green of the evergreen trees around her amongst the snow-covered rocky edges made her realize that even as desolate and vast as it seemed, there was still life and growth here.

As she turned her head slowly right and then to the left to take it all in, she knew that she could spend a lifetime trying to do just that. "The Grand Canyon is a fitting name, and yet it doesn't do it justice."

"I agree. No matter how many times I see it, it changes and becomes even more beautiful. Every season is different, or so I've been told, and every sunrise and sunset more glorious than the last." Miss Anniston's shoulders shook with a shiver. "Wait until you see your first thunderstorm." She let out a long sigh. "Anyway, let's get you inside. I know it's freezing, but I just didn't think it was fair to not let you see it first."

"Thank you, Miss Anniston." Emma Grace breathed in the crisp air and tore her eyes from the canyon. "I'm so grateful you brought me here."

"Please, when it's just us, call me Ruth. We're going to be working quite closely together. Come on, I'll show you around a bit more while your things are brought to your room."

Nodding, she allowed herself to smile. Perhaps she'd have a friend in Ruth. Years of keeping her distance from everyone made her crave a real relationship. But her heart sank a bit. Her whole identity was a façade. How could she be real with anyone?

It didn't matter. Maybe she could pour herself into exploring the canyon. It'd been so long since she'd allowed herself to even think about having an adventure. That had been what had spurred her on in her youth. Always seeking adventure. Her mind went back to her favorite books and how she'd dreamed of running away when she was a child. Once it clicked that her father and Mr. Cooper had been involved in her kidnapping—that they'd used her for their gain—she'd come up with dozens of outlandish scenarios. Anything to get away. Books had been her escape and had spurred the creative engine to life.

It was easy to dream back then and not understand the reality of life on her own as an adult. But she'd learned. And she'd grown. Her life may not be as fantastic as life was in *20,000 Leagues Under the Sea*, but it promised to be an adventure here with an entire canyon to explore. The canyon could be her best friend.

Ruth led her back toward the east side of the building. The path along the rim would be wonderful for their guests, and it was barely a stone's throw from the hotel. They walked all the way around the beautiful structure. "Here's the main entrance for the guests, with the Hopi House to your left."

The entrance for the guests was lovely indeed. She could imagine carriages pulling up to the front circle drive, with people not only seeing the beautiful hotel but also the canyon. Many might not ever want to leave, if not for it being so far from civilization.

When Emma Grace looked to her left, the boxy, large sandstone structure that greeted her was nothing like that of the hotel. With small windows and several ladders going up between the levels of roofs, it reminded her of Pueblo architecture she'd seen before, which was built to keep the desert sun out and the cool air in. It was also an impressive building.

"Mary Colter designed the Hopi House and it was completed just a couple weeks ago. She wanted it to be timeless, like the people it represents."

"Fascinating. You say a woman designed it?"

"Yes, you'll have to meet her. She is truly one of a kind."

"Is it true that there are real Indians there?"

"Yes. The Hopi people are very talented and have sold a lot of artwork already. I'm sure it will be another great attraction for our guests."

So many thoughts were on the tip of Emma Grace's tongue, but she had to bite it so she'd keep them to herself. It wouldn't do any good for Ruth to find out about her past by her spilling her knowledge and education. Over the years, that had been the hardest part, always needing to think before she spoke. Something she'd been horrible at as a child.

It had become a part of her daily routine—necessity had proven a valued teacher—but obviously, she was tired and had begun to let her guard down around Ruth. Already. Which was strange for her. She'd have to work harder at it.

They walked in silence for several moments until they'd made a circle from where they started at the train depot. Ruth pointed to the door she'd stopped at earlier. "This is the basement, where our quarters are. Most of the time, you'll need to use this entrance."

"Yes, ma'am."

"No need to be so formal when it's just the two of us." Ruth waggled her eyebrows.

"I'm sorry, it's a habit." Another thing that she'd had to work diligently at when she first went into service five years ago. And a habit she didn't want to break. The carefully crafted façade she'd kept up all this time *had* to stay in place. The reminder rang in her brain like a bell. "But I appreciate your warm welcome."

"You are most welcome, Emma Grace—may I call you that?"

"Of course."

"After your experience all these years as a Harvey Girl, you're quite familiar with the rules at all the other locations. Rules that we also follow here in a professional capacity. But things will be different since we are so remote. It's important that we all work together in the professional Harvey capacity but also learn how to work as a family unit as well." Ruth opened the door for her. "We're going to have to rely on one another more than ever before. It won't be easy living this far away from anything and everything. We don't want anyone to feel lonely or left out. That's why all of the workers have been handpicked, not only for their experience and excellence handling guests, but also for their reputations of working well with others, their loyalty, and their ability to adapt. I'm sure Mr. Harvey would be very proud of what has been built here. He always wanted to leave a legacy—something he's done and that the Harvey company continues. But I also think that El Tovar will be the crown of that legacy."

Everything within Emma Grace at that moment wanted to talk about Mr. Fred Harvey and all the times he'd dined at her family's table growing up. All the countless conversations she'd listened to as he described each place in great detail, how he organized the employees, and planned out the service. But it was another piece of her past that had to stay hidden. No one could know she'd known the man himself.

Tears pricked her eyes and she blinked them away. Mr. Harvey had been a bit of salvation for her. It was his stories that had given her hope and a way of escape.

In all honesty, he was the reason she'd become a Harvey Girl. Mr. Harvey's passion for what he did had poured out in every story he'd told. It had fascinated her when she was younger and all the facts she'd learned had helped her secure a job. He'd inspired her to be passionate about the work as well. Something an heiress was unaccustomed to.

Blinking several more times, she followed Ruth into the building. If the basement was any indication of the floors above, she had no doubt that El Tovar being Harvey's crown jewel was true. Cleaner, brighter, and shinier than any other Harvey House she'd visited, it gleamed new and modern. Their steps echoed down the long hallway.

Ruth pulled out a key and unlocked a room. "This will be yours."

A single bed, dresser, desk, and wardrobe filled the space. Ruth carried in Emma Grace's two cases that had been sitting outside the door.

"This is all just for me?" She'd had to share at every other establishment. "I thought only the head waitress had her own room."

"It's all yours." Ruth's face lit with another smile. Her eyes were the lightest of blues. The contrast with her fair skin and dark hair made her quite striking. Why wasn't the woman married? "We've decided that things will be a bit different here, as I assume you read in my letter."

"No. I apologize, it must not have arrived before I left."

"Oh, well, no wonder I see the confused look on your face. You have been chosen to be a head waitress in training, meaning that you will fill in for me when I am gone and assist me with my duties. You will, of course, still need to serve tables. But eventually the management would like to have two head waitresses, and you will be one of them."

Ruth clasped her hands in front of her. "Now, I'm sure I've overwhelmed you with all this news and the view, so I will leave you to unpack. My room is right next door in case you need anything." She held out a key. "Always keep your door locked. Best thing to do is hang it around your neck under your uniform. That way there's no risk of leaving it in your pocket if you have to change uniforms during the day. Or worse, it falling out of a pocket during your shift and then having to retrace your steps to find it later. The manager—Mr. Owens, I'll introduce you to him later—and I are the only ones who have access to a spare." She stepped toward the door. "Oh, and thank you for sending your measurements. Your uniforms are hanging in the wardrobe. All laundry is done on Tuesdays and Fridays. The iron and steamer are down the hall, but I can show you those after dinner." She smiled. "Since we don't have guests coming for a few days, the staff who are here get the luxury of eating together in the dining room and tasting all of the chef's delicacies."

"Thank you." Emma Grace looked around the room. This was a dream come true. Comfortable, homey, with a cozy atmosphere. "This is quite a surprise, and it's all so very lovely." She fingered the latch on the wardrobe and pulled the door open. Five long black dresses hung neatly on hangers, with a row of bright white aprons next to them. Seven, to be exact. Always extra aprons in case anything got spilled on them during the day. Fred Harvey had been insistent upon the highest of standards.

Without warning, a memory rushed into her mind's eye. Mr. Harvey was dining with them back in Boston. She had been, what? Ten or eleven at the time? Their butler had just served dessert. A lemon meringue pie, which was Father's favorite. The silver gleamed in the light of the chandelier as Mr. Fred Harvey looked down at his slice and asked if that was all he was going to be served. Father chuckled, but poor Jones stumbled and stuttered until her father rescued him.

"Don't mind Mr. Harvey, Jones." Father's eyes had twinkled. *"He was just making the point that they serve whole quarter pieces of pie at the Harvey establishments."*

A touch to her shoulder made the memory disappear and brought the wardrobe back into view.

Ruth's light laughter washed over her. "Don't worry, when I'm tired, I often daydream as well."

"I'm sorry. Would you repeat what you said?" Emma Grace felt the heat rushing into her cheeks. Not the greatest impression to her superior.

"It wasn't anything important. I was just explaining about the water closet and bathing chamber, which are also down the hall. But why don't I show you those before dinner? Unless you need them now?"

"Before dinner is fine. I'm sure I can find them on my own if I need to. Thank you."

"Of course. All right, then, you have about an hour, so feel free to unpack and lie down to rest your eyes for a little bit. I'll come knock before dinner."

"That would be wonderful." She stifled a yawn. "I slept very little the past few days."

Ruth nodded and gave an understanding look. "I'll be back in an hour."

"Thank you. For everything."

The door closed behind Miss Anniston, and Emma Grace plopped onto the bed. Leaning back, she draped an arm over her forehead and let her mind go over everything. Was she really at the Grand Canyon? It seemed so . . . surreal. But here she was. With an unexpected promotion to boot. It was a beautiful place. And very far away from anything and everything . . . and every*one* she'd ever known.

Allowing her eyes to close, she relished the warmth of the room and the softness of the bed. Perhaps she wouldn't have to move again. She could just stay hidden here forever.

BOSTON, MASSACHUSETTS

"I know they say it can't be done, but I'll find her."

He always found them. Not that he went around bragging, but everyone knew it. That's why they came to him.

Hands behind his back, he casually strolled around the room as if he didn't have a care in the world. The fancy desk and polished bookshelves were an obvious attempt at show-casing the power and wealth of the owner of the office, but it didn't fool him. A man was a man, no matter his status. He couldn't care less about the prestige of anyone who hired him. He did a job. That was it. Lifting his chin, he turned back to the desk and the full chair behind it.

"Glad to hear your confidence in the matter because it's been five years and everyone else has come up empty. I'm tired of waiting." The man—his new employer—let out an exasperated sigh. Fingers drummed the leather arm on the chair. One eye twitched. "I really need her found—*alive*. It does me no good if she's not. I expect results this time."

"That's what I deliver. Results. Mark my words . . . I'll find her. Before the year is up." He placed his bowler back on his head and turned to leave. The best way to make an impression was to have the final word.

After the door was shut behind him with a solid click, he buttoned up his overcoat. The wind had quite a bite to it, but he put his mind to the task at hand. This wasn't an easy case, proven by all the men who'd failed. But that only spurred him on. With a guarantee of all his expenses covered—plus a nice stipend to get him started and a hefty finder's fee in addition to all that—Peter calculated the profit. Even if he found the woman faster than he guaranteed, he'd still find himself sitting pretty.

Maybe one day he wouldn't have the reputation that he had. The people he found were the lowlifes. Not him.

Brisk steps brought him back to his tiny office. Quite a contrast from the one he'd just exited. But he found there was no need to spend funds on anything extravagant. People hired him because he was good at what he did, not because they liked him or thought his office was fancy. And frankly, he didn't care what people thought of his means or status.

The musty smell of a room being shut up for too long with the windows closed to keep the heat in made him long for fresh air. No matter. He'd get plenty of it on this new search. All he had to do was buy a train ticket, grab his travel case, and head west.

His instincts would handle the rest.

3

Moving his camera stand a few feet to the left, Ray took in the view, trying to memorize everything he saw. Never in his life had he seen anything that could rival the magnitude of this place.

When they'd checked into the El Tovar a few hours ago, he had done nothing more than see his room before grabbing his camera equipment and heading out to the overlook. The railroad had been genius. To build this luxury hotel a mere twenty feet from the rim of this glorious canyon was visionary. Ray could only imagine what it was like in the different seasons. With the snow dotting the landscape around the rugged rocks, everything glistened. What would it be like in the heat of summer? How would the colors shift?

The light before him changed. Just a few more minutes and the sunset would be upon them. If only his camera could capture all the colors.

Crisp clouds moved at a brisk pace from west to east across the blue sky. Pinks edged the clouds on the west side, giving them the most glorious glow. He lifted his watch out of his pocket. It was getting close to the dinner hour, but he wanted to see the sunset on the canyon for himself.

For once, he was thankful for the trip Dad sent him on. All the other times, he had to sit through tedious meals and take copious notes on things that didn't really interest him. But for his father and the company, he'd endured, understanding that one day all this would be worth it.

As he watched the sun slip lower and lower into the west, his thoughts went back to years prior. Before he'd gotten his life straight with the Lord. Back when he'd been just like all his other rich friends, eager to spend the family fortune and live off everything that had been amassed by their fathers and grandfathers. Caring little about working or how the business had been run. Concerned only about how he could take his father's place at the helm and have enough money to burn.

With a hard shake of his head, he sent the memories back to where they belonged. He wasn't that person anymore. But they kept pushing to the forefront. Vying for his attention.

In his mind, a red hoop bounced in front of the headlamps of his 1901 Locomobile. Tires screeched.

"Ray." One of his father's men broke through the scene replaying in his mind. "You've been out here quite a while. Aren't you freezing?" Michael had his hands shoved into his coat pockets, his hat pulled down low.

Shaking off the vestiges of the all-too-vivid memory, Ray pasted on a smile. "Have you not seen the view out here? I could look at it all day long, every day for a year, and not get enough of it." He looked back through the viewfinder in his camera to distract himself.

A few of his father's men who had been with the company a long time remembered what he'd been like. It had taken a good bit of time to prove he was different and earn their respect. But the past few years, Dad had hired a whole slew of younger men—all a bit like sharks circling the waters, always on the hunt. The three men with him were like that. And Ray wasn't sure what he thought of them. They'd risen up in the ranks of seniority faster than he could comprehend.

"How many photographs have you taken?" Michael stepped closer to the edge, which gave them only a hint of safety when looking at the depth of the canyon in front of them.

"Not enough. Even though it won't do the picturesque scene justice, I can at least try." Perhaps the light would play off the clouds and colors in the canyon and shade the photo nicely. But it would all be grays and blacks and whites. Not the glorious colors before him right now.

Even if there was a way to take color photographs, he doubted that they would be able to capture the beauty and grandeur. This was something a person had to experience themselves. Something he would definitely have to convey to his father.

"It is truly magnificent, I agree, but the delicious smells wafting from the dining room are making us all go mad with hunger. We secured a table by the window, so you can still take in the view. Besides, I don't think your father would appreciate you freezing to death trying to take pictures." Michael's laugh sounded a bit forced.

Watching the sun make its final descent, Ray nodded. "There will be plenty of other chances to see the sunset. I wouldn't want any of you to starve on my behalf." No matter if they were his father's right-hand men, they still had to wait. Because of him. The boss's son. And that wasn't a good way to earn their loyalty as a leader. He wasn't better than them and didn't want them to get the impression that he *thought* himself to be better than them. So, he lifted his camera off the wooden tripod and tucked the bag of glass plates under his arm.

Michael reached out. "Let me carry something."

Not wanting to risk damaging one of the plates, Ray handed him the tripod. "Just unscrew the legs and you can fold them up so it's easier to carry."

They headed for the front entrance, the arched windows in the stone face greeting them from the porch. A warm glow emanated from the multiple fireplaces within the welcoming Rendezvous Room. Dinner did sound very appealing, especially now that the sun no longer cast its warmth on his face and he realized how cold his limbs had become. A shiver worked its way up his spine.

"I don't know how you stood it out there for so long." Michael opened the door for him with his free hand.

"I was too enraptured with the scene before me until we started packing up. Now I'm downright frigid." He walked across the patterned carpets over to the grand staircase. "Here, hand me the tripod and I'll get this put away in just a moment." He looked down at his clothes. "I better change for dinner as well."

"That's all right. I'll head up with you. I need to change too. The boys will hold our table, I'm sure."

Taking the plush red-carpeted steps two at a time, Ray journeyed up to the third floor as fast as he could. His stomach rumbled with every step. The smells from the dining room were quite enticing.

As he approached his room, Edgar opened the door. "Mr. Watkins, sir. I have your dinner attire laid out."

"Thank you, Edgar." Ray nodded at Michael, who was unlocking his own door, and entered the room. How his valet knew exactly when he was coming was beyond him. The man was impeccable at his job. But why Dad insisted that they have servants travel with them was also something he didn't understand. It was all about appearances to his father. Having the wealth wasn't enough for him. He wanted to make sure that everybody knew it.

It was one of the things that bothered Ray the most since he'd come to know the Lord. While the Good Book didn't say that being wealthy was evil, it certainly did state that the *love* of money was the root of all evil. There were so many good things that they could do with their fortune, but every time he brought up a new charity or way to show philanthropy, it ended in an argument.

Edgar silently helped him change out of his day suit, and Ray mulled it all over. If he were in charge of things, what would he change? The ever-present need Dad had to have the Watkins name be as big as all the other wealthy names that rolled off people's tongues. That would be first. Second, he wanted to help show the world God's love. Would that mean funding missionaries? Churches? He had no idea. Maybe that's something he should start speaking to someone about. But who? Their reverend back in Chicago was of a like mind with his father. And Reverend James had passed away.

"There, sir. If you won't be needing anything else, I shall retire until you call for me this evening."

Adjusting his jacket sleeves at the cuffs, Ray gave the older man a smile. "That's quite all right, Edgar. I am perfectly capable of getting myself ready for bed. Why don't you take the rest of the evening off? It's been quite a grueling journey, and I'm sure you would like to enjoy some time to yourself."

"Of course, sir. Many thanks." While he didn't quite smile, it did give Ray hope that there was a bit of joy within the man somewhere. Working for the Watkins family could not be an easy task. Mother and Dad could both be quite difficult. "Oh, I almost forgot. This telegram arrived for you earlier." The older man handed him the paper and nodded his head.

"Thank you." Who would be sending him a telegram? Ray closed the door behind Edgar and opened the paper.

Send photographs of the art. Especially the Harvey Collection.

—Father

He tapped the paper against his palm. Did Dad forget that he'd already asked him to take pictures of the art? Odd. Ray tossed the paper onto his bed and shrugged. Age and stress must be getting to the old man.

"Another train has arrived with another crowd of visitors. The hotel is completely full." Emma Grace stood straight in the dining room with her hands clasped in front of her and smiled. "Are you ready for the evening hustle and bustle, Caroline?" The whispered words to her new trainee sounded a bit too loud to her own ears, and she glanced at their head waitress.

But Ruth was whispering her own encouragement to other waitresses-in-training. They'd lost several of the new staff when the girls discovered how remote their new job would be. Out of twenty-five girls, they'd had to replace four. Three of them had offers they couldn't refuse and married men in Williams. Marriage was the reason why they lost most of their waitresses at all the Harvey establishments. The other girl returned home from the Williams depot without ever journeying all the way out to El Tovar. Granted, it wasn't very appealing if all she saw was the barren terrain as the train chugged into Arizona Territory. If only she'd taken the time to see the view of the canyon . . . but one had to travel miles and miles through endless trees and desert-like landscape to get there.

That reminded Emma Grace that she'd overheard several men talking about a hike down into the canyon. Since there was a trail, she couldn't wait to try that for herself.

"My hands are shaking." Caroline's words pulled her attention back. "What if I spill something on somebody important?"

"You'll do fine. You've been a Harvey Girl for several months now and I haven't seen you spill a drop since you got here. Just follow my lead." Emma Grace lifted her chin and stood straighter as guests were shown into the vast room and to their tables. Many of them oohed and aahed over the room and pointed to the enormous log walls and immense beams in the vaulted ceiling. Then, as they caught their first glimpse out the windows, many of them tried to contain themselves, but most couldn't. No matter how many times a person saw it that first day, the canyon overwhelmed them.

Several of the new waitresses suppressed giggles. They'd all done the same thing. It had been a relief when Ruth told her that the new waitresses were at least seasoned Harvey Girls. If they'd been completely new? Well, that would have been a disaster. Trying to train them on top of trying to keep their attention.

"I'm thankful for my experience as a Harvey Girl, but it was not at a place like this. These people are all wealthy. They're a different class of customers. What if someone really important comes in and I'm not ready? What if President Roosevelt were to come? Or the Rockefellers?" She let out a tiny gasp. "Or John Jacob Astor?" The young girl was working herself up into a frenzy and positively quaking in her boots as her voice squeaked.

"Straighten up, Caroline." Using a tone that brooked no argument, Emma Grace looked her trainee in the eye. "It doesn't matter who they are. They're our customers and they deserve the best—the Harvey best. Rely on your training. There's no more time to doubt yourself or to worry about it. It's time to serve." Emma Grace took determined steps toward her area, confident that Caroline could pull it together.

Emma Grace smiled and nodded as she walked past guests, but something Caroline had said began to niggle at the back of her mind. This crowd *was* the upper class. What if the El Tovar drew people here who knew her? She found herself at a place where her crowd was sure to come. A place she'd chosen. She'd been so worried about getting as far away as possible that she hadn't thought it all through. Of course, there had always been the chance that someone from her social circle in Boston could ride the train west and see her. But she'd always been in disguise up to this point. Perhaps she should wear her hair differently. And maybe use the glasses again.

Even as her heart picked up its pace, she forced herself to focus on the moment. She'd have to think about it later. Change her appearance tomorrow. "Good evening. Welcome to the El Tovar." She gave a broad smile to each guest at the table in front of the large fireplace, the most prized seating in the dining room, where two large windows flanked the stone fireplace. Guests seated at those three tables—one at each window and one in the middle by the fireplace—had the best seats with the best view. The Grand Canyon lay before them in all its glory as they dined. And those tables belonged to her.

As the waitress with the most seniority under their head waitress, she loved the privilege of choosing her tables. She'd never tire of this view, and to think she'd get to see it every day. . . .

"Our menu offers many scrumptious dishes this evening. But might I recommend the breast of chicken El Tovar, created by our very own Chef Marques." She offered coffee to each of the four guests as Caroline followed her with the water pitcher. "It is served with wild rice."

"That sounds utterly delightful." The lady was the first to speak and gave her a smile.

"I've had the pork with applesauce at another Harvey establishment and thought it divine, so I will stick with that." One of the gentlemen kept his nose buried in the menu. "With potatoes." The last part was almost a grunt.

The gentleman with his back to the fire thumbed his mustache. "I believe the roast sirloin of beef *au jus* will be my choice." His chin went up and down as he gazed through his spectacles at the menu. "Boiled sweet potatoes and Elgin sugar corn with that."

"I'm inclined to agree with you." The last man spoke and tucked his hand into his vest pocket. "I'll have the same."

"We will be back shortly with your dinner." Emma Grace turned and walked toward the large buffet cabinet that lined the west side of the room and guarded the entrance to the kitchen. Caroline followed closely and listened as Emma Grace gave the orders to Ruth, who would give them to the chef. Turning to her trainee, Emma Grace lifted her eyebrows ever so slightly. "Are you ready to be on your own?"

Caroline grinned back, her nervousness gone, at least for the moment. "Yes, Miss Edwards."

"Good. Now, why don't you offer coffee to both the window tables, and I will take the pitcher of water? Then you take the orders at the table by the right window, and I will take the left."

Ray followed the host across the intricately designed carpets into the dining room. The open dining room boasted vaulted ceilings with large beams that rose to the apex. The log trusses and beams were rough wood, which gave the room a rustic appeal. The red and blue crosses in the center of the carpets were quite mesmerizing. He spotted his group at a table by one of the windows facing the canyon.

As he approached the table, he let out a sigh. Ah yes, it had a marvelous view. Exactly what he'd been hoping for— one of the best seats in the room. He nodded to the host. "Thank you."

"You're most welcome, sir." The host laid a menu on the table and went back to his station.

As Ray took his seat, he looked at the others. "Good evening. My apologies for the delay."

"Not a problem." George dipped his chin and looked back down at the menu.

"Coffee, sir?" The waitress's voice to his right made him glance up. She was young, with brown hair. She looked a bit mousy and a good deal uneasy.

"Yes, thank you." He gave her a smile, hoping that it would ease whatever discomfort she had.

She poured him a cup and walked away with brisk steps. He raised the fine china cup to his mouth and took a sip. The warm liquid and the sandstone fireplace right next to him began to melt the chill that had set into his bones. After another long sip, he set his coffee cup down on the saucer. "Look at that view." The scene out the window in front of him was like that of a priceless painting. With a glance back to his tablemates, he found it odd that the other men weren't more captivated by it.

"I don't mind the view one bit." Ben wasn't looking out the window, though. He was watching the Harvey Girls as they glided through the room.

"I agree. Too bad Harvey has such strict rules about their curfew." George let out a low chuckle.

Listening to the conversation emanating from his father's company men made him want to turn the table over on top of them. Why had his father hired them? Because they could *act* like gentlemen when they needed to? Definitely not because they *were* gentlemen.

A twinge hit his gut. He had no place to judge. These men acted exactly like he used to.

It wasn't long ago that his behavior was no different. God had done a mighty work in his life, in more ways than Ray could count. There was hope for these guys . . . maybe he had a chance to be a positive impact on them. If he could just control his temper, he'd be doing well. God had infinite patience for Ray. He needed to pass that on to those around him.

"That one's quite the looker." George smirked and sipped his coffee. Every man at the table followed his gaze. The waitress was dressed like all the others. Black dress, high collar, with a long white apron over it. Her dark hair was piled high atop her head and she smiled as she served a table two away from them.

While she was an attractive lady, it wasn't proper for his father's men to be talking in such a manner. Time to get things back on track. He cleared his throat. "*Gentlemen*, I'd like to discuss what tasks my father has asked for your assistance on. That way I know what I can request of your services as well. No need to overlap." Ray pulled a small notebook and pencil out of his pocket.

All the men quieted. Michael tapped the table a moment

and shared a glance with the others. "Our apologies. It's been a long day—a long trip. Our discussion was improper and unbecoming to gentlemen."

"Agreed." George leaned back in his chair. "I forgot my manners."

His obvious attempt to stop their gawking had worked. Ray looked each man in the eye. No need for reprimands. He put the notebook away. "Perhaps we can save business discussions for breakfast and luncheon. It *has* been a long day." These men were different than the ones Dad usually sent with him. They were more . . . worldly. Young. Best to get on their good side, yet keep them reminded who was boss. How he was to accomplish that balance, he wasn't sure.

The difficult position of being the boss's son wasn't his favorite. Especially when he'd been given more responsibility than ever before. But he had to remember that he was representing the Watkins name.

"Good evening, gentlemen."

He turned at the voice behind him and smiled. The woman dressed in the waitress attire wasn't what he'd expected. Instead of the mousy and timid-looking young woman, this lady was self-assured. Confident.

"Good evening."

"I see Caroline has already brought you coffee. Does anyone need a refill?" She poured water into his glass and then the next with precision. Not a drop was spilled. He watched her as she rounded the table. Her light blond hair shimmered in the dining room lights. Steady hands. No jewelry of any kind. And she walked around the table as graceful as a dancer. He'd seen the Harvey Girls in action at many locations, but something about this woman was different. What was it?

Michael asked her a question about the menu's offerings,

and every man at the table listened intently. At least they seemed to be on their best behavior. Thank heavens.

Without missing a beat, she explained every dish and stood before them, waiting. "If you've decided, I can take your orders now."

As she went around the table again, she nodded and asked each man questions about their specific choices, their vegetable and dessert preferences. "How about you, sir?" She turned to Ray.

He cleared his throat. "The chicken by the chef sounds quite good."

"It's served over wild rice. Would you like anything else to accompany it?"

"The asparagus with cream sauce, please."

"Of course. And how about for your dessert?" She tilted her head ever so slightly.

"Apple pie."

With a nod, she then looked at each one of them. "I will return with your dinners shortly, but should you need anything before then, don't hesitate to raise a hand and I will come as soon as possible."

As she walked away, his entire table watched.

Michael was the first to speak. "I almost don't feel like I'm dressed well enough to be in her presence."

George let out a low whistle. "I was feeling the same thing. And she's just a waitress."

"There's nothing wrong with being a waitress." Ray's tone was sharper than he intended. "She's not *beneath* us."

"Of course not." Michael's voice softened a bit and he looked between George and Ben.

An awkward moment of silence stretched before them. This was why Ray disliked society and all its rules of classes and such. Why couldn't people simply be people? All equal?

He took another sip of his coffee and gazed back out the window. Perhaps it was best if he kept his mouth shut. It was obvious these men didn't share his perspectives.

The men chatted about the weather. How they hadn't expected winter to be in the desert landscape of Arizona. Then they talked about what it must be like to venture down into the canyon. Ray watched them and studied them. They'd all worked for his father for a while. Maybe he needed to put more effort forth into getting to know them. After all, they were going to be here for many weeks.

Their waitress returned, her arms loaded with plates. As she served their dinner, every move was quick and precise. No lingering. No flirting. No chatting. She did her job, and she did it well. And he still felt like he was in the presence of royalty. After several trips, she returned with a carafe of coffee and a pitcher of water and filled each man's cup to the brim.

"Is there anything else that you need at the moment, gentlemen?"

Each man shook his head.

Ray offered up a smile. "I think we have everything for the time being."

"I'll be back for your plates and to bring your desserts. Again, don't hesitate to let me know if you need anything." Her smile didn't quite reach her brown eyes but made her even more becoming. With a slight nod, she walked away.

Ray picked up his fork and knife and sliced into the chicken breast. Covered with a glazing of hollandaise, the golden-brown crust made his mouth water. The first bite was even better than he imagined. Not only was the hollandaise creamy and tangy, but there was a thick sherry sauce underneath and over the chicken and rice that had chunks of mushrooms cooked to perfection within it. Each bite was better than the last.

He looked up and each man seemed to be relishing their food too.

George smiled and even let out a tiny moan. "I think that's the best thing I've ever tasted."

"Agreed." Michael took another bite.

Over the course of the next forty-five minutes, they ate and enjoyed their dinners, drank coffee, and chatted about the journey. But Ray couldn't help but glance here and there at their waitress. While all the Harvey Girls were lovely, precise, and good at their jobs, their waitress was better somehow. He couldn't put his finger on why, but he was convinced of it.

Maybe he could speak with her. But why? And how would he approach her and it not be inappropriate? Maybe he could apologize for the men's comments. She might have heard them.

With his pie plate clean, Ray reached for his cup and drained the last of his coffee. "I think I shall retire to my room for the evening." He stood. "I'll see you all in the morning for breakfast."

"I forgot to tell you." Michael stood as well. "We won't be here tomorrow. Your father has several things for us to accomplish back in Williams. But we should be back the following day for dinner."

"Of course." Ray adjusted his coat to cover his surprise. They'd just arrived. Now the men were off again?

Why did his father need all of them there? It was one thing to be inquiring for the investors, but did it really take four of them to accomplish that task? The only conclusion that made sense to him was that Dad apparently had another agenda. One he hadn't shared with his own son. And that didn't sit well.

George and Ben got to their feet as well and set their cloth napkins on the table.

The men all said their good-nights and Ray watched them leave the dining room. With a shake of his head, he tapped the table and pushed thoughts of his father from his mind. This was the perfect time for him to try and speak to the Harvey Girl. He perused the room, hoping for a glimpse of their waitress. Hmmm. Where was she?

A woman older than most of the other waitresses stood in the corner. Dressed in a black skirt, white blouse, and black ribbon tied at the collar, she kept watch over the entire room. She must be in charge.

As several other guests left the dining room, Ray approached the woman. "I'd like to speak with our waitress, please."

"I'm Miss Anniston, the head waitress here. Was everything to your satisfaction?"

"Oh yes, quite." Heat crept up his neck. "I would just like to meet her. To thank her personally."

The attractive lady shook her head and smiled. "I'll pass on your thanks, Mr. . . . ?"

"Watkins. Ray Watkins." He was losing ground and fast. "I, uh, feel the need to apologize for some inappropriate comments that were made at our table. Is there any chance you'd allow me to speak with her?"

Miss Anniston shook her head again. "I'm sorry, Mr. Watkins, but no. I will let her know. Thank you for bringing it to my attention."

Ray nodded. Time to walk away, though he hated the thought.

As he turned, disappointment washed over him. He'd been so eager to speak with her, and he didn't even know her name. Why hadn't he simply said something at the table? What had gotten into him? He'd never been smitten once in his life—well, except for his fourth-grade teacher, who helped him conquer math. That woman had been a saint with the patience of the good Lord Himself, and she always smelled like lilacs.

To this day, he enjoyed the fragrance of lilacs.

Ray debated with himself as he walked across the dining room floor. He'd made a mistake going to the head waitress. Now she would be watching him like a hawk. Not the best impression he'd ever made. He considered returning and apologizing to Miss Anniston, but as he turned on his heel, several waitresses headed in his direction, each carrying a large stack of plates.

As they passed him, each one offered him a smile and a cordial, "Good evening."

Except for one.

His waitress. Whose questioning gaze bore straight through him.

As she passed, she lifted her chin ever so slightly and one eyebrow quirked up.

Ray opened his mouth to speak, but she increased her pace and walked right on by without a word or a smile.

4

Running for all she was worth, Emma Grace followed the train tracks past the hotel and into the trees. Heavy steps behind her made her surge forward. Jumping from the tracks to a rocky path, she headed toward the canyon. There had to be a place to hide. Somewhere. Somewhere he couldn't find her.

"Don't you try and get away from me. You hear me? I'll find you no matter where you go." The deep voice growled at her.

Cries tore from her throat. No! She couldn't let him catch her. Never. She couldn't go back.

She tripped over a rock and landed with her palms on the edge of the canyon. Pebbles skittered down the steep drop-off. Her vision tilted as the height made her gasp for air. Her heart raced. Tumbling down into the canyon would kill her.

Pushing up to her hands and knees, she took a steadying breath and then scurried backward. Think. Where could she go?

Hands gripped her shoulders from behind.

"No!" She tried to get free.

The hands pushed harder. Shook her.

"No! Let me go!"

"Emma Grace, it's me. Ruth." The voice of a woman broke through.

The canyon disappeared. She couldn't see anything. It was all black. Had the man caught her? Pinned down, she flailed, trying to free herself.

"Emma Grace. Calm down." The woman's voice soothed.

"No! You can't make me! I won't do it." She had to get away.

"Emma. Grace." The voice was firmer now. "You need to wake up. Everything is fine. You're safe."

The words washed over her.

With a slow inhale, she rolled over onto her back, then opened her eyes. The room was dark, with only the lamp beside her bed offering a soft glow. She released the breath and started trembling.

Ruth sat on the bed beside her, concern etched all over her face. "Are you all right?"

Words wouldn't come. She closed her eyes and tried to focus on steadying her breathing.

"Gracious, you're soaking wet. Come on, sit up. We need to get you changed." Ruth tugged at her arms.

Emma Grace gripped Ruth's hands as if she could grip reality through them. All the remnants of the dream vanished. She was back at the El Tovar. Safe in her room. "I'm all right. It was just a nightmare." She wiped sweat from her forehead.

"That was some nightmare. It took all of my strength to pin you down. Would you like to talk about it?"

"No. I don't remember it." The lie made her cringe inwardly, but it couldn't be helped. She'd had the nightmares a few times over the past few years, but since she'd shared a room, the other girls had been able to awaken her sooner.

This time, the man in the dream had gotten a lot closer.

Rubbing the back of her neck, she tried to push it out of her mind. But that didn't work. She swung her legs over the edge of the bed. Sweat had indeed soaked her from head to toe. "I think I might actually go take a bath." But as she went to stand, her knees buckled.

"You're shaking. Why don't you take a few minutes to gather your senses?" Ruth placed an arm around her shoulders. "I've heard you call out in your sleep for a few nights now, but every time I came to your door, it was quiet again. Tonight seemed to be quite frightening for you. Have you had one of these before?" The words weren't accusing, but soft and concerned.

Emma Grace didn't have the energy to come up with a decent story. If she wanted to stay here long term, perhaps it was best for her to confide in someone. Just not everything. "Yes. But I've always shared a room, so I've been awoken before he . . ." She squeezed her eyes shut. She'd already said too much.

Ruth patted her back and then slowly rose to stand in front of her. "You don't have to say any more tonight." The lines between her brows were deep, and Emma Grace could almost feel the pity. Then Ruth's expression softened. "Let's go get a bath ready for you."

"Thank you." Her whispered words caught in her throat. It had been a long time since anyone had shown this kind of care. Probably because it was the first time she'd allowed herself to be vulnerable. Every other time, she'd laughed it off with the other Harvey Girls and pretended the nightmares didn't bother her. Her carefully crafted façade had placed a wall between her and everyone else. It had been five years since she even permitted herself to think about having a real friend.

Friend.

The word made her want to cry. Was she ready to open herself up?

Doubts flowed through her as fast as a river during spring thaw.

"Come on." Ruth reached forward and grabbed her hands. "I'll make a pallet here on your floor so you won't be alone tonight. Then, after you've had a relaxing bath, maybe we can both get a little more sleep tonight."

With her friend's help, Emma Grace stood up and went to the wardrobe to fetch a clean nightdress and her dressing gown. "You don't have to do that, Ruth. I've already stolen too much of your rest. Don't worry about me."

"I won't take no for an answer. I'm sleeping here the rest of the night. Then, tomorrow evening after we're done with our shifts, I think we should sit down with a cup of tea and talk." Her tone held the ring of authority.

Emma Grace didn't argue. At least she'd have the whole day to formulate a plan and decide exactly what she wanted to share. Enough of the truth that Ruth would understand, but not enough to put her in danger.

After Ruth had plenty of hot water in the tub, she turned to the door. "I'll go get my things moved into your room."

With a nod, she watched her close the door and then disrobed and climbed into the tub. The hot water helped to ease her muscles, and she did her best to let go of the anxiety that clawed at her. But even after several minutes of soaking and a good scrubbing of her skin, she couldn't rid her mind of the question. What had made her have a nightmare tonight? It had been so real. She could feel the hairs on the back of her neck stand up as she remembered being pursued.

Shaking her head of the thoughts, she dunked her head under the water and tried to wash it all away.

When she came up for air, she knew what it was. The men

from table one. By the window. She could see each of their faces in her memory. Then one of them had spoken to Ruth after dinner. Had he recognized her? What had he wanted?

She climbed out of the tub and dried off as quickly as she could. The sooner she could get dressed and back in her room, the sooner she could find out what that man wanted.

With her things gathered in her arms, she slid her feet into her slippers and then opened the door and headed back down the hall to her room.

Ruth met her halfway. "Do you feel any better?"

"I do, yes. Thank you."

Once they were back in her room, Ruth closed the door and locked it, then gestured down at her pallet. "I tried to give you enough space where you wouldn't trip over me if you had to get up before me. But if you step on me, I'll live." Her light laughter was a nice break to the seriousness of how they'd left this room before.

"I appreciate you sacrificing your own bed for me. It's really not necessary—"

"Yes, it is." Ruth held up a hand. "Mr. Owens told me that some of these rooms have doors between them, ones not in the hallway. I'll ask him about it tomorrow. If there is one, we could leave that door unlocked or even open in the middle of the night if you think that would help."

"There's another door?" Emma Grace looked around. "I don't see it."

Ruth pointed to the wardrobe. "It might be behind that. It was smart of them to install the adjoining rooms in case there was a need for them in the future. Nobody else knows they are there. Except for Mr. Owens, of course."

"I think it would be a good idea to keep the door open once we are in for the night. That way, I won't wake anyone else up—not that I have nightmares often. But I hate that the responsibility will be on your shoulders." The thought of everyone knowing about her night terrors made her really uncomfortable. "I didn't disturb anyone else, did I?"

"No. At least I didn't see anyone out in the hall. Don't worry, your secret is safe with me." Ruth yawned and sat down on her pallet on the floor. "We've only got a couple hours before dawn, so we better get what rest we can."

Emma Grace bit her lip. "May I ask you one question?" She climbed into bed and turned off the lamp.

"Of course."

"I saw one of the gentlemen from table one speaking to you after dinner. Was he"—how could she ask this?—"complaining or upset about his service tonight?" There. That sounded innocent enough.

A sound that was almost a laugh crossed the room. "Gracious no. I think he was sweet on you and wanted a chance to talk to you, but he used the excuse that perhaps you'd overheard some inappropriate comments made by his companions and said he wanted to apologize."

Relief filled her chest as the throbbing in her temples eased. She let her body relax and released a soft breath. "Oh." She worked to keep her voice steady and calm. "I was worried I had done something wrong."

"Not at all." The rustling of sheets sounded as Ruth settled in for the remainder of the night. "I've had the privilege of watching you for a week now, Emma Grace. Your work is impeccable. No wonder the recommendations from your previous managers have been stellar. I don't think I've ever seen a Harvey Girl as poised, professional, and graceful as you."

The words rang in her ears over and over. The praise of this woman soothed the raw places in her heart.

Sinking into the soft feather pillow, she allowed her

thoughts to wander back to Boston. Back to home. Back when her family had been intact and everything seemed . . . happy.

A single tear slipped down her cheek. When she was quite small, her parents had been inseparable. Quick to smile. Full of love and laughter. But maybe that was all a dream from her little-girl mind. Because she couldn't remember much after her brother passed. There'd been a lot of sadness after Mother died. Then Father worked all the time.

She shivered in her bed.

Maybe the happiness she remembered wasn't real. It probably never was.

But as she closed her eyes, her heart ached for the family she'd adored. And one question kept haunting her. What would her parents think of her now?

The next morning, the question still bothered her. Why was she all of a sudden so worried about what her parents would think of her? They were gone. And there was nothing she could do about it. This was her life now.

With a quick stretch behind the buffet, Emma Grace put on a smile and walked out to her tables. The lack of sleep last night made her wish she could go back to bed, but that wasn't an option. Besides, a good day at work should keep her mind off everything. There wasn't a lot of extra time to think or worry during a twelve-hour shift. Especially now that the hotel was full to capacity. When they weren't serving the guests, they were polishing the silverware—a *lot* of it. Over and over again.

She pushed her spectacles up her nose, gave the tight knot at the back of her head a quick pat, and nodded to the lovely couple at table two. While it wasn't directly in front of one of the windows, it did offer the warmth from the fireplace and a lovely view. "Good morning. Would you like some coffee while you peruse your breakfast choices?"

"Yes, for both of us, please." The lady's sweet smile as she moved closer toward her husband nearly screamed that they were newlyweds.

"I'll return in just a moment to take your orders." Emma Grace filled their cups and turned toward table one. She couldn't help it that her eyes widened when she realized the sole occupant was none other than the man who had spoken to Ruth last night.

Thankfully, he was reading a paper and hadn't seen her reaction. She blinked and took a breath. "Good morning, sir. Dining alone for breakfast?"

He looked up and his blue eyes connected with hers. "Good morning. Yes, it's just me. My companions have some business to attend to in Williams."

"Oh." Not the correct response for a Harvey Girl. She scrambled to get her thoughts in order. "Coffee?"

"Yes. Thank you." His smile was genuine and helped her unease to dissipate.

As she filled his cup, she reminded herself that he hadn't recognized her or been looking for her. He was just a customer. "Do you have any questions about the breakfast choices?" She studied him. His brown hair was neatly parted down the middle. His perfectly tailored suit with blue silk tie and gold tiepin spoke of great wealth. His accent told her that he definitely wasn't from the Northeast. She'd know, because hers had been so strong, it had taken her a good year to consciously get rid of it.

"I'd like to look at the menu for a bit, if that's all right? I'm not in any big hurry this morning." There was that smile again. Warm. And it made his eyes sparkle.

"Of course. I'll come back in a few minutes." As she

walked away, she let out a breath that she hadn't even realized she'd been holding. While the man didn't scare her anymore, there was something about him. Something that made him stand out. Perhaps it was simply because Ruth thought the man might be sweet on her.

But there wasn't time to dwell on it. "Good morning." She greeted table three. "Coffee?"

"Yes. We'd also like to order toast and fried eggs." The man didn't even look up from whatever he was reading.

"For both of you?" Emma Grace tilted her head and glanced at the lady seated next to him. But she didn't look up either. Her eyes were firmly glued to her lap.

"Yes. Sunny-side up." The man answered. Still no eye contact.

"I'll put in your orders immediately." Turning toward the kitchen, she compared the customers from those three tables. What untold stories were there? And what a difference in demeanors. She could tell a lot about people from how they treated the Harvey Girls and other staff members. It fascinated her that after all her years in high society, she found it more comfortable to be among who she thought of as "regular" people. The wealthy were all too fake, in her opinion.

After putting table three's order in, she went to take the other tables' breakfast choices. The lovey-dovey couple wanted French toast and fruit. Simple and easy. Time to head back over to table one.

This time, the man's paper was folded on the chair next to him and he looked straight at her, as if he'd been waiting.

"I'm sorry. Did you have to wait too long?" She swallowed. Too many times, she'd been put in her place by the well-to-do.

"Not at all." He held up a hand, and the corners of his

lips turned up again. "I was just looking forward to seeing you again."

"Oh." Normally she quashed any flirtatious behavior immediately, but for some reason, this man didn't seem to be casually flirting like all the other men she'd met. What was he up to?

"Your hair is different this morning, and I don't remember you wearing glasses yesterday." It was his turn to study her. And the directness of his stare unnerved her a bit.

Out of habit, she pushed the spectacles up her nose. "I couldn't find them yesterday. It gave me quite a headache to work without them."

"My apologies. That was awfully uncouth of me. I meant for it to be a compliment to you. You look lovely."

No one else had said anything about her change in appearance. Funny that it would be a customer who commented on it. A wealthy, nice-looking male customer to boot. She cleared her throat and tried to quell the new feeling in her belly. "Have you decided what you would like to order?"

"Does the chef have a specialty?"

Now that they were back on familiar ground, she reminded herself to smile. She was a Harvey Girl, after all. "Yes. His croissants are quite delicious, as are the pancakes. Oh, and he makes the best omelets I've ever tasted."

"You've sold me. How about an omelet and a croissant?"

"I'll get that right in and be back with your order shortly, sir."

"Thank you." His words chased her as she turned from the table.

One of her other customers raised a hand briefly to get her attention. Perfect. Anything to get her mind off table one, its occupant, and his motives. Whatever they were.

Scurrying around the dining room, she delivered orders,

refilled coffee, water, and orange juice. When she returned with table one's food, she smiled as he thanked her and then she hurried off. Her other two tables ate quickly and left. New customers occupied them within minutes.

By the time she'd filled their coffee and taken their orders, she thought for sure the lone gentleman would be gone—not that she'd been deliberately neglecting him. Most people didn't need a lot once they received their food, and she had been very busy. But when she looked over at the table, he was still sitting there, enjoying the croissant. She'd never seen anyone eat that slowly before. While she was looking his way, she saw his hand shoot up. With quick steps, she headed back to his table.

"What can I get you, sir?"

"Perhaps a refill on the coffee?"

"Of course."

His mouth was full of his last bite of omelet when she came back with the carafe and filled his cup. He picked up his juice to wash it down and tapped the table once he had swallowed. "My apologies, I know you are very busy, but would you mind bringing me some more butter?"

"Not at all, sir. I'll be right back."

"Oh, and miss?" His words made her turn back around.

"Yes?"

"Thank you." As the morning light streamed in through the window, his eyes seemed even bluer than they had before. Maybe it was just the color of his tie bringing them out.

She gave her head a little shake and headed back to the waitresses' station. Ruth greeted her with one raised eyebrow. "How's your morning going? I see your guest who was inquiring of you last night is back."

"Yes. And he's a very nice gentleman. A slow eater, but he seems genuine enough." Emma Grace reached for a small plate that held a pat of butter hand-pressed with the El Tovar crest. "Do I need to encourage him to leave so that we have the table available?"

Ruth shook her head. "No. I've just learned that the man is Mr. Watkins. Ray Watkins Junior, in fact. His father is the richest man in Chicago, and Mr. Owens has instructed us to make sure that Mr. Watkins has whatever he wants and needs. If he wants to stay at that table all day, we must oblige him."

Wonderful. Another of the extremely wealthy crowd. Always putting money first. And whatever they wanted, they got. She tried to school her features, but it irritated her that this man was to be a permanent occupant of one of her tables.

"Is there a problem, Emma Grace?" Ruth had a way of lifting that one eyebrow when she asked a question.

"No. No problem at all." Pasting on the fakest of smiles, she headed back to Mr. Watkins.

"Here's your butter, Mr. Watkins. Can I get you anything else?" Her words were shorter than they should have been, but sometimes her temper got the best of her, which wasn't a good thing. She was a Harvey Girl. Not the daughter of a railroad baron.

He looked almost hurt as he took the plate of proffered butter. He hesitated for a moment. "No, thank you. But . . . have I offended you in some way, miss?"

Oh, great. If Mr. Owens heard about this, she could be reprimanded. She forced the muscles in her face to relax and gave him a slight smile. "No. I'm sorry, Mr. Watkins. It's simply been a trying morning."

"Good." He put a hand to his chest. "I'm relieved. It was not my intention to upset you. Please don't let me keep you from your duties."

"Thank you." She removed one of his empty plates. "Don't hesitate to let me know if you need anything else." The phrase she repeated hundreds of times a day rolled off her tongue. Good thing she'd had lots of practice. Turning on her heel, she hoped she'd smoothed things over.

"Miss?"

Once again, she went back to the table. "Yes?"

"Might I ask for some jelly or jam?"

"Of course. Grape, apple, or blackberry?"

"Blackberry. Thank you."

She spun around again to head back to the station.

"I'm sorry. . . . Might I inquire of one more thing?"

Doing her best not to roll her eyes as she pivoted back toward Mr. Watkins, she blinked several times. "Yes, sir?"

"Since my party will be here for several weeks and you already know *my* name, I was wondering if I could have the privilege of knowing yours?"

In that moment, she wasn't sure whether she should feel flattered or disappointed. Flattered because he sought out her table and wanted to know her name. Disappointed because it probably meant that she would need to deal with him for a while. And if he was as needy at every meal as he had been today? Oh boy.

But her job was to ensure that each and every guest felt welcome, so she put on her best smile. "I'm Miss Edwards. I'll be right back with your jelly." This time as she walked away, she half-expected to hear him call her name. But when he didn't, she let out a sigh.

The only thing she could hope for now was a big tip.

5

Today was the perfect opportunity for Ray to get his sunset pictures. The deep blue sky was beautifully decorated with clouds, as if the Master Painter had used a brush to spread the wispy white layers for the light to play with. Since the other men were in Williams, Ray could stay as late as he liked and not have to worry about delaying everyone's dinner. And he doubted anyone else would miss him.

Especially after he'd bugged Miss Edwards time and again at breakfast. He cringed just thinking about his behavior. Then, after realizing his faux pas, he tried to do the opposite and practically ignored her at lunch. Not the best impression. But then again, what did he know? It's not like he had taken the time to pursue women after he gave his life to the Lord.

Before that, he'd been young and stupid, and more than one young lady had tried to convince him that he should marry. Because they wanted his fortune. But he'd been too caught up in having fun to even think seriously about a woman. Why was he even thinking of pursuing one now, anyway? Because she fascinated him? Because she didn't seem to dote on him just because of his name or his fortune?

Or perhaps because loneliness had become his companion? None of those were great reasons.

He couldn't figure it out. Not that he should even try. The example of marriage his parents had set hadn't exactly been something to make him want *that* for the rest of his life. Maybe he should put all thoughts of Miss Edwards out of his mind and focus on the glorious view before him. Ray set up his tripod and placed his new Century Camera atop. Once it was stable, he removed the front case and gently tugged on the lens so that the red bellows could extend. He reached into his bag and counted. Perfect. He had at least twenty glass plates. That should give him plenty of photographs to develop after dinner. Even if he could get only one good picture out of the lot, it would be enough.

Edgar had set up a nice little darkroom for him and offered to fetch water whenever he needed it. Hopefully the man wouldn't mind staying up a bit late tonight. It would probably take the rest of the evening.

As the sun shifted behind a cloud, the rays hitting the canyon almost took his breath away.

"Quite magnificent, isn't it?"

The question made Ray turn his attention from the camera.

Hands deep in the pockets of his trousers, the man didn't look at all cold in the frigid temps. And yet all he wore was a single-breasted jacket and waistcoat that matched his trousers. Even the felt homburg hat didn't look like it provided that much warmth.

"It is probably the most amazing thing I've ever seen." He stuck out his hand. "Ray Watkins."

"Pleased to make your acquaintance." The man returned the gesture, and they shook. "Name's Frank Henderson."

"You don't look the least bit cold, Mr. Henderson." Ray rubbed his gloved hands together.

Frank's deep laughter echoed over the canyon. "I grew up in the mountains of Colorado. The cold doesn't bother me much."

"What brings you to the Arizona Territory?" Ray looked back through the viewfinder to see if the right shot presented itself.

"I'm the assistant chef at the hotel. Couldn't pass up the opportunity to work at this fine establishment."

"I should say not." He grinned back to his new acquaintance. "And I must say that everything I have eaten here has been some of the best food I've tasted anywhere."

"I quite agree. Chef Marques is a stickler about his recipes and the way he runs his kitchen. I will pass on your compliment." Frank moved a bit closer. "It's my day off, and I've been enjoying just walking the rim when your setup caught my attention. Is that one of the new Century Cameras?"

He leaned back. "Yes, it is. Are you familiar with them?"

"No. Not really, but I have become interested in photography. Have you met the Kolb brothers yet? They've been teaching me a bit about it." Frank shrugged. "One day I think it would be a fun hobby. Something to get me out of the kitchen and tasting food all the time." He patted his waist. Not that he was a large man, but he was a bit thicker around the middle.

"No, I haven't had the privilege. Just arrived yesterday. Who are the Kolbs?"

"Two fine young men. Wild adventurers and photographers." The chef pointed to the west past the hotel. "They built their house and studio on an eyebrow ledge at the entrance to the Bright Angel Trail, which takes you down into the canyon. Cameron—that is, Mr. Ralph Cameron—owns a small hotel down the trail and a few mining claims. He gave the brothers a piece of his land, and they take up the tolls for him from anyone who wants to use the trail. Then they take photographs of tourists and develop them so they can sell them back to the same tourists on their way back. Ingenious, really. But I wouldn't want to hike up and down that trail multiple times a day."

The Kolb brothers sounded like men Ray wanted to meet. "I can't say I would either. I heard it's quite the trek. Even on a mule's back. What's an eyebrow ledge?"

Frank lifted his eyebrows. "You think the El Tovar is close to the canyon? Well . . . let me tell you. Here, we're a good twenty feet from the edge. Those Kolbs—Emery and Ellsworth—built their studio on the ledge itself. It's practically clinging to the canyon wall. First time they welcomed me in, I almost didn't want to risk it. It looks like it could fall right into the canyon with a stiff wind."

"This, I've got to see."

"You should. And you could talk pictures with them. They know their stuff. And they're never afraid to try something risky to get the perfect shot." He chuckled. "As long as you aren't planning on opening up a studio here and presenting them with competition, I think they'd love to meet you."

Ray held up a hand. "Oh no. This is just a hobby. Besides, my work in Chicago keeps me pretty busy." But wouldn't it be amazing to spend the rest of his days here, looking at this view? Maybe these Kolb brothers had the right idea.

"Well, I didn't mean to interrupt your quiet. It was very nice to meet you, Mr. Watkins."

"Please, call me Ray."

"Then I insist you call me Frank."

"When is your next day off? Perhaps you could introduce me to the brothers and we could hike down into the canyon." It would do him good to get some more fresh air, and the thought of going down into the canyon excited him. He doubted any of his father's men would be interested in that.

"I would love to. I just need to clear it with my manager—Mr. Owens. Let's see, today is Saturday, tomorrow I have some errands to run in Williams for Mr. Owens . . . that would mean next time I'm off is a week from Monday."

Ray pulled the notebook out of his pocket and jotted it down. "I'll look forward to it."

Frank nodded and strolled back to the hotel.

A burst of color caught Ray's attention and he looked back at the sunset. The last rays of light shone on the clouds. If only his camera could capture the reds, pinks, and oranges. Focusing the lens, he snapped what he hoped would be the perfect shot. Changing plates, he set up for another picture. Then another. Eventually, he'd used every single one of the glass plates he had with him and the light was just about gone.

A sense of satisfaction filled him as he watched the sun dip completely below the horizon.

Packing up his camera, he couldn't wait to get back to his room and develop the photographs. His stomach rumbled. Dinner would probably be a good idea too, as long as he didn't make a fool of himself in front of Miss Edwards. Not that she would even notice.

But it wouldn't hurt to see her again. Maybe over time, he could show her that he wasn't that bad.

The wind picked up, and without the sun, the temperature dropped at a rapid pace. Time to get inside and warm up.

With his tripod in his right hand, he slung the bag with the camera over his shoulder and cradled the other bag of glass plates up against his chest. Thank goodness he hadn't ventured too far from the hotel. The weight was more than he remembered when he'd hauled it out.

He made it to the front steps and heard the chatter and laughter inside the Rendezvous Room as the door opened.

Maneuvering his way through, he bumped the doorjamb as the heavy wooden door closed behind him.

Crack!

His heart plummeted at the sound as he stopped in his tracks and looked down.

One of the legs of the tripod had come unfolded and gotten caught in the door. It was splintered beyond repair. He stared at it for several seconds and worked hard to keep his frustration muted.

"Is everything all right, sir?" The hotel manager headed for him.

"I don't suppose you have anyone who can repair this?" He held up the deformed apparatus.

"I'm sorry, Mr. Watkins, but I doubt it. Perhaps we can send for a new one from Williams. I've got one of the men headed there tomorrow."

Disappointment threatened to overtake him. But he took a deep breath and tamped it down. Nothing he could do about it now. He'd have to be more careful in the future. "I'd appreciate that, Mr. Owens. I think that's probably a good idea. Will it take long?"

"Perhaps a few days, depending on what is available." The man looked eager to please. "But I could request a rush."

A few days. It would be difficult to not have a tripod to work with, but he'd have to accept it and move on. "Thank you. Sounds like that is the best we can do."

"Yes, sir. I'll work on it first thing in the morning." The man reached out. "Might I have this as a reference? Maybe we can obtain the same model."

"Of course." He handed the man the broken pieces. The scents from the dining room beckoned him in, but instead, he strode toward the stairs. It hadn't been his best day.

The dinner rush had been grueling. For more than three hours, every table had been filled, and Emma Grace was feeling it in her back. If only she could have a long soak in the tub tonight, but the sign-up sheets for use of the bathing chamber were filled until far too late in the evening for her. Sleep was far more important at this juncture.

She hadn't slept well since arriving at El Tovar. A new place and a new job, they were bound to be the reasons for her trouble getting rest, but that didn't help her know how to make it through. Or how to actually catch up on sleep. When Ruth said that she'd been awoken by Emma Grace more than once that night, it made sense that they were both tired this morning. Something had kept her from fully resting. Then there was the nightmare.

The thought of the dream brought chills to her spine. Yes, she lied to Ruth about remembering. That was the least of her concerns at this point. Perhaps Ruth would forget that they were supposed to chat tonight.

Emma Grace could only hope.

She glanced at the clock on the wall. Almost eight thirty. One of the girls had gotten sick this afternoon, and as the assistant head waitress, it had fallen to her to finish out the shift. But she'd been on her feet since seven this morning, and it would be nice if everyone could be done with dinner now and leave.

Two of her tables emptied, which meant she only had one more and they were almost finished. All she needed to do was deliver dessert.

But on her way back to their table with two plates of peach cobbler, she saw Mr. Watkins being seated at table one. Again.

At this point, she didn't know what to think about the handsome, rich man—other than to wish that he'd sit somewhere else. At breakfast, he'd been in constant need. At lunch, he hardly even spoke to her other than to give his order and to thank her. She didn't need this kind of customer.

At least he tipped well. Very well.

Maybe he would eat fast.

After delivering the desserts, she headed over to his table and slapped on the best smile she could at this hour of the night. "Good evening, Mr. Watkins."

"Evening, Miss Edwards." He looked tired. Weary. And something else she couldn't quite ascertain. "I'm sorry for arriving so late, but I had a mishap with my camera equipment."

"You're a photographer?" It took her completely by surprise. She'd thought he must be some sort of wealthy snob helping out with the family business.

His chuckle was dry. "No. But I do enjoy dabbling in the art."

"Oh. Well, there's not a better place to practice your art than here, I'd wager." The ache in her left foot began to throb. She shifted her weight, but there was no relief. No matter which foot she stood on, everything hurt. "Is there anything I can get you this evening?"

"I'm so tired I don't even care. Maybe you could surprise me with something hearty? Oh, and please, something that won't take too long. I don't wish to keep anyone any later than need be."

He seemed genuine. Maybe he wasn't so bad after all. "We are here to serve, Mr. Watkins. I'll return with your dinner shortly."

"Thank you." He pulled a notebook out of his pocket, put a hand to his forehead, and went to studying it.

She headed to the kitchen and knew exactly what to bring him. Her new favorite was the chef's beef stroganoff. Hearty. Rich. Comforting. Perhaps that was exactly what he needed.

Several minutes later, she headed back to his table with a steaming plate. "Here you are, Mr. Watkins."

"Thank you. It smells delicious." He placed his napkin into his lap.

Noticing his glass was almost empty, she headed back for a pitcher of water. The dining room had cleared of customers except for two tables. She let out a long breath and attempted to relax her shoulders. It was a nice feeling when her shift was almost over. Water pitcher in hand, she went back to table one and filled her customer's glass. "Here—" She cut off her words when she realized his head was bowed. Was he praying?

Mr. Watkins lifted his head. His eyes looked clearer and brighter.

"I'm so sorry. I didn't mean to intrude." She gripped the pitcher's handle tighter.

"Not at all." He picked up the glass and took a long drink. "Thank you. This was just what I needed." This time his smile was relaxed and reached his eyes.

"Can I get you anything else?"

"Not unless you have a camera tripod lying around." He shook his head. "Sorry, that was a bad attempt at a joke."

She rested the pitcher's base in the palm of her hand and allowed herself to give him a real smile as he lifted the first bite to his lips. "Sorry, I'm fresh out of camera equipment. But I'm sure Mr. Owens can help you procure what you need."

"He has already offered his assistance, which is greatly appreciated. I simply am upset with myself for not taking better care. It was my own fault."

A rich man taking responsibility? That was something she hadn't heard before.

He pointed his fork to his plate. "Good choice, Miss Edwards. I think this might be my new favorite dish."

"I'm glad you like it." His sincere appreciation filled her exhausted and dry spirit. Spending all day serving the customers was tiring, but even more so when the clientele's expectations were sometimes outlandish. And today had been one of those days. It had made her detest the upper class and their hoity-toity ways. Thank goodness she'd escaped that life before she became just like them.

What was she thinking? *He* was one of that class. When his companions returned, they'd surely be demanding and snobbish toward her. Because she was just a waitress. They'd certainly had something to say about that on their first evening here. Not that she would ever admit to overhearing them.

"Did I say something wrong?" He set his fork down and rose to his feet. "You look upset."

Gracious, she needed to rein in her thoughts because apparently she couldn't keep them from her expressions. "Not at all, Mr. Watkins. It's simply been a long day."

He reached a hand out toward her as if to offer . . . what? "Please, then." He pulled his hand back. "Don't let me keep you. I don't wish to be the cause of making your evening even longer." With a nod, he took his seat and placed his napkin back in his lap. "I'm quite content with my delicious dinner. I can't imagine requiring anything else."

"Forgive me. There's no need to rush." Now she felt like a heel. What was it about this man that made her attitude swing from one extreme to another? She'd never had that issue with anyone else. It was her job to make sure that the customers felt at ease and comfortable. Somehow, she'd managed to do the opposite with him. "Honestly, I'm here if you need anything. Wouldn't you like a piece of pie?"

"Miss Edwards, you have been so gracious to me even with all my floundering and faux pas. Thank you. But I feel I should finish my dinner and head to my room." He pointed with his head to the rest of the dining room. "It appears I'm the last one here. Please don't worry about me and thank you for all that you've done. I hope you have a lovely evening."

His words made a light laugh escape. "I should be the one saying that to you, Mr. Watkins. Have a good evening." She turned and headed back to the waitresses' station and finished polishing the last few pieces of silverware. When she glanced back up at the table, Mr. Watkins was walking away. With a little wave, he nodded and smiled in her direction.

An hour later, Emma Grace sat on her bed. Did she even have enough energy to change out of her uniform? Or could she just flop back on the bed and go to sleep? As tempting as the latter sounded, she forced herself to stand back up and remove her shoes and stockings. Changing out of the apron and black dress, she tossed them in the laundry bag and grabbed a nightgown. Gone were the days of her owning dozens of day dresses and hundreds of evening gowns and gloves. Every once in a while, she missed the finery, but most of the time, she was thankful to not be burdened with it. In fact, the Harvey Girl uniform had become her favorite over the years because every one of the girls wore the same thing.

Harvey Girls took pride in their jobs and the fact that they were privileged to have the prestigious name. In a world where working women hadn't been the norm or even re-spected, the Harvey Girls broke through all the preconceived notions and had become widely esteemed as women of good moral character, manners, loyalty, and work ethic.

And while the twenty-five-dollars-a-month salary, plus room and board, would be scoffed at by the upper class, it was more than enough to take care of her needs. She even had tucked away a tidy sum over the years in case she ever needed to disappear in a hurry. Several times, she'd thought about putting it in a bank but had kept it in a locked box in her wardrobe instead. Trust was not something that came easily.

A gentle tap on her door made her shove the thoughts aside. She wrapped her dressing gown around her, went to the door, and opened it.

Ruth grinned up at her. "I know it's been a long day, but I still think we need to chat." She held a tray with a full china tea service and two cups. "And I promised tea."

Not willing to tell the woman who was essentially her supervisor no, Emma Grace ushered her in and shut the door behind her.

Ruth set the tray down and placed her hands on her hips. "First things first, I spoke with Mr. Owens and the door is indeed behind the wardrobe. He gave us permission to move it. Why don't we move it out of the way now, while we still have strength? That way, we can open the door that adjoins our rooms."

Between the two of them, they were able to move the heavy wardrobe across the tile floor.

"There." Ruth wiped her hands together and walked over to the tea tray. "It's chamomile. My mother always brought it to me when I was sick because she said it had healing properties. But I use it at night when I'm having trouble sleeping. It normally works like a charm." After pouring a cup, she held it out to Emma Grace.

"Thank you." A cup of tea sounded very soothing. Besides, it would occupy her hands during whatever discussion Ruth had planned.

The head waitress sat on the chair, her back ramrod straight as she took a sip of tea. "Now, I'm not the nosy type. I don't want you to think that I'm prying, though it is my job to keep all of the girls in line and following the rules of a Harvey House. But I truly am concerned about you." She paused and took another sip before continuing. "Emma Grace, I'd like to be your friend. We're going to be working together a lot, and we need to rely on one another. In my experience, the only way that works is if we have a deep, respectful relationship."

With a nod, Emma Grace looked at her tea. What could she say? She'd love to have a real friend, but she had too many secrets. And no one to trust.

"The nightmare that you had seemed to be very real to you. I looked over your employment card and it's exemplary. But there's nothing about your family or any history before you came to be a Harvey Girl."

Emma Grace closed her eyes. Ruth was a smart woman. How much had she figured out?

"I'm not trying to pressure you to tell me all about your past, but if you're in danger in any way, please let me help you. When I was trying to wake you last night, you told me to let you go. . . . Is someone after you, Emma Grace?"

She hated lying. Hated it. And it was so hard to keep stories straight, so she always did her best to skirt the truth. But what explanation could she give where Ruth wouldn't worry? And what if Emma Grace had another nightmare? What then? She hadn't told a single soul the truth about her past in five years. "It's nothing to worry about. I'm fine. Really." Lifting the china cup to her lips, she hoped her words would suffice.

Ruth set her cup down and folded her hands in her lap. "Look me in the eye and say that again."

As soon as she matched Ruth's gaze, Emma Grace knew she couldn't do it. "I appreciate that you care so much, but I don't wish to be a burden."

"You're not a burden. I told you that things were going to be different here. We need to be like a family. Families protect and help one another."

If only that were true. "My family didn't protect me." The words were harsh and cynical to her own ears.

"I'm sorry about that. But *I* will."

Even though the woman wasn't much over five feet in height, for some reason, Emma Grace believed her. Like a mama bear protected her cubs, Ruth seemed to have that same spunk and fire. Emma Grace couldn't lie to her. But she also couldn't tell her the whole truth. Besides, what were the chances that . . . *he* would ever find her out here after all this time?

"Look, I'm thirty years old. I've been doing this for a decade now. I doubt there's anything you could tell me that would shock me. I promise I won't think ill of you, and I promise not to say a word to anyone. But you've got to trust someone. Let me help you. Maybe it will help ease the nightmares if you tell me what caused them."

The woman wasn't going to let this go. "It's really nothing to worry about. It was a long time ago and sometimes I just have bad memories."

Ruth put a hand on her shoulder but didn't say anything else. Just rubbed circles on her back.

It reminded her of her grandmother on her mother's side. She had done that often when Emma Grace was little. And then she'd passed away. Mother not long after. It had been a long time since she'd received a comforting touch like this.

Emma Grace sighed. The safest thing she could share and still be honest was from her childhood. "I was kidnapped as a child."

"Oh my goodness." The tiny gasp proved that Ruth was more shocked than she let on.

"It was eighteen long days before I was returned to my parents. So, you can probably see why I still have the nightmares. Especially when I'm in new surroundings."

"That must have been horrible for you. I'm so sorry."

"Don't apologize. I'm sorry I kept it from you, but as you can imagine, it's not something that I share with people. Some things take a lifetime to get over."

Ruth nodded but didn't press any more. They sat in silence for several moments, sipping their tea. The clink of the china cups against saucers was the only sound.

Emma Grace drank the rest of her tea and got up from her seat on the bed. The awkward silence made her even more weary. "If it's all right with you, I'd like to get some rest now. Thank you for the tea. I believe it did just the trick."

"Of course." Ruth gathered the tea tray and went to the door between their rooms. "I'll leave this open in case you need anything."

"Thank you. Good night."

"Good night."

Emma Grace pulled back the covers to her bed and slid between the cool sheets. She turned off the lamp and pulled the quilt up and over her shoulders, listening to Ruth's footsteps in the room next door. It had been true, the story she'd told.

But it was nothing of the nightmare that pursued her now.

6

I'm looking for this woman, right here." Peter tapped the photograph. "Have you seen her? Sometime in the last five years?"

The Harvey Girl behind the lunch counter squinted at the picture. "I don't think so." She shrugged. "But I've only worked here for a few months."

He let out his breath in a rough, exasperated sigh. Sometimes he ran into people who didn't know how to use the brain they'd been given. "Well, is there someone that *has* worked here for several years?"

"Mr. Connors has been here a long time." She polished another knife. "Would you like me to get him for you?"

"Please." While his mother would remind him that he could catch more flies with honey than vinegar, he didn't care about his tone at the moment. He'd been to ten different Harvey establishments in the last ten days. All because a woman in Illinois had told him that she was convinced she'd seen Emma Grace McMurray dressed as a Harvey Girl. A fact that he was beginning to doubt. He'd scoured the

102

areas, asked questions of everyone he met, but still came up empty-handed.

He swiped a hand down his face. Not only was he in need of sleep, but he needed a shave too.

No one just vanished like this. Normally, he had a trail to follow at this point. No wonder all the others had failed. So, how had she done it? Or was she dead? The latter wouldn't be a surprise, but it wasn't the outcome his client wanted.

A portly bald man with a pipe and curly mustache followed the waitress out of the back and walked toward him. "I hear you're looking for someone?"

"Yes, I am." He held out the photograph. "This is Miss McMurray. It's imperative that I find her."

"Why is it so imperative?" The man wiped his hands on a towel and narrowed his eyes without even glancing at the picture.

"Have you *seen* her?" Peter growled and shoved his leather-encased badge under the man's nose.

"How do I even know that's real?" The man didn't flinch as his eyes flicked down to the badge.

"You don't." This was why he liked to do things his own way. "Have. You. Seen. Her?" He clamped his jaw so tight, he thought for sure the whole room could hear his teeth grinding.

"No reason to get all bent out of shape." The man leaned against the counter and glanced at the photograph again. "Can't say that I have. I don't know any Miss McMurray."

"Is there anyone else who has worked here for, oh, say the last four or five years who might know something?"

"Why? So you can be rude to them too?" The man raised his eyebrows. "I can't say that I appreciate you coming in here and behaving in such a manner. I think it's time for you to leave."

Peter tucked the picture and wallet back into his breast

pocket with a nod and headed for the door. Wasn't even worth his time to thank the people.

As he exited the restaurant, a hand tapped his arm. He looked over and an older woman sized him up. "Hazel across the street sees just about everything. Maybe she's seen your girl."

"Thank you. Hazel, you say?" He put his hat on his head.

"Yup. Across the street." She pointed a bony finger in the opposite direction of the railroad tracks and then walked away.

Well, it was worth a try. He ventured across the street and saw a woman—probably in her forties—watching him from where she sat by a cracked flowerpot. His lack of sleep and any real leads had made him testy. He should try another tactic.

"Good morning." Maybe honey would work this time.

"Mornin'." She tapped her cigarette until the ash fell onto the ground.

"Are you Hazel?"

"Sure am." She smacked. "I see they sent you over here."

"Yes, ma'am. I'm looking for a woman. Her name is Emma Grace McMurray, and I thought maybe she'd come through here in the last few years."

"There wasn't anyone named Emma Grace McMurray that worked over yonder." The lady blew cigarette smoke straight into his face.

Great. Another dead end. Wait. "How did you know I was asking if she worked over there?"

"Word gets around fast."

Huh. Word from where? He hadn't even asked that inside the Harvey House. "Would you look at a picture and tell me if you recognize her?"

"Sure." She stared at him. "But there *was* a girl named

Emma Grace. Don't rightly remember her last name. But it wasn't McMurray." Her lips wrapped around the cigarette for another inhale. "I thought her name was pretty. She was here a good while back."

"How far back?"

"Oh, maybe three or so years ago."

He slid the photograph in front of her. "Is that her?"

She looked at it for a moment and tilted her head. "Nah. That ain't her. She had real dark hair." She pointed to the photo. "Not blond or light like that." Her voice cackled as she coughed and laughed at the same time. "And she definitely wasn't all fancy-rich like that girl there. Nah, Emma Grace was sickly-looking. Way too skinny, like she hadn't eaten in a month of Sundays. And scared of her own shadow, that one. Always kept to herself and kept her chin down."

Didn't sound much like the lively and stubborn Emma Grace McMurray that had been described to him. But what if it was? How many Emma Graces could there be? And the timeline would be correct. "Could you take a second look, just to be sure?"

"Of course." She leaned forward and looked at the photo. "I don't know. The eyes look similar. But I really can't tell for sure. Nah, I don't think it's her." Lifting her gaze, she shrugged. "Sorry. Why are you tryin' to find this gal, anyways? Is she in some sort of danger?"

"You could say that. You could even say it's a matter of life and death."

The dining room lured Ray with the smells of Harvey's famous coffee, bacon, and fresh baked goods. But as much as his stomach growled for attention, Ray was more focused on sitting in Miss Edwards' section again. Perhaps this time, he could talk to her like a normal person—not some fool who either pestered her or ignored her.

Since his father's men weren't back yet, he looked forward to another morning of quiet. Sunday had been a wonderful day of rest for him. But the entire day, he hadn't been able to stop rehashing every conversation he'd had with the fascinating Harvey Girl.

Wanting to scold himself for his previous behavior, he shook his head and tried to put it behind him. Today was a new day.

He stood next to the host with his hands clasped behind his back.

"Would you like the same table, Mr. Watkins? Mr. Owens has reserved it especially for you."

"Oh?" Ray tipped his head to the right. "That's very kind of him but not necessary."

"Your father telegrammed Mr. Owens himself and we would like to make sure you are comfortable and happy with everything El Tovar has to offer." The man dipped his head a bit. "Let me go check on your table."

His father telegrammed? Again? "I assure you, everything has been more than comfortable. Magnificent, really. I'm completely content. No need to bestow additional attention or favor." He held up a hand and hoped the host could pass on the message.

Frustration began to bubble up inside him. His father needn't demand extra services. Dad liked to make sure that everyone knew who he was and how much money he had. Wanted to be named among the wealthiest. And wanted people to fawn over him. It disgusted Ray.

"Of course, sir." The man walked into the dining room.

Most of the time, he tried to ignore those particular flaws of his father, but there were times that they reared their ugly heads and it burned inside of Ray. How many times had he heard the spiel about Vanderbilt—the shipping and railroad tycoon—being a self-made millionaire? Or about Rockefeller and his Standard Oil Company, Carnegie and his steel, Astor and his real estate, and Morgan and his banking houses. His father wanted the same accolades and recognition for the Watkins name.

Lord, help me with my attitude toward Dad. There are times I don't even want to be known as a Watkins. Help me to show him that there's more than money in this life. Before it's too late.

The last thought hit him in the gut. He'd been trying to get his dad to listen for years with no luck. His hope had been to earn his father's ear by working hard and proving himself.

But so far that hadn't done any good.

He shook off the negative thoughts as the host returned. "Let me show you to your table, Mr. Watkins."

"Thank you." With a deep breath, he reminded himself to smile. Why did thoughts of his father always turn him into such a grouch? It needed to stop.

"Here you are, sir." The older man gave a slight almost-bow and walked away.

Ray took his seat. Facing the window, he allowed his gaze to roam the landscape. Even in the rain, it was glorious. In fact, the water on the canyon made colors of the rainbow distinguish themselves in the rocky layers. If only a picture could capture it. He studied it, trying to memorize how the light and water changed the scene.

"Good morning, Mr. Watkins." Miss Edwards appeared beside him almost instantaneously. "I see you are enjoying the view."

"Good morning." He turned so he could look at her. "Yes, I simply cannot get over how beautiful it is."

Her face appeared softer toward him today. Perhaps she was getting used to him. Now, if he could remind himself to act like a gentleman, maybe things would stay that way.

"Coffee?" She held the carafe close to his cup, waiting for his answer.

"Yes, please. And I believe I will have Chef's omelet again. Please give him my compliments. Everything I've had has been delicious."

"I will do that." Her eyes sparkled and then she walked away.

It was all he needed to boost his spirits.

He lifted his cup and took a sip of the coffee, savoring the strong, hearty blend. He knew Harvey had strict rules about the coffee served. It had to be made fresh so many times a day, and Ray had never had a bad cup at any Harvey establishment. This morning, it was the perfect addition to the view.

He pulled out his notebook, tearing his gaze away from the window. Last night he'd made a list of things they could do that would be good research for the investors. Once his father's men were back, they could tackle those. Hopefully, it would make Dad happy that he'd taken initiative on this project. There were so many ideas he had but wasn't sure exactly what his father was looking for or which direction the investors would wish to take.

He leaned back in his chair and watched the rain drizzle down. *Lord, I need Your direction. I want to honor my father and help the business. But I long to make a difference. To do some good with all the blessings You've bestowed upon us. Guide my thoughts and my words.*

He leaned over the table and his cup, watching the curtains of rain pass over the canyon. To the west, a break in the clouds gave him hope for some sunshine today. And as the light streaked through, it lit up the rocky walls, making them shimmer and glow.

"Here you go, Mr. Watkins. A piping-hot omelet." Miss Edwards set his plate down and refilled his coffee with the carafe in her other hand. "I hope you enjoy it." The smile she gave him was broader than he'd seen cross her face.

That head waitress—what was her name? Anniston?—appeared at Miss Edwards' side. "Emma Grace." She cleared her throat. "Forgive me, Miss Edwards. I need to speak with you immediately." The look on her face was stern and her skin ashen.

"Excuse me." Miss Edwards looked back at him, her smile gone.

He gave her a nod. Now that he knew her name was Emma Grace, he realized it suited her perfectly. Hopefully she wasn't in any kind of trouble. Miss Anniston was the head waitress, yes, but she hadn't seemed harsh or unreasonable. What could the trouble be?

He watched them cross the room and exit.

Hmmm. He'd have to wait and see.

The lovely scent of peppers and onions mixed with melted cheese and mushrooms wafted up to his nose. It made his stomach growl.

Bowing his head, he offered up a prayer of thanksgiving and then picked up his fork.

"Mr. Watkins?" The familiar voice brought Ray's head up.

"Good morning, Frank." Ray reached out a hand in greeting. "Please, have a seat."

The assistant chef sat down, a frown on his face. "I'm afraid I need to share some unpleasant news with you."

"Go ahead." He set his fork down and sat up a little straighter.

"While I was in Williams yesterday running errands, I was contacted by the sheriff. The phone line has been busy here, so he couldn't get through to you and asked if I could give you the message. I'm sorry to tell you this, but your companions are in the jail. Per the sheriff's request, I've informed Mr. Owens, but out of respect for you, I thought we should keep it quiet."

He felt his eyes widen. "Jail? Whatever for?"

"They were playing poker with some unsavory characters and things got out of hand. One of the men threatened to kill one of your men. There was a big fight. And when the sheriff investigated, he found a bunch of stolen goods in your men's possession."

Ray's breath left him in a great whoosh, and he leaned back against the chair. He'd had an inkling that the men weren't aboveboard, but he couldn't put his finger on why that thought had nagged at him. It hadn't been his place. Or so he thought.

Besides, he didn't know them all that well. But didn't Dad trust them? No matter now, he was the one here. That meant he'd have to clean up the mess. The question was, should he get his father's input before or after he visited the men in jail?

Emma Grace tread on Ruth's heels through the rotunda to the office behind the clerk's desk. Whatever Ruth had to say must be most serious indeed. Emma Grace gripped her fingers together and tried not to tie them into knots. But her stomach was already there. Had she done something wrong?

What if *he* had found her? If he had . . . then she needed

to run. Now. She'd promised herself when she left Boston that she wouldn't allow herself to be forced into marriage. Not for money. Not for any contract. Not ever. With a look over her shoulder, she tried to ascertain if anything or anyone was different.

As she followed the head waitress into Mr. Owens' office, she forced herself to breathe. In. Out. It wouldn't do her any good if she lost her wits. Ruth closed the door behind her.

"I'm sorry to interrupt you in the middle of breakfast, but this couldn't be helped. Caroline will make sure that your customers are taken care of, just in case." Ruth's features had been set and firm up to this point. Now, Emma Grace could clearly see a bit of fear in her eyes.

"All right." Her heart picked up its beat.

Ruth held out a slip of paper. "This came this morning to Mr. Owens. He's quite protective of all of us and wanted me to speak to you immediately and privately."

Emma Grace took the paper and inhaled a deep breath. Holding it, she read.

Unpleasant man questioning several Harvey estab-lishments looking for Emma Grace McMurray.

> E. M. Whitaker—Frisco
> Line Harvey Newsstand

"Emma Grace, you need to tell me. Is this *you* they're looking for?" Ruth's features softened into concern. "Or is it someone else? It scared me because I've never met another Emma Grace before . . . and . . . well, we just need to know."

"Do you know who E. M. Whitaker is?" She fisted her hands at her sides.

"No, I don't."

111

"But *I* do." Mr. Owens stepped into the room. "And you didn't answer the question." His brow was furrowed as he closed the door once again.

"Oh." Emma Grace's stomach dropped to her toes. This was it. She'd be fired and have nowhere to go. No friends in her corner. No family. Nothing except for the savings locked in her room. And that wouldn't get her very far. Not without work.

"Whitaker is a good friend of mine in Missouri. He keeps his ear to the ground and lets several of the managers know when something is amiss. Normally it's business related, but this caught my attention right away." Mr. Owens held out a hand for the telegram.

As she handed it over, her hands shook.

"Are you this Emma Grace?" His tone was flat.

A knot formed in her throat, making it difficult to swallow, but she gulped past it. She looked back and forth between Ruth and her manager. One, a new friend with the tentative roots of trust beginning to take hold. The other, her boss. A man she'd hoped would be a great protector and wonderful manager. But would he send her off? Accuse her of wrongdoing?

"It's all right." Ruth came toward her and put an arm around her shoulders. "Anything you say will be in the strictest confidence. We are here to help you, not condemn you."

The look on Mr. Owens' face was hard to decipher. Did he feel the same way?

"Answer the question, please." Ruth squeezed her shoulder.

"If Mr. Whitaker is a friend of yours, perhaps we could call him and get more information? I'll gladly pay for the call." She dropped her eyes to the floor.

"I take that to mean that you are Miss McMurray?" Mr. Owens raised his eyebrows.

She bit her lip, her thoughts racing. There was no other way. Lifting her chin, she looked the manager in the eye. "Yes. I am Emma Grace McMurray."

Ruth's tiny gasp made Emma Grace look at her. Her friend's eyes had widened, and her mouth made an *O*. Lying was *not* allowed by Harvey staff.

The manager walked around his desk and sat down. "Let's call Mr. Whitaker. I'm told we can reach Missouri now via phone lines, but I haven't tried it yet."

As he spoke to the operator to get the call to the correct location, all Emma Grace could do was stand there and look at her hands. What had she done? Would her job be at risk? Harvey rules were strict. Deception wasn't tolerated.

The seconds ticked by in slow agony.

"Everett?" A little pause. "It's good to hear your voice, my friend." Mr. Owens' voice took on a different tone. Almost lively, jovial. "I received your telegram, yes. I need to ask you a couple questions."

More silence stretched as they waited for what Mr. Whitaker would say.

"Do you know who the man was?"

Ruth squeezed Emma Grace's shoulders tighter.

"Umm-hmm. I see." Mr. Owens pursed his lips to the side. "No. I don't think so."

The office clock chimed as the room hushed once more. Mr. Whitaker must be talking a good bit.

A silent nod from their boss.

Emma Grace wanted to hold her breath, wishing there was a way to know what the man in Missouri was saying.

"Any idea where he is now?" Another nod. A humph. "All right then. Thank you." Owens hung up the earpiece. He shifted his gaze to them and leaned back in his chair. "No one knows who the man is or why he's looking for you. But a woman named Hazel in Kansas says that he told her it was a situation of life and death. Hazel lives close to the Harvey House and knows every bit of gossip around for miles."

"I remember Hazel." Emma Grace's words were soft. "I never spoke to her myself, but everyone knew who she was."

"If this *is* a situation of life and death, I think you need to tell us more. We need to know the truth, Miss Edwards—uh, I guess that's what you want to be called?" He quirked an eyebrow at her.

"Yes, please. Miss Edwards." The sting of tears hit her eyes. This couldn't be happening. "It's a very long story, I'm afraid. And I know that there are tables that need my attention. Perhaps we could discuss this later?" Somehow she had to buy herself some time to come up with a way to tell the truth without telling the *whole* truth.

"Your tables are in good hands, I assure you. Miss Anniston has it all taken care of." The man scratched his forehead. "Look, I know this must be difficult for you. But you are not leaving this office until we get some answers."

7

So, why does your employment card state that you are Emma Grace Edwards?" The manager's voice was a bit softer now, but he hadn't hesitated a moment before he began to interrogate her. "Are you in danger?"

There was no escape. No way to get away from the questions. The time to tell the truth was here. But how could they understand? "I . . . My father was murdered." It was the first time she'd said the words aloud to anyone. Her knees shook as if they couldn't support her any longer.

"Help me get her to a chair, Mr. Owens." Ruth's command made it sound like she was in charge of the whole place.

"Of course." He brought a chair over, and they eased Emma Grace down onto it.

"That's not a story you hear every day. Or live through, I guess." Ruth knelt in front of her and whispered, "I thought you said the nightmares were because you'd been kidnapped, but that it was a long time ago. . . . There's more? You didn't tell me your father had been murdered." The questions in her eyes made Emma Grace's heart squeeze. Her friend stood back up. "Why don't you start at the beginning?"

Emma Grace took several deep breaths and looked them

both in the eye. How could she be certain they would keep her secret? But did she really have a choice? She couldn't lie her way out of this one.

Lifting her chin, she closed her eyes for a brief moment. "May I ask that you both pledge to me that you will keep my confidence?"

"Yes." Ruth's answer was quick.

"Yes, of course. As long as it doesn't put anyone else in danger." Mr. Owens got up and pulled another chair up beside her and patted her arm.

"I need to know what Mr. Whitaker knows about this man looking for me."

"Not much other than a description. He didn't say why he was looking for you. And it sounded like the man knew for certain that you were a Harvey Girl—at least from Hazel's perspective. Tell us your story, and then I promise, I will do whatever is in my power to help." The manager leaned back in his chair.

The manager's promise didn't mean a lot to her. Men she trusted had made promises to her when she was young. Not one of them had been honored. But a glance at Ruth's concerned face gave Emma Grace the prodding she needed. She had nothing to lose at this point. Nothing and everything.

"My father wasn't the same after my mother died. He had always been a shrewd businessman—railroads. But after she passed, he changed. When I turned seventeen, he tried to convince me to marry one of his railroad associates. When I kept saying no, he put another plan into motion. The night I left, I found out he'd sold off contracts to men. Contracts in which they would gain a piece of the railroad if they married me in exchange for stock in their family's businesses, land, or gold. And to further entice them, he put in the contracts that when Father died, we both would then inherit it all. I found out later he'd negotiated with six men. Six men who paid substantial amounts in stocks, real estate, and money. Six men who all thought they could marry the heiress. Me." She hadn't spoken of her former life in so long, it almost didn't seem real anymore.

"Oh dear." Ruth just shook her head.

"When I confronted my father, he laughed and told me that I had no choice in the matter. I chose to leave and not give Father the chance to force me into marriage. But three days after I left, I picked up a newspaper that said my father had been murdered and that I was missing. It crushed me. I hadn't even said good-bye. Our last words to each other had been ugly." She took a deep breath. "The paper mentioned that my *fiancé*—the man who was first in line—was desperate to find me and wanted to ensure I was safe. Not knowing where else to turn, I contacted a man who had doted on me like a grandfather." She paused and bit her lip. It'd be best to not give his name. "He'd been our family solicitor for my mother's father until my father fired him. He was the only man I trusted because I knew he didn't agree with everything my father had done. Sadly, our solicitor informed me that even though all of the contracts couldn't be legally binding, whichever one was dated the earliest could be used to force me into marriage and join two business empires."

Staring at the wall across the room, she blinked away the thought. She tucked her chin to her chest and gripped her fingers tighter.

"I'm so sorry." Ruth's words were choked, as if she were about to cry.

"I know this is difficult, but I can imagine there's much more to the story. Please continue." The words were at least gentle as Mr. Owens reached forward again and patted her arm. Probably the only thing he knew to do to comfort a lady.

"I stayed in small towns, selling off pieces of jewelry I'd stashed in my reticule. They were of no use to me, other than to keep me hidden and alive. I had three different wigs made with different hair colors. I wore a different one at each new location. Switched back and forth with wearing glasses. But then the grief hit—realizing I was an orphan, that I had nothing. No one.

"So, I risked it all and called my grandfather's solicitor again from a busy train station. He told me that in the days since my father's death, the men who held contracts were in an uproar. Hiring lawyers. Bending the ears of judges who were family friends and filing suits left and right. Claiming that the contracts were valid and any one of them had to have the right to marry me and inherit, even in the light of my father's death. Especially since they'd all paid dearly to have the chance."

The more she told the story, the more the pain returned. Everything in her felt cold. "But as they fought and told the press that they would all find me and let me decide who I would marry, it didn't take a judge long to rule that Mr. Wellington—the man who held the first contract—had the law behind him."

"That's good, isn't it? Then there's only one man looking for you?" The innocence on Ruth's face touched a deep well in Emma Grace's heart. Oh, if only she could walk in such innocence of the greed of man.

"Any of the other contracts can still be legal if they find me and convince me to marry them—*Convince* being the judge's term and his nice way of saying *force*. Because that's how rich men do things." She tried to keep the contempt from her voice but failed. "It's all to gain control of my father's holdings. I've been told that Mr. Wellington wouldn't rest until he found me. That he was relentless and would stop at nothing to gain control of my father's empire. But all six of the men with contracts have a vested interest because they've already laid money on the line."

"This is truly a nightmare." Ruth rubbed her forehead. "No wonder you have difficulty sleeping. Is that why your father was killed?"

"That's what they don't know for certain. At least the last time I spoke with my family's former solicitor . . . and that was a long time ago. I was only seventeen when I left home, which made it even more advantageous for whoever was going to be my husband. They could do whatever they wanted with the money. If I had been twenty-one at the time, things would have been different for me. But that's why my father told me I *would* be married by my eighteenth birthday. He didn't want me having any say." She released a long breath and tamped down the all-too familiar anger that rose every time she thought of what he'd done. "He was worth hundreds of millions of dollars. That's why I've been running. The man who killed my father could very well be after me, to try to force me to marry him and then kill me as well. It could be Wellington . . . or it could be any one of the contract holders if they thought they'd been swindled out of the fortune."

"It could be any man who knows your father's dead and knows about his fortune." Mr. Owens shook his head and frowned. "I assume that *any* man you marry could get his hands on it, correct?"

The thought made Emma Grace shiver. She grimaced and bit her lip. "I asked why the judge couldn't declare me dead because I wanted nothing to do with any of it, but Mr. Scott told me that things weren't that simple. He couldn't—in good conscience—tell a judge that I was dead when I wasn't. He offered to help me and asked me where I was, but I hung up on him and kept running."

"Mr. Scott is the family solicitor?"

Gracious, she'd let it slip. What would he do with the information?

"What about your father's empire now?" Ruth looked as if she couldn't quite comprehend all the information thrown at her.

"There's a board handling the day-to-day proceedings of the railroads, but they aren't allowed to do anything else until I'm found. I've since learned that three of the men who hold contracts are on that operating board, so they have a vested interest to keep things running in a profitable manner."

Mr. Owens sat there with his head swinging back and forth between the two women like a pendulum. "And your plan was what? Just run away and let it all fall apart?" His tone held a hint of accusation, but for a man who understood business, she really couldn't blame him. She'd had the same thoughts.

"Fear was my biggest motivator. I wanted nothing of the money." She shrugged. "Frankly, I figured they would declare me dead at some point and I wouldn't have to face any of it ever again. But the law on presumption of death in Boston is fourteen years."

"That means nine more years. And you'd really be willing to give up your inheritance?" Her manager shook his head in disbelief.

It made her bristle. "Like I said, I want nothing of the money. I've only seen what it does to people. Rips families apart. Destroys lives."

Ruth leaned closer. "But you could also do so much good with it."

Emma Grace bit her lip before going on. "That's true. But it's only true if I'm alive. Because of my father's greed, there are six men out there who think that if they marry me, they can control his fortune. It's in the contracts—they would be at the helm. Not me. I refuse to be forced into marriage."

As her words sank in, she watched the faces of her superiors.

"Please don't think I'm selfish, but I don't want to end up like my father."

Mr. Owens' face shifted to the look of protector. "Then we will help keep you safe here, Miss Edwards."

"Of course we will." Ruth set her jaw.

The manager tapped his desk. "While I can't say I understand it all, I think I've heard enough for now. But as the manager here, I do need to know what made you become a Harvey Girl. And how did you get employment in the first place? We have strict regulations." Mr. Owens appeared put out at the thought he'd been hoodwinked somehow.

Emma Grace swallowed. "I brought a box with me that belonged to my grandmother. I changed the record of my grandmother's birth—I was named after her—and used her surname as my own. Emma Grace Edwards." She'd used the name so long now, that was who she was. "It wasn't hard. Her birth year was 1833, so I changed it to 1883. Please don't lecture me on the dishonesty of my actions. Believe me, I have carried the guilt for a long time.

"But I *knew* Mr. Fred Harvey. He had often dined at my home as I was growing up. The railroad and all. Before my mother died." Her heart pinched at the memories. "He was such a wonderful man. I loved hearing his stories. So, I knew exactly what to do to procure employment."

"But you lied."

Ruth looked up at the man. "With good cause, Mr. Owens. She was running for her life."

"I understand that but lying is against everything the Harvey name stands for." The man was looking less understanding and more irritated.

Which only served to make Emma Grace's anger well up. This was why men couldn't be trusted. Always jumping to conclusions, lying, and hypocritically not trusting anyone but themselves. "I don't wish to defend my actions to you, Mr. Owens. Like I said, I knew Fred Harvey. Personally. Did you?"

Her boss sputtered. "No . . . not personally . . ."

"Well, I know beyond the shadow of a doubt that he would help me if he were still alive. I am asking for understanding. Just like I would ask of Mr. Harvey. I don't think you know what those men who are after me are capable of doing. I gave up everything and would do it all over again if it meant that I was able to live a life free of the chains of wealth. You have no idea what greed and obsession do to men. Or maybe perhaps you do?" It was her turn to raise an eyebrow in his direction. "I wasn't about to be auctioned off to the highest bidder."

She gulped down the lump in her throat. "I lost my mother, my baby brother, my father, and every other relative I had. But it didn't have to be like this. Perhaps my father would still be alive today if he'd been able to let go of his greed." The surge of anger built behind her words. "I don't know who killed him, but what if they *are* after me next? I was kidnapped and held against my will for eighteen days when I was a child . . . all because men argued over who would have control of a railroad spur. Did you hear me? They *kidnapped* a *child*. For a few miserable miles of track! And now we're talking about hundreds of millions of dollars. You don't think any one of them would do oh-so-much worse?"

His face showed his horror. "My deepest apologies. I'm simply trying to understand—"

"That nightmare will haunt me for the rest of my life, Mr. Owens." Emma Grace pressed her lips together and told herself she would not fall apart in front of him. "I'm sorry that I lied to get a job. But I didn't believe I had any other choice. I have done everything else honorably, I promise. And I will continue to do so if you'll allow me." Sucking in a long breath, she lifted her shoulders. That was not the way to speak to her boss. But she couldn't pull her words back now.

She desperately needed the job. And it was all she knew. Her fate rested in Mr. Owens' hands. And her distrust probably didn't win her any favors.

He stood from the chair beside her and took his time stepping back to the chair behind his desk. Then he eased down onto it and steepled his fingers together under his chin.

Ruth patted Emma Grace's shoulder. The warmth of her friendship was the only thread holding her in her seat.

Emma Grace watched them both. A tear slipped down Ruth's cheek. Mr. Owens' features switched from horror to disgust and then softened. Several minutes passed, with the only sound the ticking of the clock.

The balding manager leaned forward. "I see no other course of action you could have taken that would have been any better. I can't say I agree with your actions in light of your inheritance, but we can discuss that at another time. Since your work is exemplary, I have no problem continuing your employment, Miss Edwards. As I said, we will do everything within our power to protect you—and not because you are worth a fortune. But because you are valuable to us for who you are."

His last words made tears spring to her eyes.

"We will speak of this to no one. All of our jobs could be on the line if word gets out." He pointed a finger at them both.

Emma Grace relaxed and closed her eyes, tears slipping

down her cheeks. Relief spread its tingly fingers throughout her midsection.

"*But* we need to discuss the safety of our customers and the rest of the Harvey Girls. If you keep any information from us that puts anyone else in danger, there will be repercussions."

Opening her eyes to look at him straight on, she nodded. "I understand, sir. Thank you."

"No one else knows?" His pointed gaze pierced through her.

Her head went back and forth in a fast motion. "No. I haven't told a soul since I left five years ago."

Ruth stood up. "Five years is a long time, Mr. Owens. I think we are pretty safe here."

"I agree. But as Mr. Whitaker informed us, there *is* someone looking for her."

"There's probably been any number of men hired to look for her all these years. But the clues can't be very fresh by this point. Maybe this man is just grasping at straws." The head waitress put on a weak smile and turned to her. "The first several days you were here, you wore your hair differently and didn't wear glasses. Since then, you've worn your hair tight and pulled back and you've worn glasses."

"Yes. I'm sorry for the dishonesty."

"That's not why I'm pointing that out. What I want to know is, what made you change your appearance here? I thought you said you felt welcomed and at home." The concern on her friend's face was more than she deserved.

"I did. I do. . . . But Caroline mentioned during her training about how nervous she was because the customers we get here are much wealthier than ones she had served before. It made me realize that I hadn't fully thought through my plan to come here—that the upper class from all over the country will be the ones who can afford to come out here and stay at this hotel. The only thing I'd been thinking about was putting as much distance between me and . . . where I'm from.

"So I did what I could to change my appearance without it being too much of a shock to people here. I couldn't risk someone from my past recognizing me. To gain control of my father's empire, one of those men has to marry me."

While she tried to keep her tone calm, her heart sped up. Mr. Wellington was a monster in her mind. He was the one with the legal contract. He was the one who met with her dad the night she left. The night Father . . . died. So it was Wellington who haunted her dreams. Chasing her down no matter where she went. But she couldn't let him find her.

"Which means . . ." Mr. Owens tapped his desk and then looked up at her, his eyes laced with fear. "They are all hoping you're alive. They just don't know where."

8

The sheriff led Ray to the small building that served as his office and the jail. "I'm sorry you had to come down here, but I'm glad you did."

"Is the telegraph office close by?" Ray swiped a hand down his face. In his hurry to leave, he hadn't taken the time to contact Dad. It would be best to get his father's opinion before he faced the men.

"It is. Do we need to stop by there?"

"Yes, I need to contact my father." He followed the sheriff's steps as they crossed the dusty street and the wind whipped up a swirl of dirt beside them. "What are the charges against the men?"

Opening the door to the telegraph office, the man shook his head. "Well, they were in the middle of a brawl when I came in on 'em. Apparently, the others at the table accused them of cheatin'. Your fellas didn't look like the fightin' type, but they were handy with their fists. Doc's got two of the other men at his place. Not sure how bad off they are."

126

The sheriff put his hands on his hips. "But then we have the theft charges."

After a brief discussion, Ray sat down to compose a telegram to his father. Who knew what the senior Watkins would think of all this. "Thank you for the information." He shook his head at the sheriff. "This might take a while."

"I understand." The man went to the door. "I'll be at the jail. I'll show you the evidence there."

An hour later, Ray walked over to the jail, his heart heavy. Dad was furious. And, of course, worried about his reputation.

"Glad you made it." The sheriff stood up and put a skeleton key into a cabinet behind his desk. When he opened it up, he pointed. "This is what we pulled off of your men."

Ray couldn't believe what his eyes were seeing. Jewels were strewn across the shelf. He blinked several times and wiped a hand down his face. The Watkins empire included many jewelry stores. What if his father's company was accused of being behind the theft?

"Each one of 'em had some stashed in their pockets."

Ray looked toward the back, where he assumed the men were being held. "I don't even know what to say."

"That's what I thought. Especially when they started spouting off about who they worked for. But I had just gotten a call from the sheriff down the line in Kingman. There was a jeweler traveling with a lot of precious stones, and he noticed half of them were missing after the stop in Williams, but he couldn't report it until the train stopped. His description of what was missing matches all that you see here. I called to confirm it this morning."

Why had the men done it? They obviously made plenty of money from the company. Ray couldn't wrap his brain around it. It made absolutely no sense.

The sheriff pointed to the telephone. "Do you need to let anyone at the hotel know anything? Feel free to make a call."

Ray picked up the old candlestick model phone. Without a rotary dial like he was used to having in his office back in Chicago, he'd have to go through the operator. He put the receiver to his ear and spoke into the mouthpiece, directing the operator to the El Tovar. How embarrassing to have to explain to Mr. Owens that his men would not be returning and to please pack up their things and cancel their room reservations. What a nightmare.

After he hung up the phone, Ray placed his hands on his hips.

The sheriff jerked his head toward the hallway. "You don't have to see them if you don't want to. When the judge comes, he'll take care of them."

"No. It's only proper that I speak with them."

"I'll take you back then." The sheriff got up and headed down the hall.

Ray followed, a million different thoughts vying for attention. He needed divine intervention here to say the right words.

When they stopped in front of a cell, Ray shoved his hands into his pockets.

Michael stood first. "Ray—Mr. Watkins." His Adam's apple bobbed as he swallowed, embarrassment and shame clear on his face.

But George and Ben simply looked irritated as they took their time coming to their feet.

George tipped his chin at him. "Are you here to bail us out?"

Ray cinched his lips and gave a slow shake of his head. "No. I'm sorry, but I'm not."

With a slump of his shoulders, Michael sat down hard. "I had a feeling you would say that."

128

None of them looked like the men he'd traveled with. They were rumpled. Disheveled. Unshaven. Filthy. Which made him wonder, which image of the men was true—the polished businessmen, or this one in front of him now?

George narrowed his eyes and approached the bars. "It's the old man, isn't it? You heard from him?"

"Yes, I did." He maintained eye contact and was saddened by the anger he saw there. "What you did was a bad representation of my father's business. It was wrong. Illegal and immoral. And then you hurt men in the process. That's unacceptable."

A surly grin lifted Ben's lips. A look he'd never seen on the man. "What exactly did the old man say?"

"I regret to inform you that he said you are all fired and will have to fend for yourselves here."

"Figured as much." George crossed his arms over his chest and sat back down on a cot in the corner.

"My father built his company on morals and ethics. You, gentlemen, disrespected the Watkins name. You broke the law. Now you have to reap the consequences."

Bolting back to his feet, George charged the bars and gripped them with both hands. "You really don't know what your daddy does, do you?"

"Where do you think we learned our behavior, *Junior*?" Ben spat on the floor.

———— | |————

Stretching out in her bed, Emma Grace yawned. No light peeked into the room from the window high up near the ceiling. Even though her room was in the basement, it was nice that someone had thought to at least put some small windows in. It made all the difference in the world to her. Her body was awake, though, even when she could tell it was still before sunrise.

With another stretch, she rolled over onto her side and glanced at the clock. 6:10. Wouldn't it be glorious if she could actually sleep in? The thought made her chuckle to herself. She was too accustomed to the long workdays.

But today was Thursday. A day off.

It made her smile. She hadn't taken one in the two weeks she'd been there because she'd volunteered to fill in where they needed help. It had kept her busy. Something she wanted to keep her mind off things.

But Ruth had insisted. Now Emma Grace had a whole day off, and then on Monday there was another one on her schedule. Another requirement from the head waitress. Ruth said she had been looking far too weary and stressed.

Thankfully, the nightmares hadn't returned, even after the discussion with Mr. Owens and Ruth at the beginning of the week. But she felt the strain on her body. It was hard to relax when her worst fears were coming to light. Someone was actively looking for the person she used to be.

Maybe today, she could forget all of that and simply enjoy the day. She'd been longing to spend more than a minute or two over at the Hopi House. The Indians who lived and worked there were refreshing to be around. Warm, genuine, giving. It didn't matter that people were coming and going, they kept working at their art and welcomed people, sharing stories of their people and heritage.

Decision made. She'd go watch the sunrise from the rim, then spend the day at the Hopi House.

After that, she could explore a bit more of the rim and watch the sunset. Sometime soon she'd like to explore more, but there were rules about the Harvey Girls venturing down into the canyon on their own. She'd have to look at the schedule and see who had a day off lining up with one of hers. Someone who was brave enough to hike down the steep trail.

Excited to get the day started and have a change of scenery, Emma Grace dressed casually for the day. Rather than pulling her hair back into a tight bun, she braided her long locks and threw the braid over her shoulder. Placing a wide-brimmed hat over top, she smiled into the mirror on her dresser. She pushed her glasses up on her nose. She was a far cry from the Emma Grace McMurray of Boston.

With one hand, she grabbed her key on its long chain and put it around her neck, while the other hand opened the door. She exited and locked the door and headed for the stairs.

After the conversation with Mr. Owens and Ruth, she'd come back to her room and had a good long cry. The effort she'd poured into staying hidden had exhausted her. She was so ready to just live her life and stop worrying about the past.

But that wasn't an option for her.

This was the life she'd chosen when she ran away.

With a shake of her head, she pushed the thoughts back. The only way for her to survive would be to find some happiness in her surroundings. Ruth's friendship was stronger since the confrontation. It felt so good to have someone in her corner. Each night, they'd had tea together and chatted. Not about anything consequential, just about their days— funny things the customers said or did, who left the largest tips, who needed the most attention. Normal, regular chats for a couple of Harvey Girls.

Refreshing. That's what it had been. Soothing for her soul. As she ventured out into the rotunda, she decided against breakfast and headed through the Rendezvous Room to the front doors. Buttoning up her long wool coat, she prepared for the chill that would surely accompany her outside.

The dark of the night was just beginning to hint at the start of a new day.

With brisk steps, she headed for a spot behind the Hopi House that had become her favorite place to sit. She pulled her gloves out of her pockets, then wrapped her scarf around her neck several times.

The canyon was quiet this morning. No wind. No chatter of tourists. Just a star-filled sky giving way in the east to the sun. The stars over the canyon were her favorite. Like a black velvet blanket stretched as far as the eye could see with millions of shimmering lights dancing on top. When she'd lived in Boston, she'd never seen stars like that. And here, there was just something about sitting on the edge of the great crevasse and looking up to the sky. The first time, it had made her dizzy. Now, it was her favorite thing to do.

Taking careful steps, she crept to the very edge and lowered herself to where she could sit and dangle her legs.

For some reason, as the sun began to peek over the eastern horizon, her thoughts recalled words. Words she hadn't thought of for so long.

> The spacious firmament on high,
> With all the blue ethereal sky,
> And spangled heavens, a shining frame,
> Their great Original proclaim.
> The unwearied sun from day to day
> Does his Creator's power display
> And publishes to every land
> The work of an Almighty hand.

She was transported back to when she was a little girl. Back when Mother made sure they all attended church each Sunday. That big cathedral of a church where all the wealthiest of the city went. She could hear her mother's voice—clear as an angel's—beside her, singing her favorite hymn.

> What though in solemn silence all
> Move round the dark terrestrial ball;
> What though nor real voice nor sound
> Amid their radiant orbs be found;
> In reason's ear they all rejoice,
> And utter forth a glorious voice,
> For ever singing as they shine,
> 'The hand that made us is divine.'

Funny how she could remember the words and the tune even after all these years. Her mother had been gone a long time.

Too bad God left with her. It's not like she knew Him all that well anyway, but for a little girl, she'd been devastated by the loss.

The sky began to change quickly now, and the canyon awoke. The birds who endured the cold winter nights began to sing their early morning songs. Life began to whisper "good morning" around her.

The sun streaked the sky with pinks and lavenders that changed the colors of the canyon walls every few minutes. Emma Grace shoved every thought of church, God, and hymns to the back of her mind and tried to imagine how she would paint the scene before her.

For a couple of years, she'd had a tutor teaching her art. They'd dabbled in oil painting for a while and then water-colors. The oils had been her definite favorite. If only she'd had more talent. She'd love to be able to paint what she saw in this moment.

Footsteps sounded to her left, which made her heart speed up its pace. She shifted her gaze in that direction so she could see who was approaching.

"Ah, Miss Edwards." A familiar voice greeted her.

"Mr. Henderson, how nice to see you." Her heartbeat relaxed at the sight of the assistant chef. "You must not have the breakfast shift today?"

"You would be correct." He pointed beside her. "May I join you?"

"Of course. As much as I'd like to claim the whole canyon as mine, I think there's plenty of room for us both."

His soft laughter echoed in the still morning air as he took a seat several feet away. It almost made him look like a big kid when he scooted to the edge and let his legs hang over the rim as well. "How generous of you. What brings you out here? A much-needed day off?"

"Yes. This view calls to me. The sunrise is amazing."

"I will never tire of it."

The light grew and chased the stars away to the west. "I agree with you. I don't see how it could ever be boring."

"I love watching the Creator at work." Mr. Henderson's voice conveyed his smile.

She didn't even have to look to see it. What was it with people and the Creator? First Ruth, and now the chef. Several of the other Harvey Girls kept inviting her to some makeshift church service too, but she'd declined them all.

"I take it you don't believe in God?"

This time, she turned to him and searched his face. Honest. Friendly. He seemed sincere, and as she'd worked with him for a while now, he'd always struck her as respectful and hard-working. "It's not that I don't believe in God. I just don't think He really cares. I mean, how many people are there on this planet anyway? There's not enough time for all of us." She shrugged and waited for his response. Surely he couldn't have an explanation.

"Sounds like you've been hurt."

She let out a humph. "More times than I can count."

"By people, right?"

"Of course. God too."

He nodded and looked down into the canyon. "How did God hurt you?"

"He abandoned me." She didn't want to sound pitiful or angry. She was simply stating the facts.

Mr. Henderson didn't respond. How could he? There was no excuse he could give, no platitude he could convey, no Scripture he could recite that would change her mind.

A couple of birds in the tree to the left had begun their chitter-chatter.

Emma Grace was thankful for the break in the silence. Had she offended the man? Maybe she'd said too much.

"Look over there." Mr. Henderson pointed to the other rim of the canyon. The sun had shown through a crack in one of the canyon's many divides and lit up the other side with a streak that shone like pure gold. "I've never seen anything like it. No wonder the miners are always coming here searching for treasure."

"There are mines here?"

"Oh, several. The Orphan Mine is the one you'll hear the most about. These rocks are supposedly filled with ore."

That surprised her. "Why would they allow mining here? It's too beautiful to destroy."

Mr. Henderson held up his hands. "Don't look at me. I have wondered the same thing myself." He shook his head.

Questions filled her mind. "Mr. Henderson, I'm curious. . . . How would they even attempt it? How do they get down to wherever they're mining?"

He held out a hand to her—like a gentleman offering a handshake. "Please, call me Frank. Mr. Henderson can be reserved for when we are on duty, but it seems like such a mouthful."

She took his hand and shook it. "Then I insist that you call me Emma Grace." Raising her eyebrows, she crossed her arms over her middle. "Well?"

"Oh yes, the mines. I don't really have any answers, other than the fact that Daniel Hogan is the one who filed for the Orphan copper claim. His miners use a trail called the Battleship Trail—named for a rock formation—but he also built another trail, if you can even call it that. I hear it's nothing more than a rope, a couple of crude ladders, pegs shoved into holes, and toeholds that he chiseled into the wall of the canyon. He calls it 'the slide' while everyone else likes to call it 'the Hummingbird Trail.' Apparently, he's quite good at using it and claims it's a lot faster."

Emma Grace leaned her head a bit over the edge and looked at the sheer cliff. "Faster or not, I don't think I would be brave enough to try this Hummingbird Trail. But I do look forward to trying the Bright Angel Trail soon. I hear it's quite magnificent."

"I'm taking one of our guests down the trail on Monday. It's beautiful, but it is quite a hike to come back up it. That's the hard part."

"I have another day off on Monday. Miss Anniston insisted, since I haven't taken any time off." She bit her lip. Was it too forward to ask? While she and Frank worked together, she really didn't know him all that well. "Is there any chance I could accompany you on Monday?"

Frank slapped his thigh. "That's a splendid idea. I don't think Mr. Watkins would mind that one bit, seeing as he always reserves one of your tables." He gave her a knowing look.

"Oh, it's Mr. Watkins you're accompanying?" It made her swallow hard. Not that she disliked the man. "He likes the view. And I do have the best tables."

"He's really quite down to earth. We had a chat about photography one day, and since then, we've had several opportunities to discuss everything from faith to art to food."

"I see. Well, as long as you don't think he will mind."

"I think it would be a nice outing." He looked away and then rubbed his hands together. "There's not any chance that Miss Anniston is off as well? We could invite her along." When he glanced back at her, there was a glimmer of hope in his eyes.

"No. I'm sorry. We can't both be off at the same time."

"Oh yes. Of course, you're the assistant head waitress. I should have thought of that." He scooted back and lifted himself to his feet. "Well, it has been a lovely morning chat, Emma Grace, but I'm afraid I must attend to other things so that I will be ready for the lunch rush." He dusted off his trouser legs and gave her a nod. "I look forward to Monday."

"Me too." She gave him a smile. "Thank you for allowing me to come with you."

"You're welcome. You are going to love it." He waved his good-bye.

There were times—every once in a while—when she felt comfortable around men. Mr. Henderson was definitely one of them. He didn't seem to put on airs, he was honest, and he was funny. How interesting that he and Mr. Watkins had spent so much time together.

Normally people of Mr. Watkins' class didn't associate with the working class. Then again, Mr. Watkins had surprised her with his actions on multiple occasions. And, of course, Mr. Owens wouldn't deny the man any request, even if it was wanting to spend time with the staff.

What would Mr. Watkins be like out of her normal world? Where he was the guest, and she was the waitress?

He'd been gone a couple days this week. Mr. Owens had informed her he was away on business, but he would be returning. Their manager seemed anxious for his return, wanting to make everything perfect for the son of the wealthiest man in Chicago—not that she could blame him. That was his job.

But the longer she was around staff who catered to every whim of the rich simply because they had money, the more she disliked this whole cultural divide. Why couldn't they simply take care of the guests because they were customers? That's what good service was about and what Mr. Fred Harvey himself portrayed in every business plan—that no matter who the customer was, they deserved the best of the Harvey service.

Emma Grace had been on both sides of it: being the richest of the rich and working herself to the bone to keep herself clothed and fed. If God were really up there, and if He truly cared, why didn't He break down the barriers between all people? Didn't the Bible say that He loved everyone the same?

With a shrug, she got to her feet. It didn't really matter. Maybe it was a question she could ask Ruth or Frank next time they brought up God. Probably a question that would make them squirm and perhaps never bring up religion with her again. Frank hadn't responded to her question today, after all.

As she walked back around to the Hopi House, she let herself get excited about the hike on Monday. Thoughts of Mr. Watkins flooded her mind again. It irritated her that she couldn't seem to banish him from her thoughts. He popped up all too often.

Before, she'd thought it was because he sat at her table.

She saw him at every meal. But now, he'd been gone a few days. What kept bringing him to mind?

She opened the wooden door to the Hopi House and ducked as she walked through. Even though it was probably an inch or two higher than the top of her head, her instincts always made her slouch down, just in case.

"Welcome back to Hopi House." A beautiful dark-skinned woman greeted her from where she sat on the floor, weaving a basket. Feet bare. Dressed in the traditional garb Emma Grace was getting used to seeing. Her long black hair was plaited on either side of her head. "Come." The woman beckoned to her with a smile and a wave of her hand. "I will teach you how we weave."

Not needing another invitation, Emma Grace returned the smile and removed her long coat. Without thinking twice, she sat on the floor next to the woman and arranged her skirts to cover her legs. "You recognize me?"

"Yes." The woman pointed to her chest. "I'm Chuma. You work over at the hotel and came in last week sometime while I was making jewelry."

She nodded. "You are very observant. I'm Emma Grace. Thank you for your warm welcome."

Chuma grinned, showing a missing tooth on the bottom. She was young, probably around eighteen. "I teach you how to weave. Okay?"

"Okay." Clasping her hands into her lap, she leaned forward to see what Chuma was doing. Her hands moved with a quickness that attested to years of experience. The peaceful atmosphere around Emma Grace made her feel safe and wanted. She let everything else fade away and focused on Chuma's delicate fingers.

The day passed in Emma Grace's many failed attempts at weaving. She'd lost count of how many times she'd had to start over. But with great patience, her new friend encouraged her to keep at it. By the time her legs had fallen asleep from sitting on the floor for so long, she had completed the entire bottom of a basket with a whole inch of lopsided woven reeds making the sides. With a giggle, she held it up for Chuma's inspection.

"Very good." Her chin bobbed up and down while her smile stretched across her face.

It made Emma Grace laugh harder. "You're being nice."

"Yes, I am. But I tell the children the same thing when they begin."

"And when exactly do they learn?"

Chuma's eyes sparkled. "When they've passed four winters."

"You mean a four-year-old knows how to weave?"

Chuma giggled. At that moment, one of the Hopi children ran over to Chuma and held up her completed basket. The little girl had started at the same time as Emma Grace that morning. Her long lashes fluttered against her chubby cheeks as she lifted her basket. The Hopi woman took the offering, and the child came to Emma Grace's side, tilted her head, and patted Emma Grace's cheek. "You practice."

With a skip in her step, the child ran off while Chuma and Emma Grace laughed until tears slid down their faces.

9

Please accept my sincerest apologies." Ray handed over the stolen jewels. He hadn't wasted time with pleasantries, just spilled out the honest truth, hoping the man would forgive them. The deputy who'd accompanied him from Williams stood at the door.

Mr. Krueger inspected each piece, a frown furrowing his brow. For several moments, he didn't speak. Then he placed the jewels into the safe, closed the door, and locked it. Turning back toward Ray, he lifted his chin. "Your father and I have done business together for many years."

"Yes, sir. I know."

Mr. Krueger held up a hand. "Please let me finish. While your father is a brilliant businessman and has had some marvelous ideas, this was too much of a coincidence for me. Other questionable thefts have happened around your father's men. I hate to say it, but yes, it sounds fishy. I know it's not the best position for you, but please relay to your father that I will no longer be able to conduct any transactions with him." The jewelry store owner shook his head.

Ray stepped forward. While he understood exactly where the man was coming from, he knew that his father would be furious to cut these ties. "Mr. Krueger—"

"No, son. There's no changing my mind. I think it's best that you simply leave." The man put a hand on his shoulder and gave a gentle nudge toward the door.

Ray picked up his bag and exited. Nothing could be said to fix the situation. He'd done the right thing by coming in person, but that wouldn't matter to Dad. As he walked to the train station and parted ways with the deputy, who had other business to attend to, he thought through the best way to word a telegram. But no matter what he said, Dad would blame him.

Later that morning, the train's gentle sway did nothing to relax Ray as he rode back to Williams. His thoughts hadn't given him any rest since he'd gotten word that Dad's men were in jail. Now, every muscle in his neck and shoulders screamed with the tension. Going over the events didn't help, but that was all his mind wanted to focus on.

Everything had happened so fast. The judge demanded to hear their case the very day Ray had gone to visit his father's men in jail. But Michael, George, and Ben had attempted to schmooze the judge when they appeared before him. Not a smart choice. The judge was the most hard-lined, no-nonsense man Ray had ever met. Things were definitely different out west. Especially in the Arizona Territory where the reputation of Tombstone loomed.

The worst part was that one of the men involved in the brawl had died, and the judge made it clear that he hated murderers and thieves.

In a swift ruling, they were sentenced to ten years in jail for the theft, and then a trial would take place about the murder. Not that it would be much of a trial. The judge also made that clear. But which man would end up taking the murder sentence? Or would they all?

It was such a shame.

His dad hadn't reacted with compassion either—something that *did* surprise Ray just a little. Compassion hadn't been something his father had shown him much of, but these men had been loyal to his father for years. Dad always treated his men differently. Yet, when he'd said he washed his hands of them, he'd meant it.

Ray had asked the sheriff and judge for permission to deliver the stolen jewels back to their owner so he could apologize. The sheriff didn't look all too trusting—and why should he? The men in jail worked for Ray . . . well, technically, for his father's company. But the judge had approved it and sent him on his way with a deputy escort.

Ray hadn't realized how difficult it would be to apologize for something he hadn't done. But he'd felt responsible and wanted to do the right thing. He just hadn't thought through how Mr. Krueger would react. And the impact his words would have on Ray—especially the part about the other questionable thefts.

That part couldn't be reconciled in Ray's mind. How could that be a coincidence? Another matter he would have to speak to his father about. And it probably wouldn't go well.

Wiping a hand down his face, he let out a long breath. Every muscle in his body was weary and tight all at the same time. His neck felt like he'd tied it in knots last night as he tossed and turned. He hadn't found sleep because George's and Ben's words kept echoing in his mind.

"You really don't know what your daddy does, do you?"

"Where do you think we learned our behavior, Junior?"

The implication was obvious, but was it just a desperate

attempt to clear their names? To blame someone else? Should he mention *that* to his dad? The fact that his father's men would slander him so easily did not bode well.

"Classic criminal behavior" was what the sheriff called it.

Shaking his head, Ray sat up straighter. Maybe the lawman was correct. He wasn't responsible for other people's actions and decisions. He was only responsible for his own. Something he understood all too well. He needed to shake this off and move on.

Alone in the railcar, he leaned back against the seat. Nothing could be accomplished with worry about the unknown. Perhaps he and Dad needed to have a talk, man to man. He could air his concerns, and Dad could tell him that it was all contrived. A fact he should know, anyway.

He closed his eyes. Yes. That's what he should do.

He took several deep breaths. Maybe he could sleep for just a little bit . . .

"Bring my horseless carriage around, please, Jones."

As Ray watched the servant retreat, fury burned inside him. Once Jones was out of earshot, he let the words he'd wanted to say to his father spew out in a torrent. "You'd think after all these years, after everything I've done to appease him, he could at least allow me to come alongside him in the business. But no. It doesn't matter what I do, it will never be good enough. He'll never think of me as anything other than a child."

"Then I suggest you stop acting like one." Mother's sharp voice sliced through him.

His heart raced as he turned to face her. Dad was a force to be reckoned with to be sure . . . but Mother was even worse. "I . . . didn't realize you were home."

"That was quite obvious, my dear." The words that were an endearment to most people fell on him like sharp icicles.

She used words as weapons. And no one ever dared to go up against the fierce Eleanor Watkins.

"Now . . . are you quite done with your tantrum?" Lifting her chin, she looked down her nose at him.

Swallowing the lump in his throat, Ray looked away. Then, with a deep breath, he forced himself to look at her. If he didn't keep eye contact, she'd rail at him some more. He clenched his jaw and stared.

"Don't look at me like that, Ray. I'm not against you. Your father is a tyrant, yes, but he knows his business well. In due time, he will hand over the reins to you and all my hopes for you will be fulfilled."

The fact that she called Dad a tyrant almost made him laugh. It was amazing he'd survived childhood in this home. "Fine, Mother. Your concern moves me." He kept his tone flat.

She patted his arm and shifted toward the door. "I'm always here for you. Now, be a good boy and do as your father asks." The words slithered over him and made him shiver.

He wasn't twelve. Nor did he believe that his mother actually cared about him and would be there for him. Ever. The woman was shrewd and vicious.

The rumble of an engine made him shake his head of the thoughts. Jones brought Ray's brand-new 1901 Locomobile around the curved drive and up to the house.

An outing was in order. Maybe even to Canada. The thought was ludicrous, but appealing nonetheless.

He nodded at Jones. "Thank you."

"You're welcome, Mr. Watkins."

Ray wiped at the seat, climbed into the automobile, and shifted it into gear. He took off down the driveway entirely too fast, but he didn't care. The bricks of the long drive made the tires bounce and jostle at this speed.

He needed to let off some steam, and right now, this was the only outlet he had.

As he rounded the corner to the street, a red hoop rolled out in front of him, followed by a towheaded little boy with his stick.

"No!" Ray pulled on the brake as his heart pounded in his chest.

The tires screeched.

The automobile lurched.

A hideous thud echoed.

Ray woke with a start. Bolting to his feet, he forced air into his chest. Thankfully, there was no one else in his first-class car this morning. He paced the aisle for several minutes, hoping to vanquish the memory. The dream always played out like a motion picture. He had no control over it. Just had to watch it in horror. And while he knew in his heart that he wasn't the same man he'd been then, deep guilt and regret threatened to pull him back into the darkness.

The darkness his parents banished him to.

The darkness that God had rescued him from.

The little boy had miraculously lived. Thomas Wright. A name Ray would never forget. The child's arm had been broken, but other than that, he was relatively unscathed.

Mrs. Wright had called it a miracle.

Dad called it foolishness.

While his parents yelled at him and gave him the silent treatment for weeks when they were in private, in front of the newspapers and their friends, they always talked about the bad parenting skills of the Wrights.

Ray and Eleanor Watkins declared to anyone and everyone who would listen that it wasn't *their* son's fault that a child ran out in front of Ray Junior's car. *"Children should be home at that hour of the evening. What kind of parent al-*

lows their child to roam the streets when night is falling?"
And so on and so forth.

Mother and Dad went back to their normal lives the very next day and encouraged Ray to do the same. But he couldn't.

So, he visited the Wrights. Every day. They treated him more like family than his own did. And when little Thomas told Ray how God had saved him that night, Ray couldn't help but begin his own search. He'd sought out Reverend James, and he'd found new life. Forgiveness. Peace.

Ray walked back to his seat. As he lowered himself to sit, he reached for his leather satchel. A gift from Mother when he'd gone off to college.

He ran a hand over the smooth, buttery leather and then lifted the flap. The contents were in neat order, as he knew they would be. He'd always been meticulous and a perfectionist, probably because Mother was that way and required it of him. But after the accident, he'd found that the best way to calm his nerves and quiet the chaos was to organize. His day. His belongings. His desk. His satchel.

Reverend James encouraged him to give that over to the Lord too, something Ray struggled with on a daily basis. His mind handled things better when everything was neat and in order and when his day was planned out. But the good reverend reminded Ray that he needed to be willing to listen to God's plan and not be so focused on his own. Because Ray could plan out his entire life, but if that wasn't God's will, what good did it do him?

Before the accident, Ray dreamed of following in his father's footsteps and one day being at the helm of the Watkins empire. But after he got saved, that dream changed. Oh, he still tried to honor his father by doing his best for the family business, but he had this feeling deep inside that God had something else in store for him. Until he knew what that was, he was committed to his father's company. But he could feel a yearning . . . some kind of stretching and growing going on inside.

Since there hadn't been any messages sent down from heaven to tell him what to do, Ray pulled out his notepad and got to work. If Dad wanted detailed reports, then he would write them. And Ray would keep making lists of ideas for how they could use the money they had to help other people. So far, Dad hadn't been inclined to listen to any of his ideas, but God could change his father's heart. Of that he was certain.

The first few days after telling the truth had been some of the worst Emma Grace had ever endured. Worry and fear followed her around like rabid dogs nipping at her heels.

But Ruth's positive tone and constant encouragement chiseled at the wall of fear Emma Grace had built around her heart. It didn't even bother her that Ruth had shared her favorite verses of Scripture. In fact, they'd been comforting.

Frankly, she was too exhausted to live in fear anymore. Tired of the façade. Tired of hiding. Not that she wanted to be found. That was the last thing she wanted, but she needed friends. She needed a family. Ruth reminded her over and over that she didn't have to carry all of this alone. Wouldn't it be nice if that were true?

Emma Grace wanted to believe it could be.

Then, yesterday morning, before their shift started, Ruth pulled her off to the side and said Mr. Owens had done some more investigating and didn't think there was any reason for Emma Grace to worry. The man that had been inquiring about Emma Grace McMurray seemed to have disappeared and hadn't asked around at any other Harvey establishments.

Emma Grace finally felt like she could breathe again.

Now, the dining room hummed with the sound of conversation and silverware clinking against the china. She had gone from table to table for the past eight hours. Her feet ached, but the dinner rush was still in full swing.

Where were all these people coming from? Granted, there were trains arriving every day, but it wasn't like there were all that many accommodations at the Grand Canyon. At least not decent accommodations that most of these wealthy people would consider using. She couldn't imagine many would want to rent the tent cabins during the winter weather they'd been having. But the hotel had been completely full, and Mr. Owens said that reservations were booked for the next several weeks.

The flood of customers in January might be a surprise to her, but at least she could enjoy the tips and know that there would be plenty to keep her busy. Not that she ever doubted that for even one day since joining the Harvey Girls.

The guests at table one left, and she had an inkling that Mr. Watkins would be its next occupant. He'd been weary last night when he returned to the hotel, but as he ate a late dinner, they'd had several moments to talk.

Refilling coffee and water for her guests, she admitted to herself that their conversation had been nice. Maybe he couldn't be lumped into the same category as her father.

A small cringe hit her stomach. It wasn't good to think ill of the dead, no matter what he had turned into after her mother's death. There were days she felt a measure of grief over the loss of them both. She had some lovely memories of when she was a child. Before the kidnapping.

Mr. Cooper's face flashed before her eyes as she returned

the pitcher and carafe to the waitresses' station. She blinked back the memory. She'd been fooled by that man and told him she hated him after they'd returned home. His chuckle and pat to her shoulder did nothing to win her over.

When she'd stomped off to tell her father that she refused to go anywhere with Mr. Cooper ever again, Father told her that she would be spending all her time with Nanny Louise anyway and that he had much more pressing matters for Mr. Cooper to attend to.

In that moment, she'd known. Mr. Cooper being her driver for those weeks had all been part of their plan. And for that, she vowed never to forgive either one of them.

The yeasty scent of fresh baked bread brought her attention back to the moment as Caroline carried a basket of rolls to the station.

"You're doing an excellent job, Caroline."

The younger girl's smile lit up her face. "Oh, thank you, Miss Edwards. This is the best job I've ever had."

"I'm glad." She returned the smile. "I feel the same way. I noticed on the schedule that you have Monday off. Do you have any plans?"

"Other than resting my sad little feet? No." Caroline giggled.

Emma Grace filled a smaller basket with some of the bread for table two. She lifted her eyebrows. "Well, it won't be resting your sad little feet, but how would you like to accompany me and a couple of others down Bright Angel Trail? I hear it's quite incredible."

"Goodness, I don't know." The words were drawn out, and her face paled a bit. "I have a bit of a fear of heights. Do you think I could manage it?"

"I think you can. And I'll be right there beside you the whole time." She sucked in her bottom lip. She didn't want

Caroline to feel pressure from her. That was the last thing she wanted. But rules were rules: Emma Grace wasn't allowed to go down into the canyon unless one of the other girls went with her. "What do you say?"

"Well . . . as long as you promise not to leave me by myself, I'll do it."

"I promise." She reached for a plate of butter.

"Won't it be colder down there?" Caroline picked up some silverware.

"Actually, I've heard it's warmer down in the canyon. Several people even said it almost feels like spring weather once the sun comes out and warms the path. But I would dress plenty warm, just in case. I need to bring this to my table, but thank you for agreeing to go. I've really been looking forward to trying the trail." With brisk steps, she headed to table two, just in time to see Mr. Watkins being seated at his usual table.

After she delivered the bread and butter, she turned to him. "Your men didn't return with you?"

The smile in his eyes diminished, and his jaw clenched for a moment. "I'm sorry to say they won't be returning."

"Oh, I hope that doesn't hinder your plans." It was odd that he hadn't mentioned that last night. Of course, he'd looked exhausted.

He tilted his head back and forth for a moment. "It's really up to what my father has planned."

"Will he be coming from Chicago?"

"At some point, yes." He leaned back in his chair and rested his elbows on the arms.

She jolted. "I'm so sorry, I just realized you don't have water or coffee. I'll be right back."

As quickly as she could, she went back to the station and grabbed a carafe and pitcher. When she came back to the table, he was straightening his silverware. Strange. She'd seen him do that once before. She poured the coffee and water.

"Thank you." He took a sip of his coffee. "What are the amazing specials coming out of Chef's kitchen this evening? Actually, you don't need to tell me. I would love some more of that beef stroganoff if that is available."

The fact that he liked her suggestion the other night made her smile. "It is. I'll bring it right out. Would you like anything else?"

"Plenty of bread, if you don't mind. The aroma is making my stomach rumble."

"Coming right up. With butter, if I remember correctly? Blackberry jelly too?"

"Of course." He lifted a finger toward her. "You are quite amazing, Miss Edwards. Thank you for remembering and taking such good care of me."

His compliment sent a warm feeling through her as she walked away. It was nice to be appreciated. She placed his order and then prepared his basket of bread and condiments. As she headed back to table one and Mr. Watkins, she saw that her guests at table three were leaving. The boisterous group had been eating for more than two hours. Their table would be quite the mess to clean up. But Eli was the busboy for her tables this evening, and he would have it ready for customers in a jiffy.

"Here you are." She set the basket on the table.

"Thank you." He reached for his butter knife.

"Has Mr. Henderson told you that I will be going with you on your hike down Bright Angel Trail on Monday?" Feeling rather bold, she finished it with a smile. Just in case he had a problem with it, she'd rather hear about it now.

The broadest smile she'd ever seen crossed his face and

made his eyes light up. "No, I hadn't heard. I'm so glad you can join us."

"Are you certain? I don't wish to intrude. Caroline and I can go on our own."

"Nonsense. That is the best news I've heard all day."

She lifted her eyebrows. "You must have had a pretty awful day if that's true."

He made a face, and she couldn't help but laugh.

"Miss?" The gentleman from table two caught her attention out of the corner of her eye.

"Excuse me, Mr. Watkins. I'll be back with your dinner shortly."

"I look forward to it."

After seeing to the needs of the other table, she welcomed the guests who had been seated at table three. The evening carried on in a usual bluster of busyness. But after Mr. Watkins arrived, things felt different.

Every time she returned to table one, he shared a fact with her about their upcoming hike—which he admitted came from a sheet of paper he'd obtained from Mr. Cameron, who owned the trail. Even so, it lifted her spirits that he would seek to bring her a bit of joy as she worked.

While she was careful not to linger too long with guests or pester them with any personal questions, per Harvey House rules, she *was* able to answer topics broached by guests. So, she didn't feel guilty in the slightest talking with Mr. Watkins, and it helped make her shift fly by.

For that, she was grateful.

When he stood to leave, a sense of loss filled her. No matter, the day had been a long one—but thanks to him, an enjoyable one. Besides, she'd see him tomorrow and then they'd have a chance to see each other all day on Monday.

The thought made her smile as she finished up her evening

chores in the dining room. When everything was finished, the line of girls in their black dresses and white aprons headed to their quarters, chatting and laughing along the way. The camaraderie they had built here was different than other Harvey Houses. As much as Emma Grace had kept to herself, they still included her. Which made her long to embrace this group that had begun to feel a bit like family.

She shook her head as she walked down the hall to her room. What had gotten into her? For years, she hadn't let anyone close. No one. Now, she found herself opening up like a rosebud getting ready to bloom. Ruth, Caroline, Mr. Owens, Frank.

Then there was Mr. Watkins. Tonight, she'd found herself watching him. Noticing his manners. His sharp wit. And his good looks. The man was kind to everyone, a trait not often seen in the ultra-rich. The difference was startling. And, for some reason, he was paying attention to her. Acting as if he wanted to know her better.

Why would that be so bad? If Frank Henderson had befriended the man, he couldn't be a cad, could he?

Even as tired as she was, the excitement of Monday gave her renewed energy.

Unlocking her door, she allowed herself to sigh. It had been a good day.

"Are you as tired as I am?" Ruth's voice sounded behind her.

Emma Grace turned to her friend. "Yes." She let out an exaggerated moan.

"Good thing I had sense to sign up for the tub tonight. My shoulders are screaming at me."

Emma Grace laughed and opened her door. "Well, enjoy a soak, Ruth. You deserve it. I am going straight to bed."

"Good night." Ruth's singsong voice floated toward her.

"Good night." Emma Grace closed her door behind her and leaned up against it. For the first time since she ran away, she actually felt at home.

It was a great feeling.

She untied her apron and pulled the pins from her hair. As she turned toward the wardrobe, she noticed a piece of paper over by the door. Hopefully Caroline wasn't backing out of their hike already.

Bending over to retrieve it, she put a hand to the small of her back. Ouch. Maybe she should have signed up for the tub too.

The sheet of paper was folded in half, and as she flicked it open with her fingers, her breath caught in her throat as she read the words.

I know who you are.

10

"I know who you are."

The voice's haunting whisper chased Emma Grace up the stairs. Her nightgown wrapped around her legs with every step.

No matter how hard she pushed, she couldn't go any faster, and each step seemed higher to reach than the last, until she was climbing them like a ladder, using her hands and feet. But the threat behind her kept her moving up, up, up.

Swallowing the pulsating lump in her throat, she climbed. Sweat poured from her brow.

But when she reached the top, she didn't know which way to go. Halls stretched out in every direction. There had to be some safe place to hide. Somewhere.

She ran down a hall, grabbing at doorknobs, but none of them would open any of the doors.

Her bare feet sank into the carpet as she turned around and ran as fast as she could down another hall.

The very last door creaked open. Had she found a place to hide?

"Emma Grace!" Someone patted her face. "Emma Grace." They patted much harder. "Wake up!"

Ow. Her cheek stung. She opened her eyes and blinked several times.

Ruth hovered over her bed and let out a whoosh of breath. "It's okay. You're awake now."

"What's going on?" She grabbed at the neck of her nightgown, her palms sweaty, her heart racing. The room was dark except for a shaft of light coming in from where Ruth had left the door between their rooms open.

"You were having a nightmare." Ruth sat down on the bed next to her. "You didn't scream this time, but I heard a crash and came in. You must've knocked your books off the table. You were thrashing about on the bed and moaning, so I thought it best to wake you."

Emma Grace scooted up to where she could sit against the wall and pulled her knees to her chest. Her heart still hadn't calmed down to its natural pace. And she couldn't remember the nightmare, only the feeling that she was being chased. She peeked over at the nightstand. The note lay there. Taunting her. "I'm sorry I woke you."

"No, don't apologize. I'm glad you did. Is something bothering you? Was it the same dream?" Ruth's gaze followed where she'd been looking.

"I don't know." She put a hand to her forehead. "I just remember this awful feeling that someone was after me."

Her friend crossed her arms over her chest. "What's in the note?" One eyebrow shot up.

Emma Grace stared long and hard at the door. She should have known Ruth would figure it out. The woman's job was to observe everything. "Go ahead and read it." She closed her eyes and heard the swish of the paper as Ruth opened it.

"Where'd you find this?" Her voice had a hard edge to it.

"On the floor. Last night after I came in. Someone must have slipped it under the door."

"So that means it was someone here. In the hotel." She refolded the paper and tapped it against her palm. "Why didn't you tell me?"

The question cut to Emma Grace's heart. "I . . . well . . . you were taking a bath." There wasn't any excuse other than her own fear. She'd been so upset by the note that she hadn't been able to think straight. For several hours, she'd huddled in the corner of her room. When her limbs became numb and cold, the shivering started. It had been sometime in the middle of the night that she'd managed to undress and climb into bed. Sleep had come only because her body was exhausted. But it hadn't lasted very long.

Her friend gripped her shoulders. "Look, I know you're scared. But you have to trust someone. You can't go through this alone."

"I do trust you. . . . I guess I was just in shock."

Ruth scooted onto the bed and leaned against the wall too. "This is what I think. I think you've had to do everything on your own for so long that you're not used to people being there for you or reaching out to you."

The words held weight.

"And here's what else I think. You're so busy trying to be brave and take care of yourself that you've shoved God back because you don't think He can be trusted."

"He can't be." That much she was sure of.

"I disagree. Have you tried?" Ruth pushed. But she sat there all relaxed, like this was a normal conversation. She wasn't angry or upset.

"Humph. Not in a long time."

"'I sought the Lord, and he heard me, and delivered me from all my fears.'" Ruth got up from the bed. "It's from Psalm thirty-four. You know, my pastor back in Kansas used to say all the time that fear isn't from the Lord. Because

God is love. He's peace. He's comfort and strength. Fear is the opposite of all that God is so it's obviously from the devil. I think you've shut God out, and He's just waiting for you to open the door back up." She crossed her arms over her chest.

The words about God sounded completely different coming from someone Emma Grace had come to respect. They weren't hollered down on her from a raging reverend in his fancy attire and gold rings. "What was that verse again?"

"'I sought the Lord, and he heard me, and delivered me from all my fears.'"

Emma Grace closed her eyes and whispered them back to herself three times. At this point, she was willing to try just about anything. Even trusting God.

A knock sounded through the other room, on Ruth's door. Ruth looked at the clock. "I was thinking it was still the middle of the night, but it looks like it's time to get up. I'll be right back." She shuffled through the door and back into her room. As the head waitress, she had to deal with all sorts of questions and issues from the girls before their shifts started.

Hushed voices carried through to Emma Grace, but she couldn't hear what they were saying. She said the verse to herself three more times. How she longed for the Lord to hear her and deliver her from these nightmares.

God, if You're really there . . . what? What could she possibly do to earn His attention? *Please hear me.*

Nothing happened. Oh well. It's not like she felt she was deserving of God's help.

Ruth peeked her head back into the room. "You'll want to see this."

Emma Grace got up, put on her dressing gown, and followed.

Four other waitresses stood in the hallway: Margaret,

Leah, Elizabeth, and Jane. Ruth held up four pieces of paper in front of her face. Just like the note Emma Grace had received. With the same words. "It looks like you don't have anything to worry about."

The head waitress addressed the other girls. "When did you find these?"

"This morning." Margaret bit her lip.

"Just now?"

All the girls nodded.

"I see. Well, likely someone is playing a prank. This type of behavior isn't allowed, so rest assured, I will get to the bottom of this." Ruth's gaze swung to Emma Grace's. "I promise."

⊣ ⊢

Every muscle in her body ached. Probably from crouching in the corner for so many hours last night. Add to that the lack of sleep and the idea that someone was pulling a prank on several Harvey Girls, and Emma Grace wanted to go back to her room and stay there. For a long time.

But that wasn't an option.

The Sunday brunch was almost over, and she couldn't wait to get away. Hopefully most of her customers were so busy enjoying the day that they hadn't noticed the difference in her demeanor.

Except Mr. Watkins. He noticed. Even commented on it, but she had pasted on her same smile and told him not to worry.

If only she could convince herself of that.

As soon as her tables were all empty, she headed over to Ruth. "I really need to go to my room and lie down."

The head waitress's brow creased with worry. "It's fine. You go on and head down. I'll come check on you in about an hour. I'm praying for you, Emma Grace."

With a nod, she headed toward the stairs. While it touched her that her friend would pray for her, none of the faith talk made any sense.

Back at her room, she changed out of her uniform so she wouldn't wrinkle it and laid on her bed. In a simple day dress, she curled her legs up under her skirt, draped her arm over her forehead, and closed her eyes. Why would anyone send a note like that?

A light tapping on her door made her sit up. Had she fallen asleep?

She must have because her mind didn't want to wake up. But she sat up and went to the door.

Cracking it an inch, she saw Ruth and relaxed. "Come on in."

"I'm sorry, did I wake you?"

A yawn kept her from answering for a moment. "It's all right. I guess I didn't realize I'd fallen asleep."

"You needed it, I'm sure." Ruth came in and sat on the chair across from the bed. "I spoke to Mr. Owens just a little bit ago about the notes."

"Oh?"

"He wants to speak to each worker individually and get to the bottom of it. He thinks it's a prank by one of the girls. Every house I've been in, we've had one who just doesn't like to follow the rules and will get into all kinds of trouble just for attention. It must be a coincidence that you received one."

"But what about the fact that I found mine last night? The other girls didn't get them until this morning."

"The other girls all share rooms. And it's not like they are on their guard for any reason. It was the end of a long day and I'm sure they were just overlooked. They probably got them last night too. They just didn't *see* them."

Maybe Emma Grace was getting too worked up over this. Maybe it wasn't a coincidence that the girls showed up with their notes right after she'd asked God to hear her. Maybe she *could* relax.

"Listen, I was going to ask you to come with me for a little bit. Before the dinner rush."

Sunday was the only day the Harvey Girls weren't required to be in the dining room the entire day. They served at brunch and then at dinner. Emma Grace glanced at the clock. "All right. What did you have in mind?"

"Let's go chat with Frank."

Grabbing a sweater and her coat, she followed her friend out the door and then locked it. "Why Frank?"

"Because he leads us in a small worship service on Sunday mornings. He taught this morning on a passage in Psalms that I think might comfort you."

"Oh." Was she ready for more religious talk? Just because she'd asked the Lord to hear her didn't mean she was ready to be preached at left and right.

As they walked out to the rim, the view helped her to relax. Why was it that she could simply look at the canyon and feel like all was right with the world?

To her surprise, Frank was sitting near the spot where they'd watched the sunrise the other day. With his legs dangling, a book in his lap, he turned to smile up at them.

Ruth put a hand to her throat. "Mr. Henderson, aren't you a bit concerned to be sitting on the edge like that?"

"Not at all, Miss Anniston. In fact, a good friend showed me this technique."

Emma Grace laughed and took her seat next to him while Ruth looked on in complete shock. "Well, I don't think I will be joining you." She scooted back to a little bench and sat down.

Frank leaned toward Emma Grace a bit and pointed over his shoulder with his thumb. "I do believe Miss Anniston is too proper to sit with us."

"Oh, hush, Frank Henderson. Just because I choose to sit on this nice, comfortable bench doesn't mean I'm too proper. Besides, I much prefer looking at the back of your head."

He let out a loud laugh. "I didn't realize you'd made that a habit, Miss Anniston." He rubbed a hand over his hair and turned the back of his head toward Emma Grace. "How do I look? Is my hair combed?"

Emma Grace enjoyed watching the two of them spar.

"Oh, pshaw." Ruth huffed and gave Frank a look any good schoolteacher would be jealous of. "You do like to goad me on."

"I'm always up to the challenge." He raised his eyebrows and waggled them. "Well? Are you too good for the likes of us?"

"I'm perfectly content where I am, thank you very much." Back ramrod straight, she folded her hands in her lap and lifted her chin.

It all made Emma Grace laugh some more. "You two are incorrigible. How long have you known each other?"

Frank gave a wide grin. "She's had to endure my antics for at least a year."

"Two," Ruth corrected. It looked as if she had to really work to not crack a smile.

"Forgive me. *Two*." Frank gave an even more dramatic expression as he pronounced the word. "When I discovered we'd both been assigned to the El Tovar, well, that just made it all the sweeter. She's always correct, you know."

Emma Grace put a hand over her mouth to stifle her laughter.

Frank laughed with her and then handed her the book that he'd been holding. "I know you've been hurt and that you're searching for answers. But I want to be your friend. So, as a friend, I didn't want to preach at you, but Ruth approached me this morning after our service and said you might need to hear about these verses on fear. And since Spurgeon is a much better theologian than myself, I thought it'd be best to just lend it to you so you can read it for yourself. You're a big girl, capable of making your own decisions." He got up to stand. "Take care of it. It's one of my most prized possessions."

"All right. I will." She pulled the book to her chest.

"There's a bookmark in there to show you Psalm fifty-six. I talked about verses three and four this morning."

"Thank you." She looked at the spine. *The Treasury of David* by C. H. Spurgeon. Volume III.

"Would you care to join me for a walk, Miss Anniston?" His voice was kind and teasing.

"I'd be delighted." Ruth laughed. "Oh, won't the rumors fly now. We'll be back in a little bit, Emma Grace."

"All right," she called after the two. How interesting that they left her in peace. No lectures. No smooth words trying to convince her of something. Nothing. Just a book.

She turned the volume over in her hands. The gold lettering reminded her of all the books neatly displayed in the library at home. Her father collected nice editions not to read but to keep on the shelves to impress people. Even though this book was a lovely edition, she could tell it had been read a good deal. Pored over.

Getting to her feet, she decided to go back to the bench and sit, not wanting to take any risk of dropping the precious book over the edge of the canyon. It had been kind for Frank to leave it with her.

She opened the book to where he'd placed a satiny bookmark. In pencil, there was a line underneath verse three and verse four.

Out of respect for her friends, she lifted her face to the sky. *All right, God. I asked You to hear me. Now I guess I need help understanding. If You're really there.*

She began to read.

Verse 3. What time I am afraid. David was no braggart, he does not claim never to be afraid. . . .

Marking the spot with her finger, Emma Grace puzzled over it. And then she read it again. For some reason, she'd thought that everything she'd heard from the sermons of her youth didn't talk about anyone being flawed, afraid, or sinners. Christians were expected to be perfect and thus show the world that they were perfect. But David—King David—was afraid? It gave her a sense of comfort.

She read on.

We are men, and therefore liable to overthrow; we are feeble, and therefore unable to prevent it; we are sinful men, and therefore deserving it, and for all these reasons we are afraid. But the condition of the psalmist's mind was complex—he feared, but that fear did not fill the whole area of his mind, for he adds, I will trust in thee. It is possible, then, for fear and faith to occupy the mind at the same moment. . . . It is a blessed fear which drives us to trust.

She left her finger on the page and closed the book. "It is a blessed fear which drives us to trust." She spoke the words to the wind. "God, I don't know how to trust. I shut that door a long time ago. But I do want courage. I don't want to live in fear."

It came naturally to be talking to God. Even though she

wasn't convinced He was listening. Was she doing it right? She opened the book back up and another sentence jumped off the page.

To trust when there is no cause for fear, is but the name of faith, but to be reliant upon God when occasions for alarm are abundant and pressing, is the conquering faith of God's elect.

If she remembered the stories from Sunday school as a child, David—before he was king—had been best friends with the king's son. And when that king found out that David was to succeed him, he tried to kill David. Sitting here now, Emma Grace realized that David must have been not only afraid but also hurt. And he probably didn't trust easily either, not after that.

What a difference in Mr. Spurgeon's writings from the words that had been yelled from the pulpit in her youth. It was a connection she'd never felt before. If the Bible was really like what Mr. Spurgeon wrote about, she found herself wanting to read more. But she didn't have a Bible of her own. Not anymore.

The verse Ruth shared with her repeated in her mind. *I sought the Lord, and he heard me, and delivered me from all my fears.* Could it really be that simple?

All right, God. I don't know what to think, but I can't ignore You. I asked You to hear me. I'm really trying to seek You. So now, I'm going to ask for deliverance from my fears too. I know I'm not good enough to deserve Your favor, but I'm tired of trying to do it on my own.

The afternoon sun was warm on his face as Ray strolled over to the Hopi House. Even though the inside was closed on Sundays, many of the Hopi people were outside showcasing their crafts to the guests.

As he rounded the corner to the north side of the building, he was surprised to see Emma Grace seated on the ground with several Hopi children, while another woman looked over her shoulder.

"No, no, no." The woman's black braids swung back and forth as she picked up Emma Grace's project. "Over, under, around, and *then* through." Her fingers moved with precision.

Emma Grace's forehead had a deep V etched in it. "Hmmm. It seems I'm always forgetting one of those steps. One of these days, I'm going to be able to keep up with Sunki." She smiled down at a little girl beside her.

"I'm afraid that will take much practice."

Ray couldn't help but chuckle and then all eyes turned to him. "My apologies, Miss Edwards."

She narrowed her eyes at him, but her smile was still there. "Maybe you need to show us how quickly *you* would pick up on this art." The challenge in her words was wrapped in laughter.

Two of the little Hopi girls waved him over.

How could he resist? As he stepped over to them, he realized he was the only gentleman around. But what did it matter? The children coaxed him to sit, and without giving it another thought, he plopped himself onto the ground with them. "Where do I begin?"

The Hopi woman pointed to herself. "I'm Chuma. I will teach you."

Emma Grace raised her eyebrows. "Good luck." She held up what appeared to be the start of a small basket. "You don't want to know how long it has taken me to get this far."

Ray rubbed his hands together. "I'm excited to learn."

167

"It's much harder than it looks." Miss Edwards was back at it, her focus narrowed on the reeds in her hands.

Chuma came over beside him and sat down. "This"—she demonstrated—"is how to weave." Her fingers flew so fast that all he could do was blink. "See?"

"Oh, I see very well." He raised his eyebrows. "But I do believe you might need to show me that one more time. Slower. *Much* slower."

Laughter floated around him as the Hopi children covered their mouths with their hands.

Miss Edwards' little friend Sunki leaned toward him. "Chuma teases you."

He looked up at the Hopi woman, and she winked at him. "I am sorry Mr. . . . ?"

"Watkins. But please, just call me Ray."

"Mr. Ray." She smiled broadly at him, showing a missing tooth on the bottom. "I like to tease. I will go slower. Now watch."

Twenty minutes later, he'd watched over and over again as she demonstrated. But to his great frustration, he hadn't been able to get any of the reeds to do what he wanted.

He looked over at Emma Grace. Her face was serious. Studious. She hadn't made a lot of progress since he sat down, but it was a lot better than what he was doing. Leaning closer to her, he whispered, "How long did it take you to get that far?"

She blew out a breath and pushed her glasses up on her nose. "This is probably my fourth or fifth try. This one is less crooked than the others, so I'm determined to at least finish it." With a glance to the materials in his hands, she smiled. "I see you're struggling to get it started."

"That, Miss Edwards, is an understatement." He offered up his meager handful of reeds.

"Oh no. It's a badge of honor once you get it going, I wouldn't want to take that away from you." Merriment twinkled in her eyes.

"You're enjoying this, aren't you?"

"Immensely." She nodded at the girls in the circle around them. "You should have seen how many times I've been outdone by a five-year-old. It's your turn."

As if on cue, the smallest girl of the bunch stood up and sidled up next to him. Shaking her head, she giggled. "You need help."

"Apparently so." He laughed along with her.

Two little chubby hands took his and directed his fingers to hold the reeds between. Then the little girl deftly wove together the bottom of a small basket. It took her barely a minute. "You do it now."

His heart cinched when the little girl stood up and patted his shoulder. Taking her place back with the others, she didn't even look back. Ray watched them interact with one another and continue weaving. Marveling at the creation in his hands, he realized he better finish it. Or at least attempt to. But that might take a year.

"They're beautiful people, aren't they?" Emma Grace's words were hushed, and she never lifted her eyes from her own work.

"Yes, they are."

11

For the first time in days, sleep had come last night uninterrupted. If anything was a sign that God had heard her prayers, it was that. At least, that's what Emma Grace told herself. The past five years of her life had been lived in a prison of her own making. Always running. Always looking over her shoulder. Never being . . . Emma Grace.

Well, that was going to change. Whether she would feel this brave tomorrow was doubtful, but today she could embrace it. At least for a few hours.

She smiled as she pulled her hair back into a snug knot. Today was a new day. A glorious day. She was going down into the canyon.

A knock on her door pulled her from her musings. She opened it a crack. "Good morning, Ruth."

"Aren't you chipper today. Looking forward to your day off, I see." The smile on her friend's face warmed her. Then Ruth leaned forward and gave her a brief hug. "I've been praying for you." It had been a long time since anyone had hugged her. A real hug. Full of caring and camaraderie.

"Thanks." Emma Grace reached for her glasses and put them on to try and cover up the emotions that had stirred within her. "I definitely feel different. I want to get rid of this fear I've been carrying around for so long. I'm tired of it."

"I imagine you are."

"But it's so very real. I admit I keep saying that verse over and over in my head. If God is there, I have a feeling He's going to get tired of me real soon." She gave her friend an awkward grin.

"Not at all. He never tires of any of us." Ruth shook her head and made a silly face. "If He did, He would have given up on me a long time ago."

"I highly doubt that. You're the epitome of a good person."

Ruth doubled over with laughter. "That's only because you've never seen my ornery side. Or my fiery temper. Besides, being a good person has nothing to do with it. If it did, then we all fail. Jesus didn't come to be the sacrifice for us all because we were good. He came because we *aren't* good. Not one of us. But He loves us anyway."

That was odd. Everything she'd ever heard preached was about being good. Doing good works. Measuring up. Good good good.

"You look confused." Ruth patted her arm.

"What you just said goes against everything I've heard preached about religion and God. I have a lot of questions."

Ruth glanced over at the clock. "Look, you need to meet up with the others, and I need to get to work. We can chat more about it tonight over tea. How does that sound?"

She gave a nod. "Thanks. My gratitude for all you've done for me has been sorely lacking in words. But know that in my heart it's there." Emma Grace grabbed Ruth's hand. "I needed a friend. And you've been there. The fact that I actually feel happy this morning—even with all that's going on—is incredible to me. I don't know whether it's because of our conversation, reading the book that Frank left with me, or even my feeble attempts at chatting with God, but my outlook is different. I'm ready to live. Actually live."

"Go have fun today, Emma Grace. Enjoy the canyon. But you might be needing this." She reached out the door and lifted a basket. "I talked to Frank and he had a couple of others in the kitchen put together a nice picnic for all of you. So he'll have that in his pack, but I got up early this morning to prepare one of my mother's special treats. She called them pumpkin cakes." She grinned. "Chef was good enough to let me have use of one of the ovens. Now, you'll want to transfer it into a pack because you won't want to carry a basket down the trail, but the guys should have one with them."

"How thoughtful! Thank you." The delight on Ruth's face when *she* was the one who'd sacrificed sleep and time warmed her heart.

"You're welcome. Now go. Have fun." Ruth waved and scurried down the hall.

As she locked her door, she couldn't help but smile. She had led such a lonely life for the past few years. Now, everything had changed.

"Good morning." Caroline's voice brought her attention up.

"Good morning to you. Are you ready?"

She lifted her arms at her sides and put them back down as she grimaced. "As ready as I'll ever be."

Emma Grace hooked elbows with her as they headed upstairs. "I'll be right there the whole time, so if you need to hold on to me, you do that. All right?"

"I'll be fine. If I want to conquer this fear of heights, I've got to face it head-on, right?" Caroline let out a nervous giggle.

She nodded, not letting on that the words struck her like an arrow in her gut. As they walked out of the hotel, Emma

Grace realized that the younger waitress had struck the nail on the proverbial head. If she truly wanted to conquer her fear, she should be facing it . . . shouldn't she? How would she go about doing that? Was she brave enough?

"Anyway, I had to change my apron *twice* yesterday. I couldn't believe that two different men spilled their coffee on me." Caroline's light chatter drifted into the chilly morning air. She tugged on Emma Grace's arm. "Have you even heard a word I've said?"

"Of course!" She looked at her friend. "Well, maybe not all of it. I'm sorry. My thoughts ran away with me for a moment."

"That's all right. We work such long hours that there's often not enough time for our own thoughts or to talk with each other. It's nice to have a day off."

"I agree."

"I tend to prattle on about anything and everything. My mom is always telling me so. I don't want to make a fool of myself with the rest of the party, so will you do me a favor and poke me or nudge me if I start talking too much?"

"Of course." With a smile, she looked at the young woman. Her bright yellow dress was lively—just like its wearer. "You look so cheery in that color."

"Thank you, Emma Grace." Caroline beamed a smile back. "While we're on the subject, I was wondering why you don't wear much color. You would look wonderful in a blush shade of pink, don't you think?"

"Um, no. I'm not fond of pink." The subject needed to be changed. Fast. "You haven't told me anything about your family. Do you have any siblings?"

Caroline's face lit up. "I have a little brother. We all dote on him." Her smile dimmed a bit. "But he's been sick."

"I'm so sorry. Where do they live?"

"Back in Kansas."

"Is it hard to be away from them?" Family dynamics were such a conundrum for her. Over the years, she'd heard plenty of Harvey Girls speak lovingly about their families, and it always fascinated her.

"It is. But I can help by bringing in a good income." Caroline sent her a smile. "What about you?"

"Look, here's the trail." Emma Grace pushed aside the question and pointed up ahead. Perhaps it would keep Caroline distracted from her question.

Mr. Watkins and Mr. Henderson stood by a building that looked as if it were perched on the very edge of the canyon and could slide in at any moment. On the left side of the house, hanging over a well-used path, was a sign reading *Bright Angel Toll Road*. It was attached to the building with a post on the other side, making an "entry" to the trail.

Emma Grace read aloud a smaller sign on top of the post, "'Footmen will please stay on trail except when passing animals.'"

"As if I would want to get off the trail for any reason! Heavens, how adventurous can people be?" Caroline's brows rose so high, they almost touched her hairline.

"Good morning, ladies." Mr. Watkins nodded at them.

"Good morning," Emma Grace and Caroline chimed at the same time.

Frank stepped forward and took the basket. "What's this?"

"Ruth sent us with an extra treat. She made them this morning—pumpkin cakes." Emma Grace licked her lips. She should have tried one on the way over, because her stomach was raw.

"How kind! I'll just put this in my pack. I also brought four canteens of water. It's a long hike to the bottom and back up."

174

"Thank you for taking such good care of us." Emma Grace realized she hadn't thought to bring anything else. How foolish of her. Her history as a city girl could easily give her away.

"It's my pleasure. Having experienced the trail, I know what to expect. Ray here has already paid the toll for each of us, so we are ready to go."

"Thank you, Mr. Watkins. That was very generous of you." Emma Grace sent him a smile.

"Please. Call me Ray." He tipped his hat. "I wasn't sure if you ladies would prefer to walk or ride a mule."

"Oh, walking is fine with me." Caroline's eyes widened. "I don't think I'd want to sit on top of anything that would make me feel any higher than I already am."

"A bit of a fear of heights?" Frank turned toward the trail.

"Oh, just a bit." Following him down the path, Caroline shot a look of uncertainty over her shoulder.

"Just stick behind me and stay close to the wall of the canyon. Ray can pull up the rear so that you ladies are protected. Once we get a little farther down, the trail widens and you won't feel like you're about to fall off." Frank's voice was calm and reassuring.

Emma Grace stepped closer to her and whispered, "Don't worry. Frank is in front of you, and I'm *right* behind you."

Caroline's head bobbed in agreement. As they traveled the first bit of trail, they dipped below the rim of the canyon. Caroline's hand reached out and touched the wall of rock beside her.

"Frank, do you think we'll make it all the way down?" Emma Grace squeezed the other girl's shoulder.

"It's several miles, so it depends on how all of you are doing. Just remember that even though this part gives us an amazing view, coming back up is much harder." The chef looked right at home traipsing down the trail.

She hadn't really thought of that. Climbing out of the canyon would probably make her sore tomorrow. But she could handle it. Every few steps, they had the most glorious view. Emma Grace couldn't imagine anything ever being more beautiful. And she had been all over the world. What was it about this rugged landscape that filled her heart? "Wow."

"It's quite amazing, isn't it?" For a moment, she'd forgotten that Mr. Watkins—Ray—was behind her.

"It is. I find myself wanting to climb that rock outcropping over there."

His deep chuckle reached her ears. "Now that's a picture I would like to take."

"Are you challenging me, Ray Watkins?" She placed her hands on her hips as she turned to face him.

He held up both of his hands as if to surrender. "No, ma'am. I would never do such a thing." But his eyes twinkled with merriment.

"Did you bring your camera?" She tried to keep from smiling and lifted an eyebrow.

"I most certainly did." He tilted his head, grinned, and took the pack off his back. "And I just happen to have my new tripod with me too."

"Caroline!" she threw over her shoulder and lifted her skirts a few inches above her boots. "Wait for just a minute."

She headed straight for the large outcropping that stood between the trail and the depths of the canyon. Thankfully, it was broad and relatively flat at the top, and she only had to climb a few feet up. Once she reached the top, she sat down and looked behind her. If she could, she would sit here all day. But there was the excitement inside her of what else she would see on the journey today.

Today, she was going to have fun. No more deep thoughts or weighty conversations. She'd always been an adventurous child—and got in trouble many times because of it. Somehow, she'd shoved that part of herself down for many years as well. Well, the least she could do was allow herself to explore.

Looking down, she saw the grin on Frank's face while Caroline shook her head at her, covering her eyes every few seconds. "I don't know what has gotten into you, Emma Grace Edwards, but you do beat all."

Ray had buried his head under what looked like a large drape at the back of the camera and held up his hand as if he was almost ready.

Out of sheer thrill, she threw her hands up in the air and lifted her face to the sky. If only she could vanquish *all* her fear by climbing a rock . . .

Then it hit her. She shouldn't have her picture taken by Ray. He knew a lot of people who could have been in her social circle five years ago. "Wait!" she called. "I want to be looking at the canyon."

"But then we won't be able to see your face." Caroline placed her hands on her hips.

"Oh, pshaw. That doesn't matter. This will be better. You'll see." She turned and sat on the other side of the rock where she was facing the canyon, her back to Ray.

"She's right." Ray's voice came out from under the drape. "This will be a great photograph. You could be on an advertisement for the railroad and the Grand Canyon." Several minutes later, Ray packed up his equipment.

Emma Grace climbed down and went over to hug Caroline. "Did I scare you?"

Her friend's pinched lips told her everything she needed to know. "As long as you didn't make me climb it with you, I'm fine."

Frank shot her a smile. "We should continue on. Otherwise we won't make it back until tomorrow." Once Ray had slung his pack over his shoulder, Frank led their little party down the trail.

As she followed Caroline, Emma Grace let everything wash over her. The view. The sounds. The freedom.

Why was it so freeing to allow herself to actually be *herself*? The notion was odd even as she mulled it over.

What had happened to her? Why had she allowed men to do this to her? Men she'd trusted. Out here, it was perfectly fine to feel strong and capable, to throw her fear to the wind. But it wouldn't last forever. She knew that.

This canyon definitely brought out so many things she'd tried to keep quashed. Maybe it wasn't so wrong to allow it all to come back up. Maybe there were people who would accept her for who she truly was and perhaps even help her. *Maybe* she could actually rid herself of fear.

What if she told those who were looking for her that she was alive? The thought was a scary one. But now that she was of age, could she simply sell her father's companies and stocks? She was the heiress, wasn't she? Was there a way for Mr. Scott to handle all of it without revealing where she was? What if she refused to live in fear of Wellington and all the others? Could she do that?

Then the memory of her last night at home came back.

She'd seen Wellington's face, at least the side of it, from the second-floor landing as she was about to make her escape. But he hadn't seen her. Of that she was sure. He must have been the one who murdered Papa. Her father had even said he'd been expecting him.

Her heart clenched at the thought. What had Wellington wanted?

Probably the same thing everyone wanted. Money. Her family had lots of it.

If she contacted her grandfather's solicitor again, would

that put anyone here at risk? She couldn't bear the thought of anything happening to anyone else because of her. Mr. Scott would surely advise her and continue to keep her secret. Was she willing to try to be rid of the past forever?

Ducking her chin, she gave her head a little shake. She was on a glorious outing. These thoughts needed to be cast away. Things were better—safer—this way where she stayed hidden.

As they walked deeper and deeper into the canyon, the gentle swish of the wind and the rhythm of their steps soothed her anxious heart.

Ray began to whistle a tune. It was the perfect thing to shift her mood.

After several measures, she began to giggle. "Are you whistling 'The Preacher and the Bear'?"

"It's stuck in my head." His voice behind her sounded a bit irritated. "I can't seem to get it out—didn't even realize I was whistling it. Does it bother you?"

"Not at all." Speaking sideways over her shoulder, she smiled. "It just tickled my funny bone. I can envision the preacher climbing up a tree."

The whistling resumed, and this time Caroline turned around, waited for her, and then fell into step beside her. She hummed along until Ray reached the chorus. With a pretty soprano voice, she sang the words.

"'Oh, Lord, didn't you deliver Daniel from the lion's den?
Also delivered Jonah from the belly of the whale and then
Three Hebrew children from the fiery furnace?
So the Good Book do declare
Now Lord, if you can't help me
For goodness' sakes, don't you help that bear!'"

By the time she finished, all four of them were laughing. They traveled on for another hour. Joking, laughing, singing, and whistling silly tunes—seeing who could guess the name of the song.

All of a sudden, Caroline stopped dead in her tracks. "Oh my goodness gracious, that man's going to fall!" She pointed with one hand and covered her mouth with the other.

Their little group huddled together as they all squinted into the distance.

Frank was the first one to relax. He let out a low grunt. "He's not going to fall. That's just the Kolb brothers, Ellsworth and Emery. They're notorious for doing wild and crazy things to get a picture. They might even ask you one day to do a silly pose for them. It's their photography business, and they've done a smash-bang-up job of it."

"But Caroline's correct. It truly looks like he's going to fall." Emma Grace couldn't pull her gaze away. The man had one foot on one ledge, while the other rested on another, and there was a huge crevasse between his feet and a good hundred-foot drop-off beneath him.

As Frank led them down the trail, she couldn't help but keep looking up in the distance to see what the adventurous picture-taking Kolb brothers were up to.

By the time they had zigzagged down so many switchbacks she'd lost count, Frank pointed ahead. "That's Indian Garden. Why don't we have our lunch there?"

Emma Grace's feet were killing her. The thought that she had to go all the way back up made her realize she should invest in a better pair of boots. Because she definitely wanted to do this again and again. "That sounds like a wonderful idea to me. What time is it, anyway?"

"Ten forty-five." Ray studied his pocket watch. "I'm so famished, I thought for certain it must be after the noon hour."

"Me too." Caroline put a hand to her middle. "But I will

take the opportunity to rest. I may not be able to feel my feet tomorrow."

"Sit down and get some refreshment. But remind yourself not to get too comfortable. Because it will take quite a bit longer to make the hike back up." The sun made Frank's freckles stand out. It made him look younger, almost like a schoolboy. He removed his hat and swiped a hand at his hair, the copper strands shining in the light. "For January, I didn't think we would work up that much of a sweat." He looked at Ray.

"Just imagine what it will be like on the way up." Mr. Watkins laughed along with Frank as they opened up their packs. Frank pulled out food and water, while Ray pulled out his camera. "We should get a picture of us to commemorate the day, don't you think?"

Caroline clapped her hands together. "That's a lovely idea." She fanned her face. "Especially since I don't think I will make that trek again. Whew."

While he set up his equipment, Emma Grace helped set out the lunch fixings.

"All right, everyone." In his left hand, Ray held a bulbish gadget, which was attached to the camera on the tripod. "Let's see if I can get it in focus." He spent several moments positioning them all and then hurried to stand next to Frank. "All right, remember it takes a bit for the process, so stand really still while I count to twenty."

Emma Grace stood stiff next to Caroline and shifted her head so that her hat blocked her view of the camera. Hopefully that would keep her face out of the picture.

She'd always hated pictures because they took so long, and she was afraid of moving and making everything blurry. Father had pitched more than one fit about it whenever Mother had commissioned a family picture to be taken. Now there was a different reason to dislike them.

When Ray reached twenty, they all relaxed and smiled.

"Let's eat." Frank rubbed his palms together. The man clearly loved food. And what chef wouldn't?

They chatted about the different birds they'd seen. Caroline mentioned how proud she was that she'd conquered her fear of heights by doing something so challenging, and Frank commented on all the different flavors in the food. It was a lively party, and Emma Grace felt more and more like she really could have friends here. She might even be able to trust a man again. Just look at Frank. He'd been more than trustworthy already and very giving. Even Ray wasn't all that bad—even though he was rich.

But if she really let herself be honest, she had to admit Ray was a handsome man—someone she wouldn't have minded meeting in her former life.

The object of her thoughts wiped his mouth and wrapped his arms casually around his knees. She'd never seen a gentleman sit so comfortably on the ground. He looked at Caroline. "What are your dreams, Miss Caroline?"

The young woman, who had been her trainee a few short weeks ago, smiled and ducked her head a bit. "Do you all promise you won't think it's silly?"

"Of course."

"Yes."

"Nothing you say could be silly." Emma Grace patted her friend's shoulder.

"Well . . ." She let out a long sigh. "I dream of meeting a man here at the hotel—one who's very rich, mind you—and he sweeps me off my feet and takes me to live in some exotic place like Hawaii. He would love my family and know a doctor who could help my brother. We'd never have to worry about medical bills ever again." Covering her mouth, she shrugged.

Emma Grace reached over and wrapped her fingers around Caroline's.

"I'm sorry to hear about your brother." Ray's voice was full of emotion.

"Thank you. But I didn't want to cast a shadow on our lovely time." Caroline picked at her skirt and then lifted her gaze to Frank. "What about you, Mr. Henderson? Any big dreams?"

The chef shoved a bite of apple into his mouth and chewed for a couple of seconds. "I'm easy. I love to cook. That's what I dream of doing the rest of my life, so you could say I'm already living my dream. God has blessed me abundantly. I'm hoping to learn everything I can from Chef Marques. He's brilliant in the kitchen."

"And you, Emma Grace?" Ray's blue eyes seemed darker under his hat. Still, they bore into her, and for a moment she forgot to breathe.

What could she say? She didn't really have any dreams anymore. With a tip of her head, she pulled at a blade of dead grass. "I'm content being a Harvey Girl. I love it."

The way he studied her made her wonder what he was thinking. But she didn't know him very well.

Frank cleared his throat. "Now it's your turn, Ray. What are your dreams?"

He picked up an apple and rubbed it on his coat. "I really love photography, though it's probably just a hobby. To be honest, I'd love to do some philanthropic work. My father has done nothing but build and grow his fortune. I'd like to help other people with it."

"That's very noble. Any idea what exactly you'd like to do?" Frank began to pack things back into his bag.

"First, I have a heart to see children be able to continue their education. Then there's the horrible amount of people who go hungry. It seems like we should be able to help with that. I'd also like to see more young couples be able to get the training they need to be missionaries and then help fund them as they go out into the world to share the Gospel." He stopped short. "My apologies, I do get excited. I don't wish to overwhelm you with my ramblings."

"Not at all." Caroline prodded, "Please continue."

Emma Grace listened to the conversation shift and move as they discussed things that could be done to help people. Ray had obviously put a lot of thought into it over the years. Frank offered his knowledge on how to feed crowds of people. Even Caroline chimed in with what she would want to fund once she married her rich beau, whoever he was. Their laughter gave them the energy that they needed to start back up the trail.

At the steepest parts of the trail on the way back up, when none of them had the breath or energy to speak, Emma Grace found herself thinking about Mr. Ray Watkins. He wasn't at all like the other wealthy men she'd known. If she weren't careful, it would be far too easy to get caught up in all his talk of philanthropy.

And his blue eyes.

EMPIRE, KANSAS

"Yep. That's her. She was a lot skinnier, but I'd know that face anywhere. She was my favorite. Hard to hide a girl as purty as that even if her hair was differn'." The barkeep wiped down a glass and set it on the shelf behind him. "I know it fer certain because I ate lunch there ever' day. Yep."

So, the mysterious Emma Grace McMurray *was* a Harvey Girl. Or at least she had been. Now Peter was certain. "Thank you, sir."

"Not a problem. Hope you find her."

He hoped that too. He nodded at the man behind the bar and headed for the door.

Once he was outside, he placed his hat back on his head and faced the cold Kansas wind. A new strategy would be in play now. First, he'd contact every Harvey House there was and inquire about a waitress named Emma Grace. If he had to spend one hundred dollars on telegrams, he would do it. If that didn't work, he'd travel to each one personally. Ticking off the ones he'd visited already, that left about sixty more.

The thrill of the chase ignited in his gut. He always found what he was looking for.

Always.

12

Frank hadn't been kidding. The hike back up out of the canyon was intense. The first hour hadn't been too bad, but now Ray found his legs screaming from the exertion. It didn't help that the chef seemed to be able to stay ahead of the rest of them without a lot of effort. And he was older.

How the ladies were managing with their long skirts was beyond Ray.

Emma Grace looked back at him and slowed her steps. "I thought my work as a Harvey Girl had me pretty strong and able to withstand hours upon hours on my feet. I guess I wasn't as prepared for this uphill climb as I thought." She placed her hands on her hips.

"Funny, I thought I might be the only one feeling I was inadequate for the challenge."

Caroline halted in front of them. "Frank? Can we stop for a few minutes? I really need to catch my breath."

Their fearless leader turned back with a smile. "Of course. Do you need any water?"

The young waitress sighed and plopped down unceremoniously on a nearby rock. "Water would be much appreciated, thank you."

Ray stepped next to Emma Grace. "Please don't think this too forward of me, but I have really enjoyed our delightful time together. Would it be possible . . . that is, I'm asking if you would be willing . . . I would really like to know you better."

An expression he couldn't decipher crossed her face. "While I don't quite understand why you would, I must admit that I would like that as well. You surprise me, Ray Watkins. You're not at all like other men of your . . . status."

"Oh?"

"I'm sorry. Did I offend you?" Her blond hair was doing its best to escape out of its tight confines. The wisps around her face danced in the wind.

"No. Not at all. I guess I'm simply pleased that you don't lump me in with all the others."

"Believe me, as a waitress, I've seen my fair share of just about every type of man."

"I can imagine. In my travels I've seen some interesting characters, but I'm betting you have seen more of mankind than I have."

"Some of the Harvey Houses I worked at in the beginning were quite a shock. But I have loved working at El Tovar so far. It really is Harvey's shining star."

Ray shoved his hands in his pockets as he looked ahead at Caroline and Frank. The younger waitress looked about done in already. Frank patiently waited.

Maybe it was the fresh air, or perhaps the view, but courage seemed to be on Ray's side today. "Tell me about your family. Do you have any siblings?"

Tiny creases in her forehead told him to tread carefully. Was family a sore spot for her?

After several seconds, she licked her lips. "My parents are both gone. It's just me."

"Oh, I'm sorry to hear that. Have they been gone long?"

"My mother died a long time ago. My father . . . it's been five years now." She looked away and shaded her eyes with her hand.

"Where are you from?" He risked the question, hoping she would open up.

"Boston." She kept her face turned away from him.

"That's a long way from here. But I always enjoyed visiting Boston when my father sent me there on business. Do you miss it?"

This time she looked back at him with a shrug. "Not really. There are things that I miss from my childhood, but not much. So, how about you? Family? I know you're from Chicago and you've spoken of your father often."

"My mother passed away two years ago."

"I'm sorry."

"I appreciate that. Most people have nurturing, loving mothers, so I'm sure it is very hard to feel the loss. And while I am sad that she had to suffer through cancer, it hasn't been that difficult to adjust to life without her. She was a . . . hard woman." He'd never shared anything like that with anyone else. Hopefully she wouldn't think he was callous.

"My mother was loving. But my father wasn't the same after she died. So, the only good memories I have are from when I was a child and when they were happy." Her eyes held a sadness that ran deep. What haunted her?

"Sounds very similar to my father. He hasn't been himself since Mother died—not that they seemed all that happy before. But it's almost like something snapped in him. He's more driven. Obsessed almost." It was his turn to look away.

He shouldn't speak so negatively about his father. It was disrespectful.

"Do you have any siblings?" Her voice brought his attention back.

He gave her a soft smile. "No. Although I remember asking my parents repeatedly for a little brother. That, or a dinosaur. I didn't get either."

She laughed along with him.

Frank waved from ahead. "I think we're ready to keep moving."

With a hefty sigh, Ray widened his eyes. "Oh boy. Are you ready?"

"As I'll ever be. But I may be grunting and groaning in an unladylike manner before too long. So, my apologies now."

"I'm quite certain that I will be grunting and groaning right along with you."

She started walking, but to his surprise, she stayed beside him.

Hopefully it was because she wanted to continue their conversation. At least as long as they could breathe and talk at the same time. There were bound to be some more passages ahead that would take every ounce of effort just to keep going.

"What inspired your interest in photography?" Her question made him smile. Not only had she initiated the conversation, but she had homed in on one of his favorite subjects.

"I went to an art exhibit several years ago, and there was a photographer who was showcasing his photographs from a trip to Africa and then another to the Alps. It inspired and uplifted me, so I ordered some equipment, studied as much as I could, and started to dabble in the art. And it truly is an art. Some people are genuinely gifted at having the eye for it, and those people amaze me."

"I wouldn't even know where to start." Her breaths came a bit shorter as the incline increased. "But I can imagine you could stay here an entire lifetime and never take all the pictures you'd like."

"That is true. I've attempted to get some good sunset pictures, but I haven't quite mastered it yet. None of them have turned out quite like I hoped. But I've also been taking pictures for my father's investors, so that has taken a bit of my time."

"Is that why you were over at the Hopi House with your camera?"

"Yes. The art displayed is exquisite." He took longer steps and slowed down a bit. Every muscle in his back and legs was unhappy with him at the moment. "Did you know that Fred Harvey had a priceless collection of Indian artwork on display in there? Navajo blankets, an ethnographic collection of the Hopi people, Pomo baskets, Eskimo handiwork, and a room filled with rare buffalo-hide shields. It's incredible. The Navajo blankets won grand prize at the Louisiana Purchase Exposition last year."

"I didn't know that! I love the Hopi House. It's been my favorite place to visit. The people are so sweet, and Chuma keeps trying to teach me how to weave. Of course, you saw that."

"Trying? You did better than I did. You actually had something that looked like a basket." He couldn't help but laugh.

"So far, she hasn't been successful. But she is patient and tells me I will learn. I don't know if that's a command or just hopeful thinking. Chuma says that weaving rugs will be next. I can only hope that I'll be better at that."

The rest of the hike passed in long stretches of silence as they climbed, followed by snippets of conversation that gave him a glimpse into her world.

The more time he spent with her, the more he longed for even more of it. She was fascinating. Completely different from any of the other women he'd known.

When they arrived back at the hotel, exhausted and exhilarated, Mr. Owens handed him a telegram.

"Thank you." Ray nodded at the man as he turned to his companions from the day. "And thank you for a wonderful hike. I hope you all have a restful night."

The others said good-night and he opened the paper.

Coming now. Please make sure my rooms are ready and ensure that the kitchen has fresh ice cream made each day.
—Dad

Ice cream? Since when did his dad eat ice cream—much less every day? His behavior was getting odder by the day. What was going on?

———— ┤ ├ ————

With sore legs and a full heart, Emma Grace walked down the stairs with Caroline to their quarters. The day had been better than she'd even imagined. Not only was the canyon gorgeous, but she'd truly enjoyed the company.

As much as she wanted to keep her heart hardened against all men—especially men of wealth—Ray had shown her that he was a true gentleman. Frank too. Maybe there were good and decent men left in the world. Maybe they weren't all like her father and Mr. Cooper and Mr. Wellington and every other businessman who'd dealt with her father over the years. Maybe . . . just maybe, there was a way for her heart to soften.

Trusting was a bit more difficult to imagine. But she'd made a healthy start. She had.

"I think my legs might simply fall off tonight." Caroline put a hand on the wall and leaned against it. Her flair for the dramatic never ceased to amaze Emma Grace. But it also made life so much more fun. Something she'd been desperately missing for years.

"I'm glad I was smart enough to think ahead and sign up for the tub tonight. A long soak might be the only thing that saves me." Emma Grace couldn't wait to soothe her aching muscles.

Ruth and Blanche, another Harvey Girl, were headed down the hall toward them. The ladies waved, and Ruth's face lit up. She picked up her pace and met them in a few short strides. "Well? How was it?"

"Amazing, beautiful . . . and exhausting!" Emma Grace felt the smile stretch across her face.

"Exhausting. Now that's the word I would use. That, and hard. Difficult . . . and whoever invited me to do such a thing in the first place needs to give me a foot massage." The pointed look Caroline gave Emma Grace made all the girls laugh. "I'm serious, I can't believe I agreed to go with you." She clung to Blanche's arm. "I'm afraid of heights, you know."

"Oh, stop it." Emma Grace placed her hands on her hips. "You loved it and you know it." Their giggles echoed down the hall.

"I did." Caroline ceased her dramatics. "It was really quite unbelievable. I'm glad I went, but don't go asking me to go again. Especially after you climbed that rock. I think I lost ten years off my life because I was so scared for you."

"Wait . . . you climbed a rock?" Ruth's face had turned protective and concerned. "What on earth would you do that for?"

Holding up her hands in defense, Emma Grace put on her

most innocent look. "I wanted to see what the view looked like." She bit her lip. "And there *might* have been a gentleman who said, 'I'd like to see that,' and I *might* have taken that as a challenge."

"You do beat all, Emma Grace." Blanche shook her head, one hand on her hip. "I can't imagine climbing on top of a rock while I was already on a trail on the edge of a canyon. Weren't you scared?"

"No. It was really quite safe. And it did have a spectacular view."

"Mr. Watkins even took a photograph of her. We should ask him tomorrow if he developed it so we can show everyone." Caroline was all smiles now.

"Well, I have an appointment with the tub." Looking at the women around her, Emma Grace couldn't help but feel like they really were becoming a family here. A wonderful, sweet family.

As Caroline and Blanche headed to their rooms arm in arm, their chatter washed over her. Oh, to be young and carefree like that. No fear. Dreaming of marrying a rich man and going off to live in exotic places. Not that she wanted to emulate her trainee, but it was nice to think that there was hope for other people to not become cynical and tired of the humdrum of life.

"You seem deep in thought." Ruth grabbed her elbow. "It was a good day?"

"Yes. A very good day." Why did she allow her thoughts to turn to the negative? She'd just had one of the best days of her life. Probably *the* best since leaving Boston. "Frank is such a gem. I know you know that since you've worked with him for so long, but he's like . . . he's like the big brother I always wanted."

Her friend laughed.

"And Caroline, oh my goodness that girl is comical. She had us all in stitches time after time. Especially when we were climbing back up and conversation would lull because we were all huffing and puffing our way up the trail. She'd make a comment and it would get us all laughing again."

Ruth quirked one eyebrow at her, an expression Emma Grace had come to expect. "And what about Mr. Watkins?"

It was a very good question. One she'd pondered every time the silence had accompanied them as they hiked. "He's a very nice man."

"Oh? Just a very nice man?"

"What exactly are you asking?" Emma Grace retrieved her key from around her neck to unlock her door.

"It's no secret that he always sits at your table."

"And?"

"And . . . well, I was simply wondering if you had the chance to get to know him any better today. It sounds like you all had fun."

"We did." She opened her door and went in.

"I didn't mean to intrude on anything personal, I promise." Ruth put her hands on the doorjamb and studied her. "I'm just used to all my girls ending up married before too long. Especially one as pretty as you. Contract or no contract."

While all the Harvey Girls signed contracts to remain single for a certain amount of time and to uphold the values that Harvey insisted on, Emma Grace knew how often the girls got married. She'd seen dozens of them get hitched over the past five years. "Don't worry. I will fulfill my contract. I'm planning on staying right here. Forever."

Ruth reached out one of her hands to grab one of Emma Grace's. "I wasn't saying that you wouldn't, and I don't wish to offend you."

"I'm not offended. It's fine. It's just been a long day." She stood there, gripping the door with one hand and timidly holding Ruth's outstretched hand with the other.

With a squeeze, her friend let go. "Why *haven't* you married, Emma Grace? Because of your past and your father's business?"

"Mostly, yes. But also because I wouldn't give any man a chance to know me."

"But I've seen girls get proposals the first time they meet a man. You are definitely beautiful and one of those women who I can imagine would have generated a lot of interest."

"I turned everyone down. Immediately. I knew the Harvey way and how to treat customers, but I never allowed them the chance to flirt. One man even told me he was scared of me because I looked like I would run at any minute. That was when I realized I wanted to find a place I could stay for a long time. A place I could feel safe and not look over my shoulder all the time. But I knew that would never happen. Even so, as soon as I heard about El Tovar, I jumped at the chance, always hoping in the back of my mind that this could be the fresh start I'd wanted." As she peered at her friend, her stomach sank. Their conversation had gotten awfully personal again. "What about you? Why haven't you married? You're such a lovely person, Ruth."

Pink crept into her friend's cheeks. "I guess I just haven't met the right man yet."

"Frank seemed awfully interested the other day when he asked if you could come on the hike." She waggled her eyebrows.

"Oh stop. We've known each other a long time. Frank is just a good friend." Ruth's voice squeaked a bit as she ducked her head.

"Uh-huh." Emma Grace sent her a grin.

Ruth's face grew redder by the second.

"I'm sorry. I won't tease."

"Well, you make me feel young, Emma Grace. I'm glad you're here. And I'm thankful that you had a good day." Ruth turned to head to her room. "I hope you sleep really well."

Emma Grace leaned forward. "Ruth?"

"Yes?"

"Thank you. For everything."

"You're welcome. I thank God every day that He brought you here."

As her friend left, she pondered the last statement. Was that what had happened? Had God brought her here? It didn't seem fathomable that the God of the universe would care about her. Especially when there were so many other important people to take care of.

And she'd felt abandoned by God ever since He'd neglected to rescue her from her kidnapper. Then after Mother died. Then when her father got obsessed with his fortune, completely ignored her, and then tried to marry her off. Where had God been?

God, there's so much I don't understand. I'm trying. I really am. That verse Ruth told me has run over and over in my mind. It says that I need to seek You. Am I doing that correctly? I want to have the peace she's always talking about. And I desperately want to be rid of this fear. But I don't see any way out of it.

Her mind spun, and it made her feel muddled. Frank had mentioned earlier when he'd blessed their picnic that he always started his prayers by thanking God. Maybe she should try that.

All right, God. I don't think I'm doing any of this right, but I'm hoping You will forgive me because I'm new at this. I do want to thank You for bringing me here. For giving me this job—a way to take care of myself. And for giving me the wonderful day today. It is so incredible to see the majesty of the Grand Canyon. So, thank You for that. Help me, Lord. Help me to do what's right. Help me to know how to get rid of this fear. And Lord, if You want me to come forward and tell the truth, give me the strength to do that.

13

The lunch hour couldn't come soon enough for Ray. He paced outside the Hopi House, waiting for the chance to see Emma Grace again. All week he'd been praying about pursuing her. Praying for her heart. Praying for the Lord's will. He'd had several good conversations with Frank and knew that she was searching. And while he didn't wish to be unequally yoked, he felt a tug toward her. Like maybe he was supposed to help.

Frank had reminded him that God didn't need his help. He'd also encouraged him to step back for a few days and give her some space. It would give his own mind time to pause and reflect.

Ray had done just that. The past few days had been tortuous for him, but he was glad he'd listened. He'd even asked to sit at other tables for a few days. Which had made him miss Emma Grace even more, and he was certain it had completely confused her, given the looks he'd seen across the dining room.

Thankfully, it had been a really busy week ever since Dad's telegram. The next day, his father had sent a second telegram with a list of everything he wanted accomplished before he arrived, plus everything he demanded the hotel have for him. Yes, demanded. When had Dad started using such harsh language? Granted, things hadn't been the same since Mother passed, but he thought for sure that Dad would loosen up at this point.

His father had been investing in anything and everything. All because he wanted to be known. At least that's what Ray took out of it.

The deeper he got in his study of the Word and his relationship with the Lord, the more distant he felt from his father and what he wanted for the Watkins empire. Because Dad just didn't make sense to him anymore.

The thing that really put him over the edge was that his father's men stole all those jewels. If Ben's words in the jail were any indication, Ray didn't know his father. "*Where do you think we learned our behavior, Junior?*"

Not if the implication in those words was true.

Was it a coincidence that Dad not only knew the jeweler and had worked with him, but then his own men knew what train the man would be on and stole from him? It seemed almost too easy. And no one would have been the wiser if the guys hadn't decided to play poker and try to cheat at that too.

Ray looked at his watch for the umpteenth time and felt a little thrill of relief knowing that he could finally go in and see Emma Grace. Pushing thoughts of his dad aside, he went inside.

As the host greeted him, he asked for his usual table.

The older man grinned, something Ray hadn't seen very often. "This way, sir."

"Thank you." Ray couldn't help but smile. He couldn't wait to see her face.

There she was. Walking toward him in her pristine dress and apron. Her glasses made her look studious and a bit more serious, but what enchanted him the most was her eyes. She could convey a world of emotion in her eyes. No matter how hard she tried to keep to herself.

"Good afternoon, Mr. Watkins." She looked as puzzled at his presence now as she had by his absence. "How have you been?"

"Quite well, Miss Edwards, but very busy. I'm sorry for my absence."

"Why have you been giving up your favorite table? You've still been coming in to eat." She poured him a glass of water. It didn't seem to bother her to get to the point, a fact that made him think she was comfortable enough with him to speak her mind. That was a good sign, right?

It was now or never. He was tired of waiting. "Actually, under the advisement of a good friend, I've been spending a bit of time praying about this, and I would like to ask you if you would be free in the evenings for a walk."

"Why did you need to pray about that?" Was she offended? Standing there with the water pitcher in one hand and coffee carafe in the other, she looked at him as though he might have mixed up his words.

He took a moment to go back over what he'd said. "Well . . . I didn't want to jump in too soon or stick my foot in my mouth like I just did, apparently. I don't wish to put you in any uncomfortable situation. I simply want to get to know you better. Just like we talked about on the hike."

"Oh, I see." She filled his coffee cup, but her brow was still furrowed.

"My friend also said it would be good to give you some space for a few days since I had dominated your time and energy. That was why I gave up my table." His nervousness came out in a soft laugh.

"Does your friend know me?"

"Yes, he does."

Understanding registered on her face. "Ah, so it was Frank. I see. It makes sense now. That was very sensitive of him to think of that."

"Does that mean you agree to walk with me in the evenings?"

She pursed her lips. "You're inviting me to walk with you every evening? What if there's another gentleman I've already agreed to spend time with?"

His heart sank as heat rushed to his head. He hadn't thought of that. "Oh, well . . . I don't wish to monopolize all your time. I—"

"I'm teasing you, Ray." Her tone was a bit hushed. "I will gladly accept your invitation. I have to be honest, though, the weather may not always permit it, and there might be times my workload will keep me late."

"I don't mind. I'll wait. Perhaps when the weather is foul, we can sit and visit in the Rendezvous Room? Or maybe the Music Room?" He hoped his eagerness wouldn't overwhelm her.

"I'll have to change out of my uniform, but yes, that would be lovely." The smile she bestowed on him was brighter than any he'd ever seen on her face. "Is the invitation good for this evening?"

"Yes. I'll be here for dinner and then I'll wait for you. If that's all right?"

"I'd like that." After a glance around the room, her features were serious again. "Now, Mr. Watkins, I must ask what you would like to order for luncheon today."

He sat up a bit straighter and looked at his menu. That's right. He was here for luncheon. But he couldn't focus on it. "I tell you what, you've done an excellent job surprising me with sumptuous meals in the past. Would you mind choosing something for me? I admit to being a bit distracted by a lovely woman." He had no idea if he was handling the situation correctly, but when her cheeks flushed, it gave him a boost of confidence. Perhaps there was hope for him yet.

"I will gladly do that for you. I should probably attend to my other tables now. I don't want to get into trouble because I've neglected our guests."

"Please. Take care of them. I'll be here."

She walked away with a smile on her face. That was all the encouragement he needed to make it through the rest of the day. Tonight, he would get to spend time with her.

As he watched the bustling dining room around him, he admired the hard work the Harvey Girls put in every day. The coffee that all Harvey Houses were famous for was always freshly brewed, with the guests' cups filled continuously. The place was spotless, with everything in order, and the traffic of the busy kitchen all seemed to move in perfect rhythm.

His stomach rumbled as the scent of freshly baked bread wafted over to him.

Emma Grace brought him a generous basket of it and a plate of butter. Then she deposited a large bowl of French onion soup. "I thought it might ward off the chill of the wind today."

As he enjoyed his meal, Emma Grace appeared a few extra times. They didn't take time for much conversation, but he appreciated her smiles. She was a wonder and to think that she'd agreed to take a walk with him.

He left the dining room with a new spring in his step.

"Son!" His father's voice caught him off guard.

He turned, and sure enough Dad was standing at the front desk.

"I didn't know you were coming in today, Dad. But I'm

so glad you're here." Stepping forward, he went to hug his father, but his dad simply held out a hand to shake. Well, this was new.

"Good to see you too, son." He tucked a newspaper under his arm. "Come, we've got lots of business to attend to."

"Of course. I understand." He didn't really, but there was no use trying to get his dad to relax after the long and grueling train ride. There was no use *ever* trying to change his father's mind. He led his dad up the stairs to their rooms. "Here we are."

"This is a fine hotel. Yes, a fine hotel indeed." His dad bobbed his head up and down as he looked around the hall. "Here, I have something to show you."

Unlocking his door, his dad handed the newspaper to him. "Can you believe it?"

"Um . . . believe what?" Ray flicked open the paper and saw a headline about a murderer at large.

"Not that." Dad's exasperation was evident, and he stabbed at the paper with a finger. "This, right here."

"'America's Richest and Their Philanthropy,'" he read aloud. Ray scanned the article but couldn't find what would be perturbing Dad to such an extreme.

"It's a shame. I've had my lawyers contact that horrible reporter. To think that Carnegie, Vanderbilt, Astor, and Rockefeller have all been named and there's not one mention of *me* as one of the richest men."

Should he state the obvious?

But his dad went on. "It is well known that I am the richest man in Chicago. My name should be listed with these other men. There are not many others in our league, son. I expect to be recognized."

"I understand how you might feel slighted, Dad, but—"

"There's no 'but.' And this isn't just a *slight*. I deserve

203

to have what's rightfully mine." His face was now red and mottled.

Ray read the article in full while Dad paced the room and continued his rant. Once Ray finished it, he folded the paper neatly and laid it down.

"See? Not one mention of me."

"I know that this is frustrating for you. . . ." But what could he say? His father was off his rocker and fanatical about wealth and recognition. Was there any way to temper it? The best he could do would be to tell the truth. "But this article is about these wealthy men and their giving over the years—not just the fact that they are the richest. Carnegie has given away ninety percent of his wealth."

"Well, that's just ridiculous. Who cares about them giving it away?"

"Obviously the readers of the paper, Dad. People don't just want to know about rich people and how they've accumulated more or how they live. Times have been hard. We just came out of a two-year recession. It left many without anything. Those people want to know how the rich are giving back to their communities, to charities, to churches, all of it. Maybe it helps them to feel better about themselves when they see how the wealthy give too."

"Are you saying I'm not good enough because I don't give? Well, that's preposterous. Just because I've been smart in my investments and don't throw all my money away doesn't mean that I'm not equal to Carnegie or Vanderbilt."

"No one is saying that you aren't, Dad." There was no way to appease his father when he got like this. "I was just pointing out that the topic of the article wasn't their wealth but what they gave away."

Dad looked like he might explode, but then his face changed and he waved a hand at Ray, as if he was dismissing him. "I still don't like it. But I'll deal with it later. Please tell John to unpack my things once he's up here." He turned and headed toward his bed. "I'm going to lie down. Confounded article gave me a headache."

Another oddity. Dad never rested in the middle of the day. But Ray would take the time to go to his room and pray. Something wasn't right, and he had no idea how to fix it. "Would you like me to wake you for dinner?"

"Yes, and make sure that they have everything I've requested."

"Of course." Ray let himself out and went to his own room. The problem before him required a good deal of thought. He went to his photography equipment and pulled it all out. The best way he worked through an issue was to put things in order or reorganize.

The picture of Emma Grace up on the rock with her back to the camera was quite remarkable. The expanse of the canyon before her. But it was the picture from their picnic the other day that made him smile wider. Obviously camera shy, she'd hidden the majority of her face with her hat. The silhouette of her face drew him in. He wanted to know everything about her.

As he placed the pictures back on the desk and then sorted through the glass plates, his thoughts went back to his father's oddities of late. He mulled over his options. Maybe he could speak to other staff of his father's, perhaps even his secretary back in Chicago or, better yet, to John about his father's changed behavior. The valet knew the senior Watkins quite well after all these years.

With the words of Ben and George repeating in his mind, along with the telegrams, and now Dad's behavior, one thing was certain: Dad wasn't himself. And he wasn't getting any better.

———| |—|——

Emma Grace dashed from one table to the next as the dinner rush was even busier tonight than usual. And there were two girls sick, which didn't help matters. Now she had extra tables and had to assist Ruth with the head waitress duties since she was also in charge of tables. What a night.

The good thing about it all was that she had something really wonderful to look forward to tonight.

The walk with Ray.

Not that she had any dreamy expectations. She was determined to find out whether the man was as trustworthy as he seemed. Besides, she wasn't sure she wanted to pursue anything more at this moment. She'd made a commitment to the El Tovar and Harvey. She'd been perfectly content to think that she would remain single and waitress for the rest of her life, or at least until she was too old for Harvey's standards.

But all that changed during the picnic. She had to admit to herself that Ray drew her in. He was interesting and not like all the other rich men she'd known. She couldn't help that her stomach filled with butterflies now when he looked at her. The fact that he had taken the time to get advice and to pray about pursuing her actually made her feel wanted and special.

As if she'd conjured him by her thoughts, she spotted Ray in the host's hallway outside the dining room. He was later than usual. Then she noticed an older gentleman with him.

Oh boy. That must be his father. Ray had said he would be coming.

With a deep breath, she carried the food to table two. Table one had finished their dinner and the table would be open soon enough. Then the Watkins men would be seated and she'd get to meet Ray's father. The question was, what would he think of her?

The gentleman at table three lifted his finger in the air. Attention back on the job at hand, she hurried over to see to his request.

"What can I get you, sir?"

"My wife simply suggested that we needed to thank you. Your attention to detail has been lovely this evening." The man smiled over at his wife.

The woman tipped her head at him in a sweet and loving manner. "You see, it's our anniversary, and we decided to splurge and come out to the Grand Canyon to celebrate."

"Happy anniversary and thank you for your kind words. It is my privilege to honor you in such a way. Would you like to end the evening with a piece of pie or perhaps a slice of our chef's famous coconut cake?"

"That cake sounds wonderful. Let's try that." The wife patted her husband's arm.

"A very good choice. I'll be right back with your dessert."

Armed with the couple's compliment, she watched as their host seated Ray and the man she presumed was his father. She couldn't help but grin. So far, the night was going quite well, even if it was busy.

After putting in the order for the cake, she headed to table one. "Good evening, Mr. Watkins." She nodded at Ray.

"Miss Edwards, I'd like to introduce you to my father, Mr. Ray Watkins Senior."

"It's a pleasure to meet you, Mr. Watkins." Even though all of a sudden she felt nervous, she made sure to smile and look the man in the eye.

He looked away. "I'd like some water and coffee. Cream and sugar."

She blinked. No "nice to meet you" or anything. "Of

course, sir. I'll be right back with those." Turning on her heel, she felt the flush build in her face. Was the man intentionally rude? Or just too good to speak to a lowly waitress?

She made her way back to the table with water and coffee. Maybe she needed to prepare herself for the worst. With a stiff spine, she returned to table one. As she poured the water and then the coffee, the senior Mr. Watkins didn't even say a word of gratitude.

Out of the corner of her eye, she looked at Ray.

"Thank you, Miss Edwards." His smile was the same as it always was for her. Warm and kind.

"Have you gentlemen decided what you would like for dinner?"

Ray's father was quick to speak. "I'd like the chef's special for tonight. Along with the asparagus and the pickle platter."

"Of course, sir. Would you also like to order dessert at this time, or would you like to wait?"

"I assume there is Harvey's famous apple pie?"

"Yes, sir."

"Good. That is what I want. With vanilla ice cream." He turned to his son. "You did tell the manager that I insisted on ice cream being made fresh daily?"

"I did, although it isn't necessary. Chef Marques is impeccable." Ray smoothed his napkin into his lap.

"Don't argue with me in front of the staff, son." Mr. Watkins wouldn't even look at her.

The staff? Well, he was correct. She *was* the staff. "I'll make sure that the kitchen knows exactly what you would like. And for you, Mr. Watkins?" She shifted her attention to Ray.

"I do believe the roast beef sounds good. With creamed potatoes and carrots. I'll have the coconut cake for dessert. Thank you, Miss Edwards." While he seemed genuine enough, it was easy to see that he was on edge. Was it because of his father? Or because of her?

"I'll be back with your dinners shortly, gentlemen." No sense lingering for conversation. It was obvious that Ray's father didn't want her around.

The evening passed in a weird and strange way. Never had Emma Grace felt so awkward in front of anyone until Mr. Ray Watkins Senior was at her table. No matter what she did, it wasn't good enough for him to even acknowledge her. Ray even apologized to her at one point, to which his father scolded him. It was all so very odd.

But it didn't matter. Not really. As far as Mr. Ray Watkins Senior was concerned, she *was* only a waitress. She suspected his attitude would instantly change as soon as he knew who she really was. But why even give him that chance? He'd probably still look down upon her for lowering herself to the status of the working class. She should have known. Mr. Watkins Senior was exactly like every other rich man she'd known. Just like her father. They didn't deserve the attention they received.

Every harsh thing she'd ever thought about her own father came rushing back to the surface. All rich men were alike. Greedy. Selfish. Snobbish.

Until she'd gotten to know Ray.

But if Ray's father didn't like her, then what would he think when his son told him that they were getting to know each other better? What if the older man didn't approve? Would he take that out on Ray? And was Ray prepared for the consequences?

At this point, money didn't matter to her. But what if, underneath it all, it actually *did* matter to Ray?

As she went back to table one to refill their coffee, the senior Watkins was standing. "I believe I'll retire for the evening now." He straightened his exquisitely tailored suit and nodded to his son. "Let's discuss business tomorrow morning over breakfast."

Ray stood with his father. "Yes, sir."

His father walked away without even acknowledging her, his chin lifted ever so slightly.

"You'll have to forgive my father." Ray sat back in his seat and shook his head. "He hasn't been well for some time now. I guess I hadn't been willing to see it."

"Oh? He looks healthy enough." She refilled his coffee so he could enjoy his still-uneaten cake.

"I'm afraid it's a sickness of his mind." The sadness in his voice touched a deep place within her. "I haven't wanted to say anything or even allow myself to think that it is true, but it's become all too apparent to me now that he's here."

"I'm sorry about that." She turned to go.

"Wait." He cleared his throat. "Are you still able to join me for a stroll this evening?"

It didn't matter how the rest of the evening had passed, the eagerness in his tone made everything inside her zing to life. "Of course. I'm looking forward to it."

An hour later, she stepped out the hotel's doors. The evening was clear and cold. Emma Grace hadn't even bothered to change out of her uniform. She'd simply wrapped her coat around her and met Ray out by the Hopi House.

"I'm so glad you agreed to join me." He looked like an expectant boy on Christmas morning. "Are you warm enough?"

"I am. Thank you for asking."

They moved forward in an easy stroll and took the path on the rim.

"I don't think I'll ever want to leave this view." His voice was low and hushed.

"I agree. When I came here, I had planned for it to be for the rest of my life. Then when I saw the canyon for the first time, I knew for certain I wouldn't want to leave."

"You'd like to stay here?" The question wasn't accusatory.

"I would. I haven't been here all that long, and already I love it. The people. The distance from the big cities. The view."

"I take it you don't like cities all that much?"

"Not anymore." Their steps on the dirt path were the only sound for several moments.

"Is it because you grew up in Boston?"

She shrugged. "Probably. . . ." She couldn't tell him her real thoughts on the matter or why. Emma Grace looked at Ray from the side. He didn't push or insist on any explanations. He simply waited. "What about you? You said you didn't think you'd ever want to leave this view, but don't you need to return to Chicago at some point?"

He let out a long sigh. "You know, my whole life all I ever wanted was to be able to follow in my father's footsteps and be at the helm of his business. But then, a few years ago, I had an experience that changed my outlook on life. Ever since, I've been a bit unsettled. And the closer I get to the Lord, the more my dreams change. The thing is, now I don't know how I would tell my father that, especially since I've noticed the decline in him."

"What was it that changed your outlook?" Her curiosity was piqued. "Or if I've overstepped in asking, I'm sorry."

"You haven't overstepped. I brought it up. But I will warn you that it's something I haven't shared with anyone else other than a trusted pastor. Not since it happened."

"All right. I appreciate the fact that you trust me with the story, but you don't need to feel obligated. I understand you don't know me very well." Though she was giving him a way out if he didn't want to tell her, now she really wanted to know what it was that had turned his life around.

"After I graduated from college, I came home quite full of myself, convinced that I was ready to take over for my father. I was your typical spoiled rich boy." He took a long, deep breath. "I'm ashamed of who I was back then, but I'm glad that God loves each one of us and forgives us no matter what we've done. Or what we've *been*." He stopped walking. "Do you mind if we stop? As much as what I have to say is difficult, I don't want to hide from you. And I need to see your face as I share the rest."

"Of course." She turned to face him and tucked her hands into her coat pockets. Whatever it was, it sounded pretty intense. Was she ready for this?

"One evening, I had an argument with my father because I was determined that he needed to allow me to be in charge of something. He put me in my place, and I went off in a little tantrum. My mother then scolded me as well. Then I ran out the door and demanded that Jones—our butler—bring my new automobile around. He did. And I took off down the drive in a rage."

He looked down at his feet. "Looking back, I'm ashamed. How I acted. How selfish I was." His head came up, and he stared into her eyes.

She saw all the pain and heartache there. His need for forgiveness was plain on his face.

"Our home is tucked into one of the wealthiest neighborhoods of Chicago, and it's at the top of a hill. The drive is quite long." He blew his breath out between his teeth. "I picked up speed down and around the drive, completely uncaring about anything else. Until I saw a hoop cross the drive and I knew there was a child with a stick behind it. Everything rushed at me in that moment as I pulled the brakes. My whole, selfish life. My attitude. My greed. It was horrifying. And then . . . I hit a little boy with my automobile."

She gasped, and her hands flew to cover her mouth. Tears sprang to her eyes.

"The boy lived." Ray held up his hands and then put them back at his sides. "I have to tell you that before I continue. Not that it makes what I did any better. But it was the most horrible thing I've ever endured. I was reckless, and I put that child in danger."

It took several moments for her heart to slow down. What an awful thing to go through.

The look on his face was broken. Grief-stricken.

She reached out and touched his arm. "So . . . what happened?"

"I took the boy to the hospital and waited with his family. They were angry at first, as they had every right to be. But when the news came that Thomas was going to be all right—he had a broken arm and a lot of bruises—the couple sat down in the waiting room right then and there and started thanking God. I don't have to tell you that I wasn't a good person back then. You've probably already figured that out from the beginning of my story, but something inside me wanted whatever it was that the Wright family had.

"When I got home, my father informed me that he had taken care of everything with the police and the press and so nothing would get out about his son being a reckless driver. He was embarrassed by me. He yelled at me for a good hour and told me he'd never be able to trust me. I deserved it. And I knew it. But the next day, I went back to the Wrights'. Then the next. And the next. That little boy taught me more about forgiveness than anyone else in my entire life. A few days later, a man came to visit me. His name was Reverend

James. The Wrights' pastor." He shifted his weight. "Are you still warm enough?"

"I am." At this point, she didn't even think about the temperature. She yearned to know what had made the difference in Ray's life. "Please continue."

"That man stayed with me for six hours that day. I told him everything. How selfish I'd become, what drove me to racing down the drive. I thought that if I confessed it all, he would give me the magic formula for how to take away the guilt and shame."

"Did he?" Her heart ached to find out how to heal itself.

"Over time. It wasn't an instant fix that day. I was still stubborn and immature. But thankfully, Reverend James had an abundance of patience. We talked a lot over the next few weeks. And I spent a good deal of time with the Wright family." Ray rubbed his hands together, a deep furrow in his brow. "You see, I desperately knew I wanted forgiveness. That little boy and his family understood forgiveness. So, I asked them how I could have what they had. I was a sinner— I still am. But I needed a Savior. And I had to be willing to admit that and see my need—that I can do nothing in and of myself. I went from being an extremely selfish young man to actually being able to put others first."

"Did you feel a difference right away?" It was hard to imagine that Ray was once the young man he described, knowing the man who stood before her now. And yet, hadn't she lumped all wealthy men into the same category? Maybe this was the difference.

"I did. Although I admit that God had to work on me for at least six months to get my attitude to completely change. Like I said, it wasn't an instant fix. But faith has changed everything for me. I've learned that God loves each one of us, no matter what we've done, or who we've been, or how we've treated other people. He loves the man who murders his brother. He loves the preacher who screams about hell, fire, and brimstone. He loves the wayward child who seeks his own way and selfishly hurts those around him. That's why Scripture teaches us that we are to do two things: love God with everything that we are and love others. That's what I aim to do for the rest of my life."

She looked away for a moment. His faith was just like Ruth's and Frank's, and it was so different than what she'd grown up with. She'd never met anyone who believed this way, and somehow she was now surrounded by people who were sharing this and living it.

"What are you thinking, Emma Grace? I hope I didn't scare you away with my story." He reached for one of her hands. "I promise you, I am not that man anymore."

"No, you didn't scare me away. But I have more questions than I have answers." She glanced down at their hands. He so reverently held hers like she was fragile and precious. "May I ask you a favor?"

"Of course."

"I don't have a Bible of my own anymore. Do you perchance have one that I could borrow?"

"I will go grab it right now." The sweet look on his face did more for her heart than she wanted to admit.

14

Emma Grace was awake long before the sun arose. She'd practically been awake all night. She'd tossed and turned and spent a night in fitful unrest because her mind couldn't let go of the verses Frank and Ruth had shared with her. Because Ray's confession and story he'd shared in all humility had wrenched her heart. And because she was a broken mess.

Tears had come off and on throughout the night. Confusion clouded her judgment. All the different voices from past and present warred with each other. She'd tried to read the Bible that Ray had brought to her, but every time she read, there were more voices screaming in her head.

Every cynical and ugly thought had come out in the dark of the night. Lifting her hands to the sides of her head, she stared at the ceiling. "Stop it." Her whispered words to the room around her broke the silence that engulfed her and pressed in. Funny how that same silence had been so loud and threatening.

She let her hands fall at her sides on the bed. "'I sought the Lord, and he heard me, and delivered me from all my fears.'" As she said the words, her heart felt lighter. "'I sought the Lord, and he heard me, and delivered me from all my fears.'"

The confusion and sparring thoughts stopped. This time the silence that followed felt clean. Peaceful.

With more strength in her voice this time, she repeated the verse again and again.

The weight of the night lifted from her shoulders, and she sat up on her bed. She pulled Ray's Bible back into her lap and went back to reading. He'd advised her to read the book of John and had marked it for her.

She'd read through the entire book last night. Jesus became real to her for the first time. But then she'd allowed the negative thoughts to overcome everything else.

Flipping the pages to chapter fourteen, she took a breath and scanned the chapter until she came to verse twenty-seven, one that had stood out to her. With her finger sliding underneath each word, she read it aloud. "'Peace I leave with you, my peace I give unto you: not as the world giveth, give I unto you. Let not your heart be troubled, neither let it be afraid.'"

God, I'm struggling with my fear. I don't even know if You are listening to me but I'm seeking You. Please help me to find Your peace.

She looked down at the book in her lap. There weren't any other words to say. Ray had said that faith had changed everything for him. Not being good. Not anything else. Faith. If only she could have that same faith.

Her alarm clock's shrill ring made her jump.

It was time to start another long day.

She climbed out of bed, straightened the bedding, and set the Bible on top of her pillow. Then she remembered Frank's words about thanking God first.

As she dressed, she focused on everything she was thankful for. The more she listed, the more she realized how much had changed in the weeks she'd been at El Tovar.

She loved her work. Loved the people here. And in the evenings, she had something to look forward to—her walks with Ray. She should just strive to have a positive attitude and make the best of each day.

With one last look in the mirror, she patted her hair and pushed her glasses up her nose. Oh, to not have to disguise herself each day. It was selfish and prideful, but she longed to be able to wear her hair looser. Longed to be herself. For so many years, it hadn't mattered to her because all that mattered was hiding. The looming threat of Mr. Wellington finding her and forcing her into marriage as he stole her father's company had always been at the forefront of her mind.

While that fear still lingered in her thoughts, a new hope had sprung up.

Emma Grace closed and locked her door and headed up to the dining room. Best to focus on the hope rather than the fear. There had to be a way for her to change things. There had to be.

When she reached the dining room, the fabulous scent of the famous Harvey coffee filled her nose. That's what she needed first. Coffee. It might be the only way to combat her lack of sleep from the previous night.

Ruth was already in the kitchen, making a list for each of the waitresses that day.

Chef Marques and his staff bustled around in perfect rhythm. There wasn't any chatter, just the sounds of bubbling and simmering and the stirring of pots.

Ruth lifted her gaze from the paper she'd been writing on. "Good morning." Her eyes twinkled.

"Good morning." Emma Grace studied her friend's face. The joy that was there seemed to ooze out from her skin. That's what Emma Grace wanted. "How are things looking for today?"

"Busy as usual. But I think we will be able to keep things moving like a well-oiled machine. We are Harvey Girls, after all." Her cheeky grin made Emma Grace want to giggle.

"That we are." She reached for a cup and poured herself some coffee. "Is there anything you need me to do?"

"Could you check with Pierre about the butter? They were almost ready for us to press it." Ruth went back to her list.

"Of course." Emma Grace took a sip and put her cup back down. But as soon as she reached Pierre, he grinned at her. One of the kitchen crew already held a large tray containing the circles of chilled butter and was headed in her direction. She turned on her heel. That cup of coffee was calling to her.

Mr. Owens was speaking with Ruth when she came back. He noticed her and beckoned her with a finger.

Whatever it was, it didn't make him happy.

She stepped up to them and looked from his face to Ruth's. "Well, this doesn't bode well."

He held out a piece of paper. "This telegram just arrived." Mr. Owens' face was a bit pale as he handed her the paper. "I know it says not to show you, but I think it's only right that you should see it."

She took the paper and searched her friend's face. Ruth appeared stunned. Emma Grace told herself to breathe and opened the paper.

Urgent. Looking for young woman, early twenties, worked as Harvey Girl. Goes by Emma Grace. Important legal matter. Do not alert her to my inquiry. Her life is at stake. Respond within twenty-four hours with yes or no to her presence.

Peter Samson—Pinkerton Agent

With a gulp of air, she folded the paper and handed it back to the manager. Was this sent to scare her? How many places had the man sent telegrams to? Would he be able to find her? She swallowed before she could speak. It didn't do her any good to get worked up about it. But that didn't keep her heart from pounding in her chest. "What do you think it means?"

"I'm not quite sure." The manager nodded to the head waitress. "That's why I came to show it to Miss Anniston."

"Ruth?" Her voice squeaked, giving away the terror she was trying to hide. "What do you think?"

"I don't like it. That's for certain. It definitely sounds as if someone has come close to finding you. Whether it's someone with ill intentions or not, I don't know. But I told Mr. Owens that we needed to protect you." She patted Emma Grace's shaking hand. "And we will. I promise."

Mr. Owens' frown eased. "I agree. If this man is really a Pinkerton, why would he tell me not to inform you? Especially if your life was at stake, like he says. It makes me very suspicious. I'm not going to answer the telegram. It's perfectly valid for him to think it was never received. There's more than eighty Harvey Houses across the country. What are the odds of someone traipsing all the way out here? If he doesn't receive an answer, it's not like he'll think to come here. I think that will be the end of it."

She shook her head. "As much as I would like to agree with you, I don't think that's the case. There are millions of reasons to find me. There will never be an end to it. At least, not until . . ." She decided against saying the rest. The risk to everyone was already too great. She hadn't told anyone that she'd seen the man who must have killed her father. Or the thought that if he found her and forced her into marriage, she would be next.

"Not until what?" Ruth's eyebrows betrayed the fact that she knew exactly what Emma Grace was thinking.

"It's not important. Don't worry about me." She lifted her

chin a notch and looked Mr. Owens in the eye. "Thank you for doing such a valiant job of protecting me. I know I don't deserve your loyalty, but it is much appreciated." She turned to the waitresses' station. "I need to get back to work."

The morning passed in regular rhythm, but Emma Grace really wasn't paying much attention. She could do pretty much everything out of habit now. Not that she wanted to ignore her customers or do just enough to get by, but that's how it felt. Almost as if she were outside herself, watching her body simply go through the motions.

Her customers may not have noticed, but apparently Ruth did. After lunch, she pulled Emma Grace off to the side. "I think you need to go down to your room for a few minutes and take some time to pull yourself together."

"I'm fine." She hated to argue with her friend and supervisor, but it had to be done. "If I think about it too much, it will simply make things worse. Please let me finish my shift today. I'll have plenty of time to pull myself together tonight."

"Promise me that you'll let me know if things get too overwhelming?" Her voice was tender, but Ruth's look was stern and brooked no argument.

"I promise."

"All right. It's against my better judgment. But go ahead."

"Thank you."

The rest of the afternoon marched by as Emma Grace threw herself into her duties. She even took on extra just to keep her hands occupied. While the other girls chatted and giggled over the single male customers they'd served, Emma Grace polished the silver with more vigor than was needed.

Dinner was soon upon them, and she poured herself into seeing to her customers' needs. When Ray and his father sat down at table one, she greeted them as usual and kept it simple. Word had spread throughout the staff about Mr. Watkins Senior and his "request" for special food sent up to his room for the earlier meals, so that he wouldn't have to be bothered by people.

Apparently, the guests had heard as well, because the whispers and glances around the room couldn't be missed. But Ray's father seemed to relish it and smiled to the people around him. In a condescending way, of course. It wouldn't have surprised Emma Grace if he stood from his chair and took a bow.

She cringed at the direction of her thoughts and shook her head to banish them.

Ray sent her several smiles, and she tried to act as if nothing was wrong. His dad didn't much care for any conversation with "their waitress," so she gave him plenty of space.

At least she could look forward to taking a walk with Ray tonight. She'd spent so much time today thinking about her conundrum, that she'd finally come to a conclusion. She was ready to tell him everything.

But what would he think of her?

The only thing that consoled her was the fact that he had shared about his past already.

She'd considered talking to Frank earlier, but her heart only wanted to talk to Ray. Now she just needed to get the nerve to do it.

As soon as dinner and all the duties were complete, she went down to her room to grab her coat. Looking forward to the fresh air, she rallied her courage.

The lack of sleep and the weight of carrying this burden had become too much. It was time.

She unlocked her door and turned on the light.

As she grabbed her coat, she noticed another note on the floor.

No. She put a hand to her forehead. A pounding started in her ears.

She bent down to pick up the note and sucked in her breath.

Opening the folded paper, she read,

I know the truth.

Ray paced outside the Hopi House. He wasn't sure if it was his father's abrupt attitude with Emma Grace that had caused her to be distant, or if something else was bothering her, but he couldn't wait to see her and make sure she was all right.

The soft sound of footfalls behind him made him turn around. As he watched her approach, it became clear that something troubled her. Her arms were crossed over her waist, and her head was down.

"What's wrong?" He wanted to reach out to her and hold her—soothe whatever ailed her. But he didn't have that right.

As she lifted her gaze to him, the sadness in her eyes made him want to do whatever was in his power to take it away. "I don't even know where to begin."

He took her elbow and led her down the path along the rim to a quiet place away from all the buildings. He wiped off a large boulder and directed her to it. "Here, please sit."

She did, but then surprised him by scooting over to the edge. "I think I need you to sit with me."

"All right." He lowered himself to sit next to her, trying ever so hard to maintain space between them just in case anyone came upon them. He didn't want to put her reputation in danger.

She pulled a paper out of her pocket and handed it to him. "Here."

Taking it, he realized it was two notes. He opened the top one and read. "'I know the truth.'" As he folded it back, he opened the second with his other hand. "'I know who you are.'" His heart thudded in his chest. What did this mean? Who was she? He swallowed and turned to her.

Her hands were clasped in her lap, and she stared straight ahead. "My name is Emma Grace McMurray—not Edwards." Her knee began to bounce.

As much as he wanted to ask the questions crowding his mind, he bit his tongue and waited for her to continue.

"When I was a child, my parents doted on me, and I had everything I could possibly want. Then one day, when I was eight, I was kidnapped. All because of business. You see, my father owned parts of railroads and had built a vast empire. Apparently, there was a squabble over a certain spur. Eighteen miles of track. Guess how long my kidnapper kept me?" She didn't wait for him to answer. "Eighteen days." Her shoulders lifted and then sank with a sigh. "My father never did tell me the truth about what happened. But by that point, I didn't care to know. I only knew that men couldn't be trusted. I never wanted to be fooled by a man ever again."

It all started to make sense. Her aloof response to him when they'd first met. Her hesitance around anyone of wealth.

"My mother died shortly after. She'd taken to her bed while I was missing, and even though she was overjoyed when I was returned, the sickness had gone into her lungs. She was too weak to fight it." Emma Grace crossed her arms over her middle again.

"I'm so sorry for your loss. That must have been horrible."

A nod was barely perceptible in the scarce moonlight.

"I was still reeling from being betrayed by my own father. Even though he didn't say it to me directly, I knew he had some part in it. I saw him shaking hands with the man who kidnapped me. And my father's hired *man*"—she nearly spat the word—"handed the kidnapper a bag of money. I know that's what it was. They laughed about it and said it was just business. Thinking that, of course, I didn't understand what was going on. But I knew . . . I knew." Her voice faded, and she continued to stare straight ahead.

Ray let the moments pass in silence and simply waited. Whatever was coming seemed a lot worse.

"My father became obsessed with money after that— something I never understood because he already had plenty of it. But nevertheless, that's what he pursued. I've always been stubborn and strong-willed, so from that day on I vowed to ignore him and basically gave him the cold shoulder. He'd put me into the trust of Nanny Louise and didn't bother to care what happened to me, anyway. This went on until I was sixteen years old. Then, all of a sudden, he acted like he cared about what happened to me. He tried to convince me to host dinners for him so he could introduce me to his business partners, but I refused. I'm ashamed of how I acted toward him, but I was so angry.

"This went on for more than a year. I found out later that since I didn't cooperate, he'd started to negotiate with men— wealthy men who would make advantageous business alliances with him—to marry me. All in all, there were six men who had contracts with my father to marry me. All of them had paid substantial amounts of money or offered up real estate for this arrangement, with a promise from my father to bring them in on his holdings. When he told me about the contracts, I told him that I would never marry because he told me to, so he could just forget about his arrangements."

"I take it he didn't like that very much." Ray couldn't imagine a father doing that to his daughter, even though he knew it was common practice to arrange marriages that would benefit both parties financially in his social circle.

"Oh no. He was furious. He threatened to take away the house, servants, all my clothes, jewelry, everything, so that I would be destitute if I didn't go along with his plan. In his rage, he told me he didn't care which one I married, but I *would* marry one of them. I have no idea how he planned to get away with stealing everyone else's money, whether it was a competition or what, because I definitely couldn't marry all of them. But what he hadn't anticipated was that I didn't care a lick about any of it. Being destitute was better than being sold off to the highest bidder.

"Of course, I didn't tell him that. I stormed off to my wing of the estate, and I already had come up with a plan. I had simply been waiting for the right moment. I had a small bag packed with the plainest clothes I had and shoved as many pieces of jewelry as I could in with them, knowing I could sell them along the way. I'd had several wigs made, and I purchased spectacles. It was the best way I could disguise myself. The only piece of my former life I brought with me was a box that was my grandmother's, in which I'd kept some special mementos. I left that night.

"I knew my father was in his study. Most nights he stayed in there working and would eventually fall asleep. He'd told me who was coming—the man who was first in line in his little competition. As I was leaving, though, I saw Mr. Wellington arrive. It was the perfect opportunity to leave, since my father was occupied. I left and never turned back."

She paused in the story, but Ray sensed there was more. A lot more.

As the silence stretched, she fidgeted with her fingers.

He placed his hand on top of hers, and she made eye contact for the first time since she'd started the story.

"I'm here." He squeezed her hand. "If you need to take a break, I understand."

She blinked several times, the guarded look in her eyes fading. "Thank you." She gripped his hand between her own, and her hands ceased their movement.

She took a long, shuddering breath and continued. "I headed west. Armed with the knowledge I'd learned at our table when Mr. Fred Harvey would visit, part of my plan was to become a Harvey Girl. His stories had always captivated me, so I thought, why not? I knew enough about how he did things that I knew I could be a quick study. I also knew the basics of how to go about getting hired. I couldn't go by my real name anymore, but I had my grandmother's birth record. You see, I was named after her: Emma Grace. Her name by birth was Edwards. So, I changed the birth year and took that into the Harvey office when I went to be interviewed. I also forged glowing recommendation letters based off ones I remembered Mr. Harvey talking about, ones they'd received for girls wanting to become Harvey Girls. The next day, they gave me an employment card and I started the training."

"That explains how you became a waitress. It seems that you enjoy what you do."

"I do. It's been my saving grace. Kept me busy and kept my mind off . . . " She shut her mouth and closed her eyes for a moment, and he was content to watch her silhouette and wait in the quiet of the evening. He enjoyed the feel of his hand in hers and didn't want their conversation to end, even though he imagined it was difficult for her to open up.

"I left out a big detail." She let out a long breath. "After I left Boston, I picked up a newspaper a couple days later and discovered that my father had been murdered the night I left."

In that moment, a faint memory came to the surface. Dad had been furious because his friend was dead. Something about a business deal?

Her chin dipped and he couldn't see her face. "They never caught the man. At least as far as I know. But I saw Mr. Wellington entering my father's study that night.

"I'm so sorry, Emma Grace." He tilted his head and tried to catch her gaze. "Maybe it wasn't Wellington who killed him. After you left, it could have been anyone."

She bit her lip as she looked up at him. "Why? Unless they could get a hold of his money, what was the motive? It had to be Wellington. . . ." Tears shimmered in her eyes and she looked away.

"I don't know." He scooted closer to her and squeezed her hand. "I'm sorry. I didn't mean to make things worse."

Her shoulders slumped. "I don't know what to think anymore."

He watched her for several moments, seeing the turmoil play out over her face. What it must have been like to carry this around for all these years. "Tell me the rest."

She turned her face back toward him and gave a slight nod. "I got in contact with a solicitor—Mr. Scott—who my grandfather trusted, and he told me what he knew of the situation, but he also informed me that all those men who had held contracts with my father were now demanding legal action. Of course, all the men with signed contracts want their money returned, but they also want their hands on my father's estate, which is why they signed the contracts in the first place."

With another deep breath, her shoulders lifted a little. "Since I was nowhere to be found, things were messy. And if I don't show up for fourteen years, they could declare me dead. Which, at the time, I thought was what I wanted. But Mr. Scott told me that Mr. Wellington is relentless and would stop at nothing short of finding me. And unless I marry someone else, he has the law behind him. For five years, I've transferred from Harvey House to Harvey House, changing my hair and my appearance as much as I could, hoping that no one could trace me. It wasn't until just recently, after I came here, that I felt I might be able to look forward to the future.

"And at this point, I want it all over with. I just don't know if I'm brave enough to come forward and tell the truth. Would I even be able to put it all behind me? If it *was* Wellington who killed my father, isn't it safe to assume that he'll come after me? That is . . . if he hasn't found me already."

Ray looked down at the notes that he'd let fall to the ground. "You don't have any idea who sent those?"

"No."

He bent down and picked them up. "Does anyone else here know about your secret?"

"Ruth and Mr. Owens. There have been a couple telegrams of late. One was from someone who knew Mr. Owens and said there was some unpleasant man going around to Harvey Houses looking for Emma Grace McMurray. That was when I told them the truth. Another telegram came this morning, simply looking for a woman named Emma Grace." Her gaze shifted to her lap. "It was from a man who claimed to be a Pinkerton agent. He said my life was at stake but not to let me know about his inquiry."

"What did Mr. Owens do?"

"He said he wouldn't respond. But it does make me worry. And at this point, the nightmares, the fear, and the all-around uneasiness has made me miserable."

"You've been having nightmares?" Ray's heart felt like it would wrench in two at all this lady had gone through.

"I'm sorry. I shouldn't be telling you all of this. We've only known each other a few weeks." She stood and rubbed her forehead.

He immediately missed her presence, he reached toward her and beckoned her back. "Please, don't apologize. It means a great deal that you trusted me enough to share it with me. I know that wasn't easy." She inched closer and he took her hands in his. "Let me help you carry this burden. I want to." Had he gone too far? But his heart longed for more. Even after the shock of all she'd told him. If anything, he cared even more for her. Would do anything for her.

A shimmer of tears made the sadness in her eyes more pronounced. "I'm tired, Ray. For the first time in a long time, I want to live my life. But I don't know if I can."

15

You told me last night that your faith changed everything for you," Emma Grace continued. "I can't stop thinking about that. What was it exactly that helped you understand faith?" The pleading in her voice edged on desperation.

It was getting close to curfew time for Emma Grace, but Ray couldn't let her leave without saying what was on his heart. He understood how she felt.

"I don't have all the answers, but I'm hoping you'll hear me out."

Her eyes were filled with sadness, but he prayed he could change that. She sat back down beside him and turned to look at him this time. "Of course."

"Well, as I got to know Reverend James, he took me through the Gospels over several weeks, trying to explain it all to me in terms I could understand. One night, he showed me Mark chapter five, verse thirty-six. At the end of the verse, it says, 'Be not afraid, only believe.'"

He let his gaze go back down to her hands, and he captured hers between his own. "You see, in my eagerness to learn all I could, I had apparently tried to make it harder than it actually is. I thought for sure that I wasn't good enough, that I didn't deserve grace and mercy. There must be more to it, right?"

Her shoulders relaxed a bit. "That's exactly what has been running through my mind again and again."

"Well, it's wrong." His light laugh hopefully helped her to relax. "I'd been trying so hard to assuage my own guilt. Reverend James called it *striving*. The striving that we do as humans to work our way into grace puts us in opposition to ourselves. We're fighting and battling, clawing for every foothold, devoting all of our energy and effort into *earning* grace. But it can't be done. Because God's grace is a free gift to us. *He* paid the price so we wouldn't have to."

She shook her head. "That goes against everything I ever heard preached as I was growing up. Yes, we heard the story of God sending His Son as a baby to be born from a virgin. Then we heard about how He died on the cross. But everything else was about us doing good works so that we could attain heaven. The reverend at our church in Boston was good at yelling and scaring all of us. We definitely didn't want to go to the devil's domain, but if we didn't do enough good, that's where we were told we would end up. Fear was always talked about: We needed to fear God, fear His holy wrath, fear the consequences if we didn't do what was right."

"I know. I heard plenty of those same kinds of sermons growing up as well. That's why when Reverend James showed me that verse, I wanted to cry. 'Be not afraid, only believe.' It didn't seem possible. But then I read the verses that came before it. See, a man named Jairus had come to Jesus because his daughter was very sick. Jesus was going with him to see her when a servant came and told Jairus that he wouldn't need Jesus after all because his daughter had died. That's when Jesus said, 'Be not afraid, only believe.'

And he went with Jairus to his home and even amidst all the grief and wailing, he assured him that his daughter was not dead. When he went in and told the girl to rise up, she did." He squeezed her hands. "It was in that moment that I understood. I had heard that story in church many times, but I had missed the point. My fear was controlling me. I needed to believe. I needed to put my faith in the one true God."

She studied him for several moments.

Had he messed it all up? *Lord, give me the right words.* "I was completely broken at that point in my life. But God turned my horrible mistakes into a new life for Him."

Emma Grace looked down at their hands. "You've given me a lot to think about." Then she stood up. "Monday is my next day off. I'd like to go exploring around the canyon rim some more. Would you be available? That is, of course, if I can get one of the girls to go along with us."

Her quick change of subject told him he'd better let her deal with all he'd shared in her own time. It wasn't his place to push. He came to his feet as well and smiled. "I'd love to."

"Good." She turned her face toward the hotel. "I need to get inside before curfew."

"Of course. Let me walk with you."

On Monday, Emma Grace woke without an alarm. Ever since her conversation with Ray on Saturday night, her mind had been spinning with everything she'd heard and studied. If God was *really* like what Ruth, Frank, and Ray all described, then she wanted to jump in with both feet. But fear kept creeping in. Fear that He wasn't. Fear that He would fail her just like her own father. Fear that she could never trust again.

Fighting against all the doubt that swirled in her mind, she said the verse aloud. "'I sought the Lord, and he heard me, and delivered me from all my fears.'"

It was a good thing today was her day off and she was going out to explore, because she needed to step away from it all and just have fun.

Ruth had wanted to chat yesterday, but the timing never presented itself. Several mishaps in the kitchen had kept her running back and forth. Emma Grace had wanted to tell her about the other note but couldn't bring herself to add one more thing to the headwaitress's already overloaded schedule. It was a good thing she hadn't said anything because then Ruth would worry and probably advise her against going out to explore today. Something she desperately needed.

Including seeing Ray.

She hadn't seen him at all yesterday and hated admitting that she had inwardly pouted when she heard that Ray and his dad had taken off to Williams and he didn't even bother to leave her a note. Not that she had any reason to have those expectations.

It seemed the weight of the world was pressing in on her.

There was a man asking about her at Harvey Houses.

Then there was the mysterious guy who called himself a Pinkerton.

Wellington would stop at nothing to gain her father's money. Of that she was more certain as each day passed.

Was he her father's murderer as well? Would he kill her too? Her father's fortune was at stake, so it was entirely possible. But what if there was another threat?

It was bad enough when she thought there was only one monster after her. If there were more . . . ? She wasn't sure she could keep the fear at bay. She got out of bed and pushed the thoughts from her mind. "'I sought the Lord, and he heard me, and delivered me from all my fears.'"

Fear had become her way of life for too long, and she'd had enough.

All right, God, I need to get rid of this weight. I want to be delivered from all this fear. I just don't know how. Please help me.

As she made her bed, a sweet calm filled her. Was that God?

She definitely needed a good, long hike today. Something to get her blood pumping and her body moving so that she could forget everything else for a while.

Maybe Ray would bring his camera again and he could teach her how to use it. Or they could stop at the Hopi House and see if Chuma was available to demonstrate her weaving. The possibilities made her smile.

After she was dressed, she ran to the restroom to wash her face. All she had to do now was go upstairs to get their picnic lunch, find Blanche and Caroline, and then they would all meet Ray in the Rendezvous Room.

Ruth caught her as she was heading up the stairs. "I'm glad I got to see you before you left." She gave Emma Grace a hug. "I'm so sorry we didn't get a chance to talk yesterday. Have you found someone else to go with you today?"

"Someone else? Blanche and Caroline are coming, but you already knew that, and I'm really looking forward to it. I definitely need the fresh air."

Her friend's face fell as they reached the front desk area. "I'm so sorry, but Blanche got sick last night. I thought you knew. And Caroline agreed to fill in for Sally."

"Oh." She let her shoulders drop a bit. "That's okay. I'm sure we can find someone else to go with us."

"That's the spirit." Ruth's mouth tipped upward. "I've

got to get in there, but I can't wait to hear about your adventures tonight. I hope you have a wonderful time today." She headed down the hallway to the dining room and called over her shoulder, "Be careful! No climbing rocks today, huh?"

Emma Grace waved off her friend and shook her head. The more times Caroline told the story, the more elaborate it got. Now all the girls teased her about her mountain climbing skills.

After she grabbed the picnic lunch from the kitchen, she left notes for Mary and Bethany, the two other girls who had the day off. She would just wait to hear from them as she waited for Ray. She went and sat in one of the comfy chairs in the Rendezvous Room at the front of the hotel. She skimmed through one of the recent newspapers while the logs in the fireplace crackled and snapped as the flames licked at them.

The clock chimed the hour.

That was odd. Ray said he would meet her here fifteen minutes ago.

He must have gotten delayed.

She picked up another paper and read it front to back.

The clock chimed the half hour.

Standing up, she grabbed the picnic basket and then walked over to the front desk. Louis was manning it at the moment. "Would you mind sending one of the boys up to Mr. Ray Watkins' room and let him know I'm waiting for him? The junior. Not the senior."

"I'm sorry, Miss Edwards, but they're not here."

"Oh? They didn't return from Williams yet?" Her heart felt like it dropped down to her shoes. First no Caroline and Blanche. And now Ray.

"No, ma'am. Would you like me to leave him a note?"

She looked down at the desk and then back up to him and

pasted on a smile. "No. That's quite all right. Something must have come up."

But as she turned away, she let the storm within her rage. She really needed this day. Needed to see Ray.

But no. He was off with his father. Doing business, no doubt.

Her father's words screamed through her mind. *"It was just business, trust me."*

Just business. Right.

It was the same with all these rich men, business always came first. So, no. He didn't deserve a note from her. She wasn't about to trust anyone right now.

With a glance to the stairs, she debated going and banging on the doors of Mary and Bethany. No. She didn't need anyone.

Picnic in hand, she went in search of Frank. When she found him in the kitchen, she waved to get his attention.

Frank wiped his hands on a towel and walked over to her. "How may I help you, Miss Edwards?" The ever-present smile on the man's face made her soften a bit. He didn't deserve her foul mood.

"May I still borrow your pack?"

"Of course! In fact, I brought it for you this morning to use but forgot to get it to you." He made a funny face. "I must have gotten busy. My apologies." He tipped his head toward the back. "Help yourself to it. My hands are a bit messy at the moment."

"Thank you." She gave him a half smile and headed off to grab the pack. While she was at it, maybe she should offer the rest of the picnic to someone else.

But then word would get back to Ruth. Then Ruth would worry.

No. It was best for her to simply go on her way. She'd

carry the picnic for four. She might get exceptionally hungry, anyway.

With the pack loaded and strapped on her back, she lifted her chin and marched out the front doors. She couldn't believe that Ray hadn't even thought to leave her a note. Again.

Well, that wasn't about to ruin her day.

She would just go alone. It was better if she was by herself, anyway. Her mood needed an adjustment.

Heading out the door, she decided to go west past the Kolb brothers' studio and just venture along the rim, if it wasn't too overgrown.

The day was perfect. Sunny, not a cloud in the sky, and the temperature was considerably warmer than it had been since she arrived. She wasn't sure when spring arrived in the canyon, but she was sure it would be glorious.

As she ventured down the incline to the studio, she let her mind wander. The scent of evergreens was strong in the crisp morning air.

Two men stood outside the studio by the trailhead for the Bright Angel Trail. One leaned up against the building and the other had his foot propped up on the post of the trail, his arms crossed over his chest.

"Good morning!" the taller of the two called out.

"Good morning." She walked up to them. "You must be the Kolb brothers I've heard so much about."

"Name's Emery, and this is my brother Ellsworth." Emery picked up his camera.

"Nice to meet you. I'm Miss Edwards. I work at the hotel. I'm thinking of hiking west on the rim. Do I need to pay the toll for that?" She'd heard stories about how Ralph Cameron wouldn't abide people he thought were trespassing.

"Nope. But be careful. There are places where the edge sneaks up on ya. And there have been mountain lions in the area lately. They must be hungry." He set up his tripod and put the camera on top. "Would you like a picture before you start?"

They were already quite famous for taking pictures of guests on the trail. After taking the picture, they ran back up and developed it before the customer made it back to the top.

It made her smile to think of having something to remember her adventures. "You know what? I would really like that. As long as no one else gets to see it."

"Of course. It'll be yours when you get back from your hike. Why don't you stand over there where we can get the canyon behind you?" Emery crouched under the drape.

She stood still and held the pose while they took her picture.

"We'll have it ready for you later today." Ellsworth waved his hat at her.

"Thank you, and it was nice to meet you!" She returned the wave and headed through the scrub to the west.

The trees and undergrowth were thick in areas, and she had to watch her step because of the uneven ground, but it was all worth it to have some time to herself.

As she ventured farther along the rim, the view changed every few feet. The canyon stretched farther than her eye could see. The oranges and reds of the layers spread in ripples through the walls that stood thousands of feet above the river below. It was only at the times when she could spot the river that she realized how great the distance truly was.

Too bad the girls weren't here to see this.

And Ray.

Her anger and frustration had melted as she'd walked her way along the rim. He didn't deserve her wrath. Besides, he probably had a very good reason for not letting her know. She'd seen firsthand how difficult his father was.

But she shook off the thoughts. No sense dwelling on what couldn't be. She had the whole day to herself, and she was determined to enjoy it.

The hours passed in silence and breathtaking views. She wasn't sure how many different rock outcroppings she'd climbed, but she'd enjoyed sitting atop each one and munching on the sandwiches stashed in her pack. The only sounds had been those of her steps and a bird here and there for most of the day. As the quiet and the glorious scenery around her washed away her doubts, she took the time to talk to God. Not that she'd received any audible answers, but it was good to get her questions out. And somehow, speaking them to the vast expanse around her made her feel safe. Comfortable.

The sun began to slip toward the western sky. She pulled her grandmother's watch out of her pocket. Three o'clock. How did the time go by so quickly? Best to get back while it was still light. She wouldn't want to be on this trail after dark, that's for sure. It was hard enough seeing each step as it was!

Feeling more peaceful than she had in a long time, Emma Grace let her thoughts go back to the problems at hand. It was time to make some decisions. They wouldn't be easy. But she was tired of running and hiding. Better to come out with the truth now than live in fear for the rest of her life. She'd just have to face the consequences as they came. Hopefully one at a time.

Rustling sounded behind her, and it made her heart jump into her throat.

Turning on her heel, she looked back the way she'd come. But there was nothing there.

Nothing. No sound. She tore her eyes away and took a deep breath, then whipped her head back around to search the trees.

Again . . . nothing.

Willing herself to calm down, she couldn't shake the feeling that she was being watched. The Kolbs' words about mountain lions came rushing back. What if she was being tracked by a predator?

She picked up the pace and hummed the first thing that came to mind: "The Spacious Firmament on High." Maybe the noise would scare whatever it was away.

After several minutes, she dared to look behind her again. A gentle breeze made the short trees move and wave.

She must be imagining things.

But the hairs on the back of her neck kept prickling, so she walked even faster. What had she been thinking coming out here alone?

The rustling sounded again, and she stopped in her tracks.

Dare she look?

As she turned around, something dark blocked her vision, and she tumbled to the ground.

16

Furious with his father, Ray paced outside the front entrance of El Tovar.

How could he have been so ignorant? Once again, he'd allowed his father to walk all over him.

Dad had awoken him yesterday, stating they had urgent business that they must attend to in Williams and they needed to race to catch the first train out. Ray wanted to leave a note for Emma Grace, but Dad assured him he had already taken care of it and rushed him to the train within ten minutes.

He should have never trusted his father's words, but he'd been half asleep. They took the first train to the town, but when they reached Williams, his father told him to get a room at the hotel and off he went with several other gentlemen Ray had never seen before—something else that set Ray's teeth on edge. After the jewel theft and Mr. Krueger's words, he was hesitant to trust his father's decisions. But what could he do? He'd gone down to the hotel lobby and found the telephone inoperable, then tried to post a telegram to Emma Grace, only to find out that the telegraph line was under repair.

Hours passed as he sat in the hotel, waiting for his father to return. All the while, he stewed. Not only had he missed seeing Emma Grace, but he also missed their walk last night and, even worse, their day together today.

When Dad returned, he refused to tell Ray anything about his business dealings and only shrugged when Ray pushed for answers to why it was necessary that he come along. Dad assured him it was of import because they were meeting with an important investor later. One who—of course—never showed.

At that point, Ray prodded Dad about the note he left. But Dad shrugged and said he left a note for the staff letting them know they were gone. Of course he lumped Miss Edwards in with the "staff"—why wouldn't he? His comments about Ray's walks with a "waitress" had been snide and demeaning.

It was time to tell his father that he was interested in pursuing more than just a friendship with Miss Edwards. There was no reason to tell him anything else. If Dad knew who she really was, he'd probably try to take advantage of it for his own personal gain. And Ray wouldn't betray Emma Grace. The fact that Dad was acting odd didn't help the situation.

Emma Grace.

She was probably mad at him and rightly so. Especially when he hadn't bothered to leave a note for her himself. Why hadn't he ignored his father and gone to speak to her personally? Or at least written his own note? How many times had he reprimanded himself over the past two days?

As he paced back and forth in front of the El Tovar, he prayed she would show up for their walk. But what if she didn't? He'd asked Caroline to give Emma Grace a message that he had returned. There was a good chance that wouldn't be enough. He'd have to find her and apologize. He couldn't blame her if she was upset.

As the sun set completely, the temperature dropped, and Ray rubbed his hands together to keep them warm. She should have been back from her hike before it got dark. Maybe he'd missed her inside?

He went in the front entrance and through the Rendezvous Room. He couldn't go to her room to look for her, but maybe Miss Anniston had seen her.

Walking through the dining room, he saw it was empty except for the head waitress. "Miss Anniston, might I have a word?"

"Of course." Her smile turned to a frown as she saw his face. "What's happened?"

"I was wondering if you have seen Miss Edwards. She missed the time we normally meet for our walk."

"Oh dear. I thought she went hiking with you and some others today."

"Unfortunately, I was detained." He clasped his hands behind his back and clamped his jaw together. Anger at his father burned at the edges of his mind.

"I wonder who she went with then. I know Blanche and Caroline had to back out this morning."

"You don't think she would have gone by herself, do you?" Worry quickly replaced his angry thoughts.

The head waitress shook her head. "No. I don't think she would do anything so foolish."

"Would you mind going to check her room? Perhaps she came in and I didn't see her." He worked to keep his voice calm, but a niggling inside him told him something was very wrong.

"Of course." She wiped her hands on a towel and headed out of the dining room. "I'll be right back, Mr. Watkins."

To pass the time, he began to pace again. *Lord, please let my worry be for naught.*

"Ray. What are you doing here at this late hour?" Frank's voice brought his attention up.

"I'm looking for Emma Grace—Miss Edwards. Miss Anniston has gone to check her room for me."

"Oh? I thought you were going on another hike today."

"We were . . . it's a long story. I didn't go. And now I'm beginning to worry." With his hands still clasped behind his back, he realized they were going numb. Perhaps he was squeezing them a bit too hard.

Frank gripped his shoulder. "I'm sure she's fine."

"I have a bad feeling . . ." Ray couldn't bear to think about the possibilities.

Ruth appeared back in the dining room, out of breath and concern etched on her face. "She's not there. None of the other girls went with her today. I saw her pick up her picnic lunch this morning . . . so she must have gone out alone."

Frank yanked off his chef's coat and slung it over a chair. "Then there's no time to waste. Let's put together a search party. Ruth, would you please inform Mr. Owens and the front desk and then see if a couple of the girls would be willing to help look?"

She nodded and turned back toward the lobby.

"Meet us out in front of the hotel in five minutes," Frank called after her.

She waved in response and then untied her apron as she began to run down the hallway.

Frank gripped his arm. "We'll find her."

A few minutes later, a group of ten was gathered to help in the hunt. Mr. Owens passed out three flashlights and five lanterns, and Frank split them up into two groups.

He pointed toward the Hopi House. "I'll take this group

to the path along the rim to the east. Ray will take the rest of you to the west. Miss Edwards enjoys hiking and has been along the rim, so make sure you check all around just in case she's injured and can't hike her way back. If we find her, we'll fire two shots into the air." He turned and handed Ray a rifle. "Watch out for mountain lions too."

Prayerfully, Emma Grace hadn't run into any wildlife that harmed her. He couldn't bear the thought.

As the groups split off, lights shone in different directions as people called for Emma Grace. He wanted to run and find her, but where was she? The best thing they could do was a thorough search. It just took time. And he didn't want to waste a moment looking in the wrong direction. *Lord, we could really use Your help.*

It took more than an hour to search their way down to the Kolb brothers' studio. The two men must have heard the ruckus because they came out, Emery lifting his suspenders over his shoulders as he exited. "What's going on? Someone missing?"

"Yes. Emma Grace Edwards. She's got blond hair and probably came this way early this morning."

"Yeah, we met her. Took her picture. But she never did come back this way. At least, not that we saw." Ellsworth went back inside and brought the plate from her photograph, along with the printed picture.

"That's her." Ray looked at it and then at the brothers. "Which direction did she head in? She didn't head down Bright Angel Trail, did she?" His heart sank. That trail would be extremely dangerous in the dark.

"No. She went along the rim to the west." Emery pointed.

Ellsworth put his hat on. "We'll get some lights and help you search."

"Thank you. It's much appreciated."

Another hour passed as they searched the thick trees and scrubby bushes along the rim. Ray kept his light on the very edge so he wouldn't take a misstep and plummet down. What if Emma Grace had fallen? Would they be able to find her in time?

Voices echoed around him as everyone called her name. This wasn't supposed to happen. He should have been with her.

His heart nearly stopped in his chest. What if she hadn't gotten things right with the Lord . . . and what if . . . ? No. He couldn't allow his thoughts to go down that negative route.

As the seconds passed, each felt like an hour.

The rim of the canyon was uneven, rocky, and full of obstacles in the light of day. At night, it was ten times worse. Each step he took, he searched in every direction around him, hoping the light would fall on her.

Two shots rang out. "We've got her!"

His heart shuddered, and Ray ran toward the voices. *Thank You, God.* "Where is she?"

"Keep comin'." It was one of the Kolb brothers.

"Is she all right?" he couldn't help but yell. Then he saw her. Disheveled and banged up, but she was alive.

He rushed to her side. "Emma Grace, are you all right?" He put his hands on the sides of her face.

Her head bobbed up and down in his hands. "I'm so glad you found me."

"Emma Grace." Ruth's soft voice invaded the quiet of her sleep.

She opened her eyes and blinked away the light. Head pounding, she placed a hand over her forehead.

"Mr. Owens needs to ask you a few questions." Her friend's face hovered above hers. "Do you think you can manage that?"

Emma Grace dipped her chin down in a nod and then pushed herself up to a seated position. Every muscle and bone in her body ached. "Could we turn off the light?"

"Sure. There's enough light coming in through the window." Ruth went to the door and let their manager in.

"It's good to see you are all right, Miss Edwards." He pinched the bridge of his nose. "I'm sorry to intrude, but the sheriff in Williams telephoned this morning and wanted more information."

"I'll do my best, but there's not much that I remember." She rubbed her eyes with her fingers and hoped the fog would lift.

He stepped forward. "Last night you said that a couple men came upon you and threw something over your head, is that correct?"

"Yes."

"What happened after that?"

"They were talking about whether I could have seen or heard what they were doing. There were at least two voices. Maybe three. Then something hit me on the head, and I woke up when I heard people calling my name." She glanced at Ruth, who gripped her hands in front of her.

"What time do you think the attack happened?" Mr. Owens scribbled in a notebook.

"It was a little after three in the afternoon. I had just looked at my watch before I heard the rustling."

He let out a long sigh and exchanged glances with Ruth. "That was not too long before the robbery. From where she was found to the Hopi House is a considerable jaunt. It would take at least an hour and a half to cover that much ground. The timeline is congruent."

"What robbery?" Emma Grace sat up a little straighter in the bed.

"I need to get this information back to the sheriff, but I'll let Miss Anniston fill you in." He went toward the door and then turned. "We are all very thankful that you are all right."

After he closed the door, Emma Grace leaned forward. "So, this had nothing to do with whoever is after me?"

With a shake of her head, Ruth sat on the bed. "No, we don't believe so. Shortly before five, three men entered the Hopi House and stole everything out of the cash drawer and some of the more expensive pieces of jewelry. Chuma was by herself inside and about to lock up. The others were outside on the roof. So, the thieves must have been watching until she was alone."

"That's terrible. Is she all right?"

"She's in better shape than you are." Ruth grinned at her. "Had they not tied her up, she probably could have caught at least one of them."

She glanced down at her lap. "So that's why they were talking about whether I had seen anything. They were afraid I would be able to identify them."

"Most likely. But, Emma Grace, I have to be honest. With as cold as it gets at night here, not to mention the wild animals, those men probably left you for dead. Mr. Owens thinks you need to stay in your room all day, just in case. They're probably long gone by now, but in case they aren't, he doesn't want them to see you."

She put her head in her hands. "You won't get any argument from me. My head is killing me." Gingerly feeling the back of her scalp, she found the lump. "Ow. I don't know what they hit me with, but I'm glad I have a hard head."

"We're all very thankful for that." Ruth laughed. "Ray asked for permission to come down and visit you and I said it was okay. Just this once. But I told him he should come before I am needed upstairs." She glanced at the clock. "Which should mean he will arrive any minute now."

Emma Grace put her hands to her hair. "I must look a sight."

"I don't think he will mind."

"Well, *I* do." She couldn't help the irritation in her voice. She wasn't sure how she wanted to respond to Ray right now.

A knock sounded at the door.

Ruth stood up to answer it. "You look beautiful." She opened the door, and Ray's worried face greeted her.

"How are you feeling?" He stepped into the room.

It was odd having a gentleman enter her private space. Not like Mr. Owens. He was her boss. She pulled her covers up a little higher. "My head hurts. And I feel like I've been dragged behind a horse for a hundred yards, but other than that, just peachy." The edge to her words couldn't be missed.

Ruth raised her brows. "I think you two might need to talk. I'll just go to my room. But I'll leave the door open between them. No funny business, Mr. Watkins."

Emma Grace crossed her arms over her chest.

"You're angry with me." Ray sighed. It was more of a statement than a question.

"Yes, I'm angry. I know I don't deserve to be in the know of everything in your life, but you didn't even have the courtesy to leave me a note. You missed our walk Sunday evening and then you stood me up yesterday."

"I'm sorry." And he really did look quite pathetic as he apologized. "Dad woke me moments before he wanted to

leave on the train. There's no excuse—other than the fact
that I wasn't thinking properly as we left. You can't even
begin to understand how sorry I am. I was so worried about
you last night. I should have been with you. There's no excuse."

Picking at a thread on her quilt, she twisted it around her
finger. "It was your father, wasn't it?"

"What do you mean?"

"Your father must have said that you had something urgent to do and so you went, right?"

"How did you know?"

"I watched my father control all of his employees for many
years. It seems like the typical thing for your father to do."

She waited to see what he would say. It didn't matter that
Ray knew that she was an heiress. She didn't want the money.
How much did his father know, anyway? It's not like they
had hidden the fact they walked together each evening. That
aside, the fact that Mr. Watkins Senior didn't approve of
her—or anyone beneath him for that matter—was clear.
Ray's father would think less of her because he *thought* she
didn't have money. That irked her more than she cared to
admit.

"I'm going to talk to him." He dipped his chin and lowered
his voice. "About us."

He used the word *us*. Her heart skipped a beat. "What
are you going to say?"

"That you are my friend and an amazing woman. And
. . . that I care for you."

The look of expectation on his face lifted her mood. "I
care for you too." She bit her lip. "But you can't tell him who
I am." Heat rushed to her face as reality flooded into her
mind. This was why she never made friends. This was why
it would have been better if she would have kept the dashing

251

Mr. Watkins at arm's length like she had at the beginning. This was why she'd contemplated shedding the façade. It was beginning to tear her apart inside. "Look, Ray, I really have enjoyed knowing you—"

"Don't you even attempt to shut me out now." He held up a hand. "I'm sorry for interrupting you, but I care too much for you to let you push me away."

"But what if it's best for all of us?"

"It's not." He leaned back against the door and crossed his arms, daring her to argue with him.

"Well, I disagree. Besides, I'm still mad at you." Even as she said the words, she knew it wasn't true.

"Disagree and be mad all you want, Miss Edwards. You're not getting rid of me so easily."

A sharp pain began to pulse behind her eyes. She took a deep breath and let it out slowly between her teeth. "Well, I'm going to have to ask you to leave because you're making my headache worse."

"I'll go. But only because I don't wish to see you in pain. But rest assured, I will be back." He poked his head into the other room. "Is that all right with you, Miss Anniston?"

"You may have ten minutes with her when I come down after lunch. But that's it—and only if Miss Edwards wants to see you." Ruth sauntered through the door.

Ray towered over her by a foot, but he nodded. "Yes, ma'am."

"Go on with you." Emma Grace shooed him out. "But this is not over. I tend to hold grudges." She kept her face down so he couldn't see the signs of how much she enjoyed his presence.

Every response was negative. No one had seen or known an Emma Grace.

Peter pulled out the long list of Harvey Houses and compared it to all the telegrams he'd received. Had he heard back from everyone? If so, and no one had seen her, he'd have to start all over. But that couldn't be. In his gut, he knew he was right. She had been a Harvey Girl. In fact, he was quite certain in his gut that she still was.

Carefully checking off one after another, he stacked the telegrams beside him. As he finished going through the pile, he leaned back and looked at the list.

There it was. Two with no responses.

One in Guthrie, Oklahoma, and the other was the brand-new El Tovar at the Grand Canyon. He looked at the map in front of him and placed a tack in each place.

Standing up, he stretched and then began to pace the room. He rubbed his jaw. If he were running away, where would he go? Someplace remote. And as far away from where he was running from as he could.

Even though Oklahoma was a great distance from Boston, it wasn't near as remote as the Arizona Territory. So that ruled it out in his mind. But he could check on the way . . . just in case.

He grinned and marked a dark red circle around the Grand Canyon in Arizona Territory.

"Gotcha."

17

"I need to go to Kingman tomorrow." Ray's father walked over to the window. "I know how tedious that last trip was for you, so you can stay here."

"Kingman? You've been doing nothing but traveling all week." He'd kept his mouth shut about all his father's comings and goings, but this was just odd. It didn't make sense that Dad would be going there—especially since the client he had in Kingman would no longer do business with him.

"Yes, Kingman. My new employees will handle what needs to be done."

"What exactly are they doing for you, Dad?"

His father adjusted his cuffs. "Just some business that Ben should have been handling."

That didn't exactly make him feel better about it. Ben had proved himself shady and a thief.

A horrible thought made its way through his mind for the fourth or fifth time since the night they'd found Emma Grace. Those men couldn't have helped with the robbery of the Hopi House . . . could they?

Shaking his head, Ray couldn't fathom that his father

would hire men to be thieves for him. Especially not men who would be violent.

It was too much to think that his father could be involved. Maybe Ray should count his blessings. With his father gone, he'd be able to spend a bit more time with Emma Grace now that she was feeling better. A week had passed since the attack and robbery, and the sheriff felt she was safe now.

Dad paced back toward him. "It should only take a few days, so you can tell your mother I will be back by the week's end."

"Mother?" Now Ray was really confused. Perhaps he hadn't heard correctly.

"Yes, son." Exasperation laced his tone. "Tell your mother I'll be back by Saturday. That way she won't worry." His father reached up and scratched his beard.

Ray couldn't believe his own ears. Mother hadn't been mentioned for years. "Dad, are you feeling all right?"

His father turned and smiled. "Never better, son. Never better." He bounced on his toes and placed his hands behind his back. "You know, I think it's high time we expand into hotels. We need more luxury accommodations, don't you agree?"

"I think maybe you need to lie down." Ray stood and walked over to his father. He should telegram their physician at home and find out what was going on.

"Whatever for? I'm not tired. I do need to speak with Henry, though. I'll need to instruct him on what to pack. Please send for him, Ray."

Another person from the past. Spoken of as if he were still here. Ray searched for how to answer his father.

"Did you hear me?" Dad looked expectantly at him.

He cleared his throat. "Uh . . . yes, sir." Ray stared at his father for several moments, but he had already walked back to the window. It didn't make sense. He left his father in the room. As he closed the door, he blew out his breath. First Dad mentioned Mother and then Henry. The valet Dad asked for had been gone for more than a decade. Henry's *son* was now Dad's valet.

What could make his father not know what year it was?

He went to the room where the valets were staying and knocked.

John opened the door. "Yes, Mr. Watkins, how may I help you?"

"May I speak with you about my father?"

"Of course, sir."

"Has he said anything . . . *odd* to you of late?"

"I'm not quite sure what you mean, sir." The man's voice was clear and steady, but in his eyes, Ray could see the hesitation. The man knew the truth.

"Has he mentioned your father or my mother as if they are still . . . here?"

The older man sighed. "Yes, sir. The past few months, he's carried on conversations with me as if I were my father."

"What do you make of it?" Maybe Ray was grasping, but there had to be someone who understood what was going on.

"I'm sorry, sir. I wouldn't know. But Dr. Prentiss visited just last month and witnessed one of the episodes. Perhaps you should inquire of him."

"John, look, I appreciate the fact that you are loyal to my father and want to protect his privacy. I simply am concerned and if you know anything that could help, please tell me."

"I'm sorry, sir. I made a promise." The man's eyes were wary.

"Ah, I see." His dad had obviously sworn the man to secrecy—and likely threatened him if he broke that promise. His dad was formidable and controlling, even when he was a bit off. "Thank you for your honesty, John." He paused. "My father requested that you come. He needs some help with packing."

"Thank you, sir. I'll be right there." The valet dipped his chin and closed the door.

Ray made his way down the stairs and then sent a telegram off to Dr. Prentiss back in Chicago. Perhaps he could shed some light on the matter. Taking the stairs two at a time, he went back up to his father's room. As he opened the door, Dad frowned.

"Where have you been?"

"I went to speak with John." Ray searched for signs Dad remembered their earlier conversation. Dad's face wasn't the same as it was before. Something was different in his eyes.

"John is *here*. He's getting my things ready for Kingman." His father was already dressed for dinner. He preened in the mirror and adjusted his waistcoat.

"I can see that." Maybe he should try a different tactic. "Are you still planning on returning by Saturday?"

"Yes, I think that should be enough time to conclude my negotiations."

"Negotiations? Are you buying another business?"

"No. Just hiring some more men. I have a large job for them to do." He reached for a glass of port and drank the last of it. "Are you about ready for dinner?"

"I'll go change right now." He turned for the door.

"Good. I'm wondering if we can have our same table but request a different waitress."

He whirled around. "What is wrong with Miss Edwards?"

"I think she's a gold digger. You pay her entirely too many compliments. And attention. I'm putting my foot down. Those walks of yours need to come to a halt." His father was definitely back to his normal self.

"That is no way to speak about Miss Edwards. She is well deserving of every compliment I give to her, and she is definitely *not* a gold digger."

"How would you know such a thing?" Dad gave him a pointed look and shook his head. "It's high time you were married. A few years ago, I thought I had a suitable arrangement for you that included a merger that would have been outstanding for Watkins Enterprises, but . . ." He shrugged. "It doesn't matter. I'll arrange a suitable marriage for you— someone who will bring as much to the table as you do."

"I would like to choose my own wife, Father." It was probably said with more force than necessary, but he wasn't expecting this train of conversation. And he definitely wouldn't allow his dad to put a stop to his seeing Emma Grace. It was ludicrous.

"You must be quite vehement if you call me *Father*." Dad looked at his watch and chuckled. "Very well, I'll let this drop for now. I don't wish to be late to dinner."

"Dad . . . listen. There is someone that I am interested in. I have been waiting for the right moment to let you know."

"It's about time you worked on it." His father clapped him on the shoulder. "You can tell me about her over dinner. How much money does her family have?"

"I sent a telegram today." Emma Grace fiddled with her gloves as she walked with Ray along the rim. Their walks had become the highlight of her day.

"Oh?"

The clouds hung low in the sky tonight. "To Mr. Scott— he's the man I told you about, my grandfather's solicitor."

Ray kept his steps in time with hers. "What did you say?"

"I spent a tidy sum, that's for certain. But I asked him if I was required to marry Wellington—you know, if he could force me—because of the contract, or if there could be a way out that would appease him."

"Did you hear anything back?"

"Only that he fears that I am in danger, but he didn't tell me how or why. He said he'd contact me tomorrow." She pulled off her gloves and shoved them in her pocket so she wouldn't wear a hole in them with all her fidgeting. "I've been afraid of Wellington for five years. I haven't even seen the man in ages, and yet, in my mind, he's some sort of monster that is chasing me. After my father was killed, I felt my only choice was to hide. But now I just want it to be over. To find answers."

"It's best to wait and hear what Mr. Scott says. Wellington may not be the only one looking for you, you know."

She scrunched her brow. It had been easier to put a face and name to the one chasing her all these years. But what if Ray was right?

He shrugged. "I'm not trying to make you worry, but you said there was more than one man who held a contract with your father. In this day and age, not everyone cares about whether or not what they're doing is legal. Whether he put them up to a competition to win your hand or not, only one man can marry you and gain control. Any one of them could be after your father's fortune. Or for that matter . . . your father's killer. Who wouldn't want to ensure their inheritance? You just happened to foil their plan by disappearing."

She reached to the back of her head and felt where the bump had been. When she'd been attacked, she thought that was the end. Wellington had found her. He had won. But then it all came out about the theft at the Hopi House. Chuma had come to see her the next day, and as soon as Emma Grace had seen that her Hopi friend wasn't hurt, she'd been able to relax a bit more.

"Does it give you a lot of pain?" Ray stopped and stared at her. His gaze was caring. Kind. Why couldn't more men be like that?

"I've had a constant headache since it happened, but it is beginning to ease."

"You really had me worried. Over the last few days, I've had lots of time to pray and to think. I can understand why you are tired of running, of living with this constant fear, the black cloud hanging over your head all the time. I don't know how you've been able to bear it." He reached forward and took one of her hands in his. "I want you to know that I will be here for you through it all. I want to help you."

"I don't know what you could do, Ray, but I appreciate it. I do." She pulled away and went to sit on a rock at the edge. "When I first came here, all I wanted was to have a family of friends who I could trust and live out my days with as I hid here. But as soon as I started feeling connected to people again, I realized what I'd been missing. And then it wasn't enough to hide here. I want more."

He came over to sit next to her. "You know . . . I didn't know what I was missing in my life until I met you, Emma Grace. I understand what you are saying." His words were hushed, but the sincere look in his eyes sent a tingle all the way down to her toes.

No one had ever treated her like Ray Watkins did. She barely knew the man, and yet she felt like she'd known him for years. How was that even possible? As she stared into his eyes, an overwhelming need to be loved washed over her. She shook her head. She couldn't go there right now. "Ray, I've made a decision I need to tell you about. You've helped me do it, actually."

"Okay." He pulled back an inch or two, like the magic of the moment had been broken. She hated that she had done that, but she wasn't ready to give credence to her feelings. Not yet. There were too many unknowns in her life. Too many risks and she didn't want to put him in danger too. Especially after she said it out loud.

"I've decided to tell the truth about who I am. No matter the consequences to me. All this time, I have lived in fear. But no more. My biggest hesitation has been about putting others in danger." She looked down at her hands. "I couldn't bear if something happened to . . . to you. Or to anyone else here."

"Emma—"

With a lift of her hand, she stopped him. "I need to finish." Pinching her lips together, she summoned all of her courage. "If I want to have a future . . . if I want to have friends and a family—*real* friends and . . . love—I've got to tell the truth. And then maybe I can do something to help others. Like Caroline's little brother. You heard how much his medical bills are piling up. Maybe I can pay back all the men who negotiated contracts with my father. To be honest, I want my inheritance after all. But I want to sell off my father's holdings and company and use the money to help other people."

He didn't react at all like she'd expected. In fact, he didn't react at all.

Instead, he reached for her hand again. "Will you stay here?"

"I'd like to. I don't want to leave a legacy like my father did. He hoarded money for years and all for what? To have his child kidnapped? To get killed? To have me running for my life? No. I don't want anything to do with the money. I just want to give it away. If I need to remain a Harvey Girl for the rest of my life in order to support myself, I will. But I will do it without hiding."

"What made you change your mind? You said you thought you would have to hide forever." His thumb rubbed circles over her fingers.

"Your Bible. And you." She pulled a piece of paper out of her pocket with her other hand. "Ruth told me a verse and I memorized it. I kept saying it over and over again: 'I sought the Lord, and he heard me, and delivered me from all my fears.' That was when I started talking to God. Seeking Him. Then when you lent me your Bible, I started looking for verses on fear. Frank gave me a few, and Ruth gave me a few, and then I found several on my own." She held out the paper to him. "But these are my favorites."

> *Romans 8:15—For ye have not received the spirit of bondage again to fear; but ye have received the Spirit of adoption, whereby we cry, Abba, Father.*
> *Proverbs 29:25—The fear of man bringeth a snare: but whoso putteth his trust in the Lord shall be safe.*
> *Second Timothy 1:7—For God hath not given us the spirit of fear; but of power, and of love, and of a sound mind.*
> *Psalm 34:4—I sought the Lord, and he heard me, and delivered me from all my fears.*

"When I was attacked the other night, I thought for sure that it was Wellington who'd come to kill me. I had been praying and talking to God and begging Him for answers to all my questions, and then I remembered what you told me about trying to do it on your own and failing. That it was simple: Don't be afraid, believe." She lifted her face to the sky. "And so I did."

18

He'd been watching her all day. As soon as the train arrived, he went straight to the dining room and asked to be seated at one of Emma Grace's tables.

The picture didn't do the woman justice. She was quite beautiful. Even with her hair pulled tightly back and those ridiculous glasses on her face.

He'd found her.

She had no idea who he was as she'd been serving him all day. There was no fear in her face.

He used his fork to scrape up the last bite of pie and then washed it down with the rest of his coffee. The dinner hour had come and gone and there were only two people left in the dining room—him and one other gentleman who seemed to know Miss McMurray quite well. Or Miss *Edwards*, as he'd learned she'd been using as her new name.

She walked over to his table. "Is there anything else I can get you, sir?"

"No, but thank you." He gave her his best smile and stood

from the table. He'd go out to the room outside the lobby and watch what she did next.

"Have a good evening." She walked away and stopped by the other table again.

He headed out to sit by the fireplace. From where he sat, he could see the hallway that led to the dining room and the stairs going up and down. If he turned his head, he could see the front door. No matter where she went, he'd be one step behind her.

It didn't take long for him to spot her walking side by side with the gentleman from the other table.

The man held out her coat for her, and she buttoned herself up into it.

Huh. They must be going outside.

Well, he would just follow them.

After they left, he watched out the window for several moments to ascertain which direction they'd gone. Then he shoved his hat on his head and followed.

The two strolled at a slow pace as they chitchatted and laughed. As they neared the driveway, an older gentleman called, "Ray!"

"Dad . . . you're back!" The gentleman with Miss Mc-Murray seemed surprised.

The father adjusted his top hat. "Yes, and I've hired some new men, so the next few days I'll be quite busy as I instruct them and train them." The older man looked twice at the woman with his son. "Miss Edwards?"

"Mr. Watkins. It's nice to see you."

"Humph."

The man didn't like Emma Grace? Hmmm. That could be useful.

"I'll see you at breakfast tomorrow, son."

"I look forward to it, Dad."

Mr. Watkins walked away.

It was time.

He stepped forward. "Miss McMurray."

She put a hand to her throat. "Who are you?"

———— | |————

Ray stepped forward and pushed Emma Grace behind him with his arm. "I believe the lady asked you a question."

The man reached into his coat.

Holding his breath, Ray prayed that it wasn't a gun. But he would gladly lay down his life for her.

The man pulled out a badge. "The name's Peter Samson, and I've been looking for Emma Grace McMurray."

Ray leaned forward and read the badge. "'Pinkerton National Detective Agency.'" He looked up at the man. "What do you want with Miss McMurray?"

"I'm here to take her back to Boston with me. There's someone who is very eager to see her."

"Who might that someone be?" He felt Emma Grace press into his shoulder as she spoke. "Mr. Wellington?"

"Miss, if you'll kindly come along with me, we will fetch your belongings."

"She's not going anywhere with you." Ray had never dealt with a Pinkerton before. How much power did they have?

"Look." Mr. Samson rubbed his jaw. "I don't want to have to arrest you, so if you'll just come with me quiet-like, this can all be resolved."

"Arrest me?" Her voice squeaked. "What would you arrest me for?"

"The murder of your father."

"What?!" Ray stepped back with Emma Grace. No way was he about to allow her to be arrested for murder.

But she came around to stand beside him. "You think *I* murdered my father?"

Mr. Samson shrugged. "I think it's possible. There are several people who do. But let's not muddy the waters. My client doesn't think you did, and he wanted you found. I found you. Now it's time to bring you back."

"I'm not going anywhere with you, Mr. Samson. How do I know that *you're* not here to kill *me*?"

"That's ridiculous, Miss McMurray. If I were here to do that, you'd already be dead."

She moved a bit behind Ray again.

Ray held up a hand. "This has all got to be some misunderstanding. Why don't we go inside and discuss this in a calm, rational manner?"

"All right. I'm a reasonable man. Let's go discuss it, but that's not to say that you are going to be able to change my mind." The man held out an arm. "Lead the way."

———— | |————

It had taken an hour to tell Mr. Samson the entire story of what had taken place over the last five years. Emma Grace was thankful that Ray had asked for Ruth and Mr. Owens to be fetched before they started because she needed all the support she could get. The private dining room was closed off to prying ears.

By the time she got to the point about the notes, she realized that she'd neglected to tell Ruth about the second one. She and Mr. Owens had assured them they would speak to all the Harvey Girls again and get to the root of it since it couldn't possibly be a prank. If one of the other waitresses had been hired to scare her, or worse, then that meant Emma Grace had been in more danger than any of them imagined.

While the Pinkerton man took copious notes the entire time and asked her question after question, his face never changed. He'd even asked for a description of the man she'd seen enter her father's study, and he'd drawn a likeness right then and there.

But he thought it was possible that *she* was guilty of murder! And he said others believed that too. Was that why Mr. Scott thought that she was in danger? Or was this all a horrible and elaborate ruse that Wellington had concocted and then spread around so that he could hire a Pinkerton to arrest her? It definitely didn't sound like he wanted to marry her.

She watched the man scribble in his notepad. Empty coffee cups littered the table.

"Mr. Samson, I've given you the truth of everything. Why do I have the feeling that you aren't being honest with me?"

The man leaned back in his chair and looked around the table. "This is the strangest case I've ever worked on." He shook his head. "I can't quite believe it."

"Well, I can promise you that I did not kill my father!"

Everyone around the table took up her defense, and they drowned out one another with their protests.

The Pinkerton held up a hand. "Hold on. Hold on!" His shout quieted everyone down. "That's not what I'm having trouble believing, Miss McMurray. I'm quite certain of your innocence now."

"Then what is the problem?" Ray placed his hand over hers and squeezed.

"Never in my life have I not been able to see the truth that was right in front of my face." The agent clenched his jaw. "But I'm afraid that the man who killed your father is the man who hired me to find you." He held up his sketch. "And I told him where you are."

19

Emma Grace jumped out of her chair and put a hand over her stomach. "So it *was* Mr. Wellington who hired you? You mean he knows I'm here?"

Ray and Mr. Owens both came to her side, and they each held one of her arms as she stood there, shaking.

Mr. Samson let out a huff. "He showed me the contract that he made with your father—the one about agreeing to marry you and then the holdings he would then own. He acted all distraught and upset that you were gone, and he said that he wanted you found alive so that he could make things right. Apparently, he'd hired several men before, and they'd all come up empty."

"Get to the part where he knows that Emma Grace is here." Ray's grip tightened on her arm.

"I sent him a telegram a few days ago when I figured out she was here. Then I sent another one this afternoon after I confirmed it."

"Then that's it. He'll come for me." Her legs wouldn't hold her any longer and she sat back down in the chair. There was the very real possibility that the man had killed her father. "Did I endanger everyone here?" She swallowed, but a lump had formed in her throat.

"No. We will *not* let him harm anyone. We have the upper hand—we know he's coming." Ray's tone was firm.

The men continued talking but her ears had begun to ring and all the sound was muffled.

Lord, I don't know what to do. Help me. Please. She laid her head on her arms on the table. There was nothing else she could do. Except maybe run again.

Ruth's voice broke the conversation among the men. "Gentlemen, I'm going to have to insist that we are done for tonight. It's late, and we have guests to take care of in the morning."

"Let me make some inquiries now that I have more details." The Pinkerton man looked solemn as he tapped his notebook on the table. "Is there sometime tomorrow that we could gather together and discuss where things stand?"

Ruth helped Emma Grace to her feet. "Tomorrow is Sunday. We could potentially meet after brunch. There will be a small amount of time where we could meet in this room again. Mr. Owens, could you arrange that, please? But for now, I'm going to take Emma Grace back to her room and see what I can do to help her sleep."

Their manager nodded and said something to the men, but she had tuned him out. The thought of being in her room all alone made her feel vulnerable. As they left the private dining room, she leaned close to Ruth. "Would you mind staying in my room tonight? It might be the only way I'll be able to sleep."

"I was already planning on it." The squeeze to her arm was reassuring but not enough to banish all the swirling thoughts that threatened to overtake her mind.

She wouldn't be able to sleep. Probably not ever again.

Not now that she knew the man who killed her father was after her. He was probably already on his way.

The night had passed in fitful sleep for Ray. He doubted he'd actually had any rest. His worry for Emma Grace and the situation surrounding her identity weighed him down like an elephant on his shoulders. For the first time in his life, he wanted to do anything and everything within his power to protect someone else.

He'd prayed for a good portion of the night. And when there were no words remaining, he just left it all at the feet of the Lord and knew that He understood.

The one thing Ray wished for was guidance. Which path should he choose? How could he protect Emma Grace and get to the truth at the same time?

He'd asked Dad this morning if he knew this Wellington fellow. But his father had been more interested in the cause behind Ray asking the question than the question itself: Did Wellington have a lot of money? Was he someone that he should go into business with? What was he worth?

Ray had wanted to pull his hair out.

Then Dad had gone off about the new men that he had just hired and that they weren't getting everything done in a timely manner. The conversation had ended with Dad heading off to bed and him mumbling to "Henry" on his way back to his room.

Ray looked over at the piece of paper on the table before he left the room. The telegram from Dr. Prentiss had confirmed Ray's suspicions. *Pre-senile dementia* was what the family doctor called it. But he said it shouldn't be affecting

Dad's work because *most* of the time, he had perfect clarity. Obviously, things had escalated. Dad didn't seem to be in his right mind half the time now, at least since he'd traveled out to Arizona. John confirmed it as well.

But Ray would have to deal with that after he made sure that Emma Grace was safe. John assured him that he would stay by his father's side and make sure that he kept him out of trouble for the time being.

Ray checked his watch. Seven twenty-eight in the morning. He paced the Rendezvous Room before sitting down near the fireplace. Peter Samson was supposed to meet him at seven thirty. At first, he'd thought the Pinkerton was out to hurt Emma Grace, but after last night, Ray hoped the man could help them.

Peter came down the stairs, his brow in a deep *V*. "Good morning."

Ray nodded in return. "Have you heard back from any of your contacts?"

The man unbuttoned his jacket and took the seat across from him. As he clasped his hands in front of him, his frown deepened. "Apparently, Wellington left a few days ago. He was heading west."

"That means he could be here at any time."

"I'm afraid so." Peter held up a hand. "But let's not get ahead of ourselves. There are a lot of variables here that I haven't been able to put together. Like I said before, this case baffles me."

"Is there anything that we can do to keep Emma Grace safe? We can't exactly prevent anyone from coming here."

"No. There's nothing more we can do. But rest assured, I plan on getting to the bottom of this. I've never left a case undone. Never."

"But if the man who hired you is the murderer? What's

your motivation for solving the case? How would you get paid?"

Peter huffed. "I've been paid a substantial amount already. At this point, justice is more important than my financial gain. I can't have my reputation tied to a criminal."

Mr. Owens crashed through the front door. "Call the police immediately!"

Ray and Peter stood at the same time.

A couple of men followed in the manager's wake, their faces grim.

Peter headed toward Owens. "What's happened?"

"We've been robbed. That's what's happened." The manager's face was fierce. "The entire priceless Harvey collection on display at the Hopi House is *gone*."

Emma Grace paced her little room. The past two days had passed in a blur of tense conversations but no solutions. Everyone had decided that it would be best for her to stay in her room for a few days since Mr. Samson had confirmed that Wellington was on the way and everyone was in an uproar about the art theft. What if the second theft was orchestrated by the same men who'd attacked her on the rim? Would they come after her again?

She put a hand to her stomach. Fear had her all tied up in knots. She closed her eyes and took a deep breath. *I sought the Lord, and he heard me, and delivered me from all my fears.* The words washed over her.

But no matter how hard she tried, the events surrounding her overwhelmed her mind.

There were the notes, and Mr. Owens hadn't found the

culprit. They'd all hoped it was a prank after the first one, but deep down she knew it was more than that. And since they weren't sure who had left them, she'd been instructed to not open her door for anyone. Ruth could access Emma Grace's room through the door between their rooms, bring her food, and do her best to protect her.

The threat of Wellington coming made everything else pale in comparison.

Wellington. The mention of his name sent a shiver up her spine.

But life at the El Tovar had to go on. The hotel was completely booked. While the theft proved a good source of gossip for their patrons, it couldn't bring their day-to-day operations to a halt. Since it was now Monday, Mr. Owens had decided his best course of action was to speak to all the staff today and tell them the truth of who Emma Grace was. Even if there was a betrayer among them, he felt that the more people who understood what was happening, the more they could look out for one another. Mr. Samson agreed.

The thought of having all the staff rally around her was lovely and comforting. Except, in truth, she had no idea what the future would hold. The monster of her nightmares all these years was after her. Tensions were high.

She put a hand to her forehead. Five years of hiding, and it hadn't helped one bit. Why hadn't she simply come forward after her father's murder? She'd been young. And afraid.

Rubbing her forehead, she placed the other hand on her hip and stood in the middle of the floor. The thought of how she'd left and the last words she'd spoken to her father made her heart ache. No matter how bad their relationship had been since Mother died, no matter how he'd treated her at the end, he was still her dad. Why couldn't they have had a sweet father-daughter relationship? Like her childhood best friend, Mary, and her father?

But that wasn't what she'd been given. Her new relationship with the Lord helped her to see that she wanted to be content with what she had. But that didn't mean the questions didn't plague her.

Back to pacing, she fidgeted her fingers. Ruth had allowed Ray to come and visit with her a few moments last evening, but it hadn't been long enough. What she wouldn't do to have his comforting presence right now. There were too many unknowns. Too many threats.

There was a soft tap at the door adjoining her room to Ruth's, and then it opened. "You're going to wear a hole in the floor." Ruth brought in a tray of tea.

"Hardly." Emma Grace gave her a half-hearted laugh. "It's tile. It would take me a hundred years to accomplish that."

"Well, at least your senses haven't left you." Ruth winked at her and poured a cup of tea. "Sit down. Drink."

"Yes, ma'am."

"Cheeky girl."

The words made her smile. "You know, my mother used to say that to me. I know I exasperated her a lot. She used words like *cheeky, stubborn, independent, tenacious* . . . then made me go look them up in the dictionary and write out the definitions so that I could think about who I really wanted to be."

"When I first met you, I would have found that hard to believe. But now?" Ruth tilted her head and quirked that one eyebrow up. "I can imagine you were a handful."

She couldn't help but laugh.

Ruth sipped her tea. "I have full confidence that Mr. Samson will help to clear all of this up. He went to Williams and he knows who Wellington is, so he can stop him before he takes the train here. And the robbery Saturday night was most assuredly committed by the men who attacked you. That must have been part of their plan—to wait until the sheriff believed they were no longer in the area and then strike for the second time. The law will find them and catch them, and I have no doubt this will be resolved soon. I just hope and pray that all of Mr. Harvey's collection hasn't been harmed. The Hopi people take great pride in working here. I can imagine it has many of them scared."

"That's a lot of positive thinking. How can you be so certain?"

"I can't, but I have been praying and have faith that the God who knows the number of hairs on our heads will make sure that this situation is resolved." Her friend sat on the edge of her bed and sipped at her tea. "However that happens."

A light tapping sounded at the door.

Emma Grace exchanged glances with Ruth, and her friend went to the door.

She cracked it an inch. "Why, Caroline . . . whatever is the matter?"

As her trainee entered, the girl wiped at her cheeks, but more tears cascaded down. "I need to tell you something."

"All right." Ruth pulled out the chair for her. "Sit down."

The girl covered her face with her hands and continued to sob. "I've done something horrible."

Ruth's shoulders straightened, and she clasped her hands together. "Go on."

A sinking feeling in Emma Grace's stomach made her want to reach out and comfort her young friend, but she hesitated. Caroline hadn't looked her in the eye since she entered the room.

The moments stretched out as Caroline sniffed and tried

to compose herself. With a dip of her chin, she stared at the floor. "I wrote the notes."

Emma Grace gasped. "What? Why?"

Ruth stiffened and moved protectively toward her. "Why would you do such a thing?"

The waitress's head ducked lower. "My brother is sick, and I've been sending all my money home to help with the bills. I . . . I came to find Emma Grace that morning you were called into Mr. Owens' office, and I . . . I eavesdropped at the door. When I heard who she was, and that she had all that money, well . . ."

"Why didn't you just ask me for help?" Surprisingly, Emma Grace didn't feel angry. Compassion filled her instead.

"You were so nice to me . . . but all the other girls could tell that you were better than the rest of us. I didn't think . . ." Caroline sobbed some more.

"You didn't think. That's clear enough. So, you thought to bribe your friend? And mentor?" Ruth's voice was stern.

"I felt so guilty after I left the first note. That's why I made some for the others . . . so you would just think it wasn't directed at you, because I didn't think I could follow through with anything deceitful. But then I received a letter from my mother telling me surgery was required, but they didn't have enough money, and I was desperate to try and get the money to help my family, so I left the other note. I intended to . . . to . . ." She cleared her throat. "Blackmail you by threatening to tell people who you were if you didn't help me financially. But that plan lasted all of ten minutes. I knew it was wrong. And I couldn't do it."

Her eyes pleaded with Emma Grace as the words spilled out. "Please forgive me. I promise I wasn't going to do anything, but I didn't want my little brother to die." She looked down at her lap. "Mr. Owens questioned all of us, and I was afraid I'd lose my job, and then who would provide for my family? I panicked. But I've felt so guilty that I had to come tell you the truth. Even if I do lose my job." She glanced up. The tortured look on her face made Emma Grace feel sorry for her.

She leaned forward and placed a hand on Caroline's arm. "I'm not better than anyone else. No one is. I'm sorry about your brother—"

"I'm so sorry, Emma Grace. Can you ever forgive me?" Caroline dropped to her knees in front of her.

"Of course I forgive you." There'd been no hesitation. No question. She'd been willing to offer it before Caroline even asked for it. A notion that both surprised and brought great comfort to her.

The younger girl collapsed into a pile of tears.

Ruth got down on her knees next to Caroline. "What you did was very wrong, Caroline. I am going to need some time to pray and think about whether or not I need to bring this to Mr. Owens' attention and what consequences there will be. But thank you for coming to us and telling the truth." She glanced at the clock. "For right now, you need to wash your face and head back upstairs. You have work to finish." While her voice was firm, it held grace. And love.

Caroline didn't hesitate to get up from the floor. Nodding her head, she wiped at her cheeks. "Yes, ma'am." She turned and went out the door.

Emma Grace watched Ruth for several moments. "You can't fire her. You can't. If she's the only support for her family . . ." She let out a long sigh. "Why does money do such awful things to people? Caroline would never have thought to do anything of the sort if she hadn't been desperate."

"But she admitted to what she planned to do."

"Yes, she did. But she didn't have to tell us that, now, did she? And she didn't actually do it."

Ruth stood and put her hands on her hips. It was her turn to pace. "This is a situation I wasn't expecting. And while it's indeed serious, I know we have much larger problems to worry about at the time." She shook her head. "Is it awful that I feel a measure of relief at least knowing where the notes came from?"

"Not at all. I feel the same." Emma Grace pulled her knees up to her chest.

"If I tell Mr. Owens, he'll want to fire her. With everything else that's going on, maybe I can simply tell him that I've handled the problem. That should be enough for him right now."

20

Ray asked me to give this to you." Ruth grinned as she
handed Emma Grace an envelope. Last night before
bed the two of them had gotten on their knees and
prayed for Caroline, her brother, and the rest of the girls.
It had refreshed Emma Grace in a way she wouldn't have
expected. And she actually slept through the night after that.

"Hurry up and open it, I've got to get back up to the dining
room, but I wanted to give this to you right away. Thought
you might need the pick-me-up."

Her heart did a little flip. It *was* Valentine's Day, after all.
But they were in the middle of the biggest crisis of her life.
She hadn't expected anything from him and didn't even think
they were much more than friends . . . although she'd dared
to hope that there was the possibility of a future together.

She tucked her bottom lip under her teeth and ripped
open the envelope.

A lace-trimmed heart was on the front of the card. Simple
and sweet. When she opened it up, she read the words aloud:
"'A valentine to the prettiest and sweetest lady I know. Love,
Ray.'"

"He's a good man, Emma Grace."

"Yes, he is." She stood the card up on her nightstand. "I just wish things were different."

"This will all be over soon. At least I pray it will be." Ruth came over and gripped her shoulders. "Just remember that we are a family now. We're going to protect you."

If only Emma Grace could believe that were possible. She'd come to the realization last night that God could very well take her home to heaven. And she'd be all right with that. She just didn't want anyone else hurt in the process.

The last few years all she'd done was run and be afraid. But the fear of death was now gone. Not that she wanted to die, but she would gladly lay down her life for her friends if that's what it took. She'd come to care a great deal for the people here.

"I'll do my best to come back down and visit you whenever I can," Ruth promised. "But you know how it goes . . . there may not be a lull for quite a while. I'll bring food at some—"

"Miss Anniston!" The voice carried down the hall and was accompanied by quick footsteps. Now that they knew who had written the notes, they'd felt comfortable leaving Emma Grace's door open so she could at least have company from the girls between shifts.

Sally appeared at the door and put a hand to her stomach. "Sorry to run in the hallway, but Mr. Owens said to fetch you and quick."

"What's going on?" Ruth headed for the door.

"I don't know, but he was with two men." Her eyes were wide. "He said to bring Miss Edwards as well."

Emma Grace shared a glance with Ruth. What could it mean? Had they caught the thieves? Or Wellington?

"Well then, let's not keep them waiting."

They headed out the door and down the hall in swift

steps. The closer they got to the stairs, the more Emma Grace's heart pounded. *Lord, You know what I'm feeling. And You know what's happening. Please give me Your peace.*

As they took the stairs up, she forced her breathing to slow. In. Out. She could do this.

Sally pointed to Mr. Owens' office. "They're in there."

"Thank you, Sally." Ruth grabbed Emma Grace's hand and squeezed. Then they walked in together.

Two men had their backs to her and were speaking with the manager.

Mr. Owens saw her and Ruth and waved them in. "Miss Edwards, Miss Anniston. Please come in."

As the men turned toward her, she did a double take at the man on the right. Every instinct told her to run.

No. She'd run for too long.

She fisted her hands at her sides as she thought about what this man had done and her anger began to build. Everything seemed to come to a standstill as she stared at the man, as if no one dared to breathe. But then she couldn't hold it in any longer.

"You!" She lunged for the man. "You're the one I saw that night! You killed him!" She slapped him as hard as she could across the face.

The other man grabbed her arms and pulled her back. "Miss McMurray, calm down."

The familiar voice stunned her, and she turned. "Mr. Scott?"

"It's me, my dear." He pulled her into an embrace. Then with his arm still around her shoulders, he turned her to face the other man. "You know . . . Mr. Wellington."

"Dad, is it truly necessary for you to go back to Williams this morning?" Ray had tried everything, but his father wouldn't listen. "I'm worried about you."

"Son, you're acting as if I'm unwell." Dad put his hat on his head. "I'm perfectly capable of running my own business and knowing when I need to go where."

That was something that Ray had begun to question, but he couldn't say that to his father. "Let me at least walk you out to the train."

"That would be lovely. Oh, and be sure to tell Henry not to be late."

Ray shared a glance with John across the room. They'd decided not to correct his father, but had that been the right decision?

"Let's be on the way then. I need to stop by the manager's office on the way out."

He followed his dad down the stairs, praying as he went. Something was very wrong. But he couldn't put his finger on it or decide how to deal with it.

As they came to the rotunda, they heard loud voices coming from the manager's office. Was that Emma Grace?

Her voice pulled him toward the open door.

A man held his hands up in front of him. Emma Grace's cheeks were pink, and an older gentleman had an arm around her shoulders. Holding her back?

The man with his hands up was talking. "I assure you, Miss McMurray, I did not kill your father. And I don't wish you any harm either. As soon as Mr. Scott came to see me, I knew I needed to come out and clear this up in person."

"McMurray." His father's hushed whisper behind him sounded . . . shocked. Ray had forgotten all about his father.

The man holding Emma Grace nodded. "I can attest to

Mr. Wellington's testimony. I wouldn't have allowed him to come all the way out here otherwise."

Ray watched her. She seemed to relax a bit and shook her head. "So, you haven't been looking for me? You didn't send Mr. Samson to find me?"

Wellington shoved his hands in his pockets. "I *was* looking for you, and yes, I hired Mr. Samson because he has a reputation for being the best and no one else could find you. But I knew several of the other men who contracted with your father. They were a bit . . . shall we say, unsavory. After I left your home that evening, I knew your father had gotten in over his head. He himself had said as much. And he was meeting with someone else that night. I don't know who, but a car drove up as I was leaving. When I heard that your father was found the next day, I knew I had to do everything in my power to find you because you were likely in danger. There were men who would do anything for your father's money. And a lot of unsavory characters were already looking for you. That's why I told Mr. Samson here that I wanted you found alive. Funny how I had to make that stipulation with the others I hired. And if one of the others tracked you down before I did? Well, to put it delicately, I didn't want you to have the same fate as your father."

Ray stepped forward. "Are you here to force Miss Edwards— excuse me, Miss McMurray—into marrying you?"

All eyes turned to him. But he could only stare at her.

The look she gave him made him feel like the only one in the room. No matter what happened, he would cherish the connection.

Wellington shook his head. "Not at all." He looked at Emma Grace. "My intentions from the beginning—well, as soon as your father told me that you weren't agreeable to the marriage and then after his untimely death—were

283

to negotiate with Miss McMurray to allow me to buy out her father's holdings. I have no wish to force marriage on her, no matter what her father put in the contract. I know there are others who would, especially since there's so much at stake. That is why I was so intent on finding her. I came to offer her a fair price on the McMurray holdings and to help clear up the debts with the other men. If she is willing to sell to me, I will gladly offer to refund those contracts plus interest."

Relief filled Ray, and he glanced at Emma Grace again. Her brow relaxed. He turned to say something to his father, but Dad was gone. Hopefully he hadn't headed to the train station without John. Ray hadn't even asked him when he would be back.

The discussion in the manager's office continued as he looked around the rotunda and took a glimpse into the Rendezvous Room. His father wasn't anywhere to be seen. Oh well, he'd find him later. Right now, he wanted to focus on Emma Grace.

They'd moved to the private dining room, and Emma Grace had listened to Mr. Scott and Mr. Wellington explain in detail everything that they knew. Mr. Samson stood in the corner with his arms folded across his chest, clearly hesitant to be convinced.

For two hours, her mind reeled with all the information thrown at her. Apparently, her disappearance had created quite a legal battle. That hadn't been her intention. But she also hadn't known that her father would be . . . gone.

Oh, Lord. Did I cause all this by the anger and rebellion

of my youth? Is it my fault that my father was killed? She couldn't bear the thought. No matter how awful her father had become, she'd never wanted him to die.

As Mr. Owens poured himself another cup of coffee, the room quieted.

She took advantage of the lull in the conversation and stood. All the men came to their feet as well.

"Would it be all right with everyone if I returned to work this afternoon?" Her fingers steepled on the table in front of her.

The expressions that met her were all serious. Concerned. Shocked.

Ruth stood and came over to her. "I would think that you would want to rest after—"

"No. I've had too much time on my hands the past few days. And frankly, this is all overwhelming. I'd like to have a sense of normalcy, if that's all right with you." She looked her friend in the eye. "Please. I'm fine. I promise."

Ruth looked at Mr. Owens. "It's fine with me, if you are in agreement. I need to get back to the dining room. Blanche is sure to have her hands full."

"Of course. Whatever Miss . . . whatever Emma Grace desires."

"Then, if you all would excuse me, I'd like to go change."

Ray stepped toward her and followed her out. "Could we take a walk this evening?"

"I'd love to."

The next morning, Ray hurried down the stairs to the dining room.

The tension of the day before had worn them all out. As much as he'd loved being able to spend time with Emma Grace on their walk, their conversation had been awkward and strained.

He couldn't blame her. Her life had been turned upside down for so long. Now, she faced some life-altering decisions. Would she sell to Wellington and put it all behind her? But today was a new day, and he was eager to see her again. Prayerfully, she'd had a good night's sleep.

The host showed him to his table, and he watched the room fill up. The waitresses moved in rhythm around the room, but he didn't see Emma Grace.

He checked his watch.

Odd. She was normally up here long before the guests came in. Perhaps Miss Anniston had sent her on an errand.

But the next moment, the head waitress made a beeline for him. "Have you seen Miss Edwards?" Her voice cracked.

He stood. "No. I was hoping that you had."

Miss Anniston put a hand to her forehead. "I missed so much of the day yesterday that I came in early to catch up. Her room was still dark when I left. I just sent Sally to check on her, and she's not there."

His heart thrummed in his ears. "When was the last time you saw her?"

"Last night. We said good-night, and I made sure the outer doors were locked." The woman began to pace. "I should have checked on her this morning."

"May I have your key? I'll go check for myself." Ray couldn't believe she was gone.

"Since these are extenuating circumstances, I would appreciate that." She handed him the key. "Maybe she was in the restroom when Sally went down. Perhaps she's not feeling well."

"I'm praying you're correct." He made a dash for the stairs. But the sickening feeling in the pit of his stomach couldn't be ignored and, he lifted up his heart's groaning to the Lord.

After checking the rooms downstairs and knocking on every door in the basement, his fear became very real. Emma Grace wasn't anywhere to be found. None of the other ladies had seen her. Ray went to Mr. Owens' office and told him that she was missing. Owens got on the phone immediately with the police and Ray left to let Miss Anniston know. They'd need to put a search party together. Again. His thoughts raced.

Wellington.

He ran back to the front desk and demanded the gentleman's room number. Then he took the stairs two at a time up to the third floor. He banged on the door. "Open up, Wellington."

The door swung open. "Is something wrong, Mr. Watkins?" He dried his hands on a towel.

Ray reached for the collar of the man's shirt. "Where is she?"

"Where is who?" The stunned expression on Wellington's face gave Ray a moment of pause.

"Emma Grace. Where is she?"

"She's missing?" The man's eyes widened even more.

"Don't play dumb with me! Where. Is. She?!" He growled out the words.

"Mr. Watkins." Rushing footsteps sounded behind him and Mr. Owens' voice registered. "I understand you are distraught about Miss Edwards—"

"This man has her. I know it!" He shoved him up against the door.

Wellington shook his head. "I told you yesterday that I would never do anything to hurt her. I promise, I don't know where she is."

Ray searched the man's eyes and the anger began to drain from him. He let go of Wellington. "I'm sorry." He stepped back and straightened his suit. What had come over him? He'd never intentionally hurt anyone in his life. Never.

"Perhaps I can help." Mr. Samson's voice came from down the hall.

"Do you know where Miss Edwards is?" Ray shifted his attention to the taller man.

"No. But I do have some light to shed on the murder of her father."

"Miss Edwards—Miss McMurray—is missing. So, unless the death of her father has something to do with that, it's beside the point."

They'd searched all day, and not one clue was found about Emma Grace's disappearance. Ray's heart felt like it dwelt in his shoes. Where could she be? Discouragement filled him, and a cloud of sadness had descended upon the entire hotel. Staff members and even guests had joined in the search. By now, everyone had heard the story of the heiress working as a Harvey Girl.

He unlocked his room and headed to the bathroom to splash cold water on his face. As he looked in the mirror, he second-guessed every move he'd made since Emma Grace had confided her secrets to him. Had he missed a clue somewhere? How had he failed to protect her?

He washed his face and then buried it in a towel. Not one to cry, he felt on the verge of tears. But that wouldn't help her right now. It wouldn't help anyone. Instead, he went back over every detail of the day.

Unfortunately, Mr. Samson's new information about the murder of Emma Grace's father had left them empty-handed as to a list of suspects in Emma Grace's disappearance. Mr. Samson had shared that he wired all his contacts in Boston and heard from the detective on the McMurray case. One of the maids from the McMurray house witnessed another man coming to meet Emma Grace's father the night he died. She had gone back to her quarters after letting Mr. Wellington out, and Mr. McMurray said he had another appointment. She'd seen the man come into the house, but Mr. McMurray had excused her since it was so late. The woman said she felt confident she could identify him if she saw him again, but when she'd been shown photographs of all the men who held contracts with Mr. McMurray—all the ones who would have a motive—she didn't identify any of them.

They were back to square one. Since it didn't seem as if her father's murderer had come for Emma Grace, the police and Mr. Owens had begun to believe that the thieves who'd robbed the Hopi House must be behind her disappearance.

But what would that mean for Emma Grace? Would they eventually kill her? What if they'd already done something horrible?

The worry ate at his stomach. He prayed for help.

"Ray!" His door opened and his father sauntered in.

"Dad! Where have you been?" He threw the towel on the counter.

"Business in Williams." He rubbed his hands together and smiled. "But that's all taken care of now."

Ray let out a long breath. He didn't have time to deal with his father's issues at the moment.

"What's wrong?"

"Miss Edwards is missing." He sat down on the edge of the bed and placed his elbows on his knees.

"That's terrible." Dad sat down beside him and patted him on the back. "I'm so sorry. Is there anything I can do?"

The words made Ray look over at his father. He'd never even given her the time of day. Why was he suddenly showing any concern whatsoever?

"Don't look at me like that. Just because she was a waitress doesn't mean I don't care for her safety."

At this point, Ray didn't care that his father's behavior was odd. All he cared about was finding Emma Grace.

21

After a sleepless night, the search had continued. Now as the sun dipped lower in the west, he fought to keep a positive attitude. The day had been the longest of Ray's life.

But no one had seen Emma Grace.

Ray paced the carpet in the rotunda outside the manager's office. They'd made hundreds of calls. Sent telegrams. The police had come. The sheriff just shook his head.

Nothing.

No clues.

A horrible cloud hung over the entire hotel. Several groups had prayed on and off all day. Search parties came in and out.

Lord, where is she? Please . . . help us find her.

Mr. Owens rushed out of his office, an envelope in his hand. "Mr. Watkins, do you know where the sheriff went?"

"I'm here." The sheriff's voice echoed through the Rendezvous Room.

Ray stared at the manager. "What is it?"

The man held out the note. "This came in the mail. It's addressed to me and Mr. Scott."

The solicitor for Emma Grace's family? That was odd. Ray took it and read,

> *I have Miss McMurray. If you want her returned safely, then you must pay half a million dollars by four o'clock today. I will be in touch with instructions.*

Ray's heart sank. "Someone has kidnapped her?" After all Emma Grace had been through, she had to endure *another* kidnapping? Would they hurt her? Or were they only after the money?

"Let me see if we can get anything from the letter." The sheriff took the paper and envelope. He turned to Ray. "Who do you suppose the kidnappers are trying to get the ransom out of?"

Wellington stood up from a chair in the Rendezvous Room. "I'll gladly pay the ransom."

"So will I." Ray stood tall.

The sheriff looked between the two. "We will need to leave for Williams on the next train if you have any chance of making it to the bank."

"Of course. Let me run upstairs and speak to my father. I'll meet you at the train."

The sheriff nodded and went back to speak to Mr. Owens.

Ray took the stairs three at a time as he raced to the top floor. Father would have to be okay with them paying the ransom. There was no way that Ray would allow his dad to say no. Not when Emma Grace's life was at stake.

He ran down the hall to their rooms and saw the Pinkerton man outside his father's door.

Mr. Samson was knocking. "Mr. Watkins, I just need to speak with you."

Dad's voice was muffled behind the door. "Go away."

Ray didn't have time for one of his father's episodes right now. "Mr. Samson, I have a key. Allow me." He unlocked the door and opened it.

Dad rushed over to the corner and crouched down with his hands over his head.

"What's wrong? Mr. Samson isn't here to hurt you." Ray watched as sheer terror washed over his father's face. "Dad. It's me. Ray." He held out his hands.

But his father curled up onto his side like a small child. "I didn't mean to kill him. . . . I didn't . . ."

———— ｜ ｜ ————

Her eyelids were so heavy.

Emma Grace forced them to lift. But it took several tries.

It was dark, except for the embers of a dying fire in front of her. Where was she? Taking several seconds to blink and look around her, the only conclusion she could come to was that she was in some sort of cave. The rock walls around her glowed orange in the firelight.

Her arms ached, and when she tried to move them, she found they were bound to her sides. She felt around with her fingers and discovered she was tied to something rough and rigid. But then a piece crumbled off. Bark? Looking over her shoulder, she noted it appeared to be a large log. Pulling forward with all her might, she tried to lift it. But it was too heavy.

Her stomach rumbled. And her lips were dry and cracked. She was so thirsty.

How long had she been here?

What happened?

She'd gone back to her room after her walk with Ray. It

had been such a weird day. She hadn't wanted to talk about Wellington, her father, or anything having to do with her past. But then they'd had nothing of importance to talk about. They'd finally decided to get some rest and start fresh tomorrow.

What had happened after that?

She couldn't remember. Everything was fuzzy after she said good-night to Ruth. Wait. She'd gotten up in the middle of the night to use the water closet. Did she go back to her room?

What day was it? Her head ached and a chill ran through her. If the fire went out, would she freeze to death? In only her nightclothes and dressing gown, the possibility was real and made her shiver again.

As fear raced through her veins, she shut her eyes. *God, I need Your help. I'm scared.*

No other words would come. But she knew God understood. If she didn't make it out of this alive, she had peace about where she was going. But it would be hard for all the others. And she didn't want any of them to suffer because of her.

Her only regret was Ray. If only she'd allowed herself to truly open up to him and tell him how she felt. He was a good man. She saw that completely now.

If she could go back and do it all over again, she'd open her heart to him and dream of a future. A future filled with family and . . . love.

Staring at the flames, her eyes became heavy.

It was so cold. And she was so tired.

22

You didn't mean to kill who?" Ray knelt next to his father.

"McMurray. But I didn't mean to." He shoved a finger at Mr. Samson. "That's why he's here. To come take me away."

Ray shared a glance with the Pinkerton. "Do you know what he's talking about?"

Agent Samson shrugged. "I have no idea. But now I'm curious." The agent stepped toward Dad. "Mr. Watkins, are you saying that you killed Miss McMurray's father?"

Dad's eyes darted back and forth. "Where is Henry? I need Henry."

Ray put a hand on his father's arm. "Dad, Henry isn't here. You need to answer the question."

Dad got up off the floor and ran a hand through his hair, his eyes wild. "No . . . no." He wagged his finger. "You can't blame me for the investors. When the ransom comes, I'll pay it all back."

Ray stepped closer. No. His own father couldn't have anything to do with Emma Grace's disappearance or her father's murder . . . could he? Adrenaline surged through him and his heart threatened to beat out of his chest. "What did you just say?"

"Don't speak to me in that tone, son. It's all taken care of."

"Dad. Do you know where Emma Grace is?"

The older man lifted his chin. "Of course I know where she is."

Ray surged forward and grabbed his father by the shoulders. "Where is she?"

But Dad crumpled to the floor and put his hands to his head. "My head! Don't hurt me!"

An hour later, Ray sat with the sheriff in the manager's office and tried to make sense of it all. The words had tumbled out of his dad in a tangled mishmash of information. His father had been stealing from his own investors—even though he'd amassed quite a fortune for himself. Apparently, he'd made some bad decisions lately and lost a lot of money. But he couldn't bear to lose the status of being Chicago's richest.

And when he saw the photos of Harvey's priceless collection at the Hopi House? He put plans in place to steal it all and sell it. Ray wouldn't even be surprised if his father's men were the ones responsible, just like with the jewelry theft. His men had been stealing all over the country, apparently.

But that was just the beginning. His father had been involved with Emma Grace's father all the way back to the railroad spur negotiations. When she'd been kidnapped. And then, supposedly, the two men had negotiated way back when to arrange a marriage between their children to join the empires.

But when Ray's dad had lunch with a friend back in Chicago who then bragged about signing a contract with Mc-

Murray to marry his daughter, Dad went to confront him. McMurray had told him he could get in on the running if he wanted to, but he wasn't first in line. Ray's dad pushed him in anger, and the man had hit his head and died.

Ray took a deep breath. "I'm shocked, sir. I knew my father was not behaving rationally. I even have the telegram from his physician at home, but I had no idea he was capable of any of this."

"As soon as he tells us where Miss Edwards—er, Miss McMurray—is, I'll have to take him to the jail. Then he will have to be transported back to Boston to face charges there."

"I understand that." Ray put his head in his hands. But Dad hadn't said anything for a while, not after his hysterics when Ray and Mr. Samson had been in his room. John was with him now, along with two of the sheriff's men, hoping to calm him enough to get information on Emma Grace's location. But what if he didn't tell them in time?

He wanted to throttle his father. But he also knew his father was very sick. From one minute to the next, he couldn't tell if his father was in reality or some invented world.

As his anger built, Ray closed his eyes. No. That wasn't right. It wasn't how God wanted him to handle the situation. Fear and anxiety weren't from the Lord. Anger toward his father's actions wouldn't find Emma Grace, and it wouldn't fix anything. His dad needed help.

Ray decided then and there he wouldn't allow the negative thoughts to prevail. Instead, he bowed his head and prayed.

Shuffling sounded around him, and he felt the presence of others, but he continued to pour his heart out to the Lord. Someone laid a hand on his right shoulder. Then one on the left. His soul lifted as he felt the prayers of others.

Several minutes later, footsteps rushed toward them. Ray

lifted his head and saw Ruth and Frank were seated with him. He turned and saw the sheriff's men.

"We know where she is. Let's hope we're not too late."

Curling her legs up into the tightest ball she could form, Emma Grace shivered and watched as the last embers of the fire died and turned to black. Her head felt like it was in a fog. How long had she been here? At the edges of her memory, she'd thought someone had come back several times. But she'd been asleep each time. Had she dreamed it? Maybe they'd come to tend to the fire? To check and make sure she was still tied up?

But she was awake now. And there wasn't a fire to tend anymore. She was so cold.

This was it then. No light. No heat. No way to escape.

Her arms had gone numb from their awkward position. And her fingers felt like ice. She couldn't even feel the roughness of the log behind her anymore.

For the first time in her life, she wasn't scared of death.

But for the first time in her life, she truly wanted to live.

Maybe that was what that verse in Philippians meant. *. . . to live is Christ, and to die is gain.*

Funny how things finally made sense to her. Too bad she didn't get a chance to tell Ray how she felt about him. Or to thank Ruth for her friendship—real friendship.

What would it have been like to work here the rest of her life and have a family with her co-workers? What would it have been like to be free from her past and her father's contracts? Free to marry whom she wished?

Tucking her forehead down to her knees, she blew her

breath into the thin fabric, hoping it would thaw out her nose and cheeks.

Frank had reminded her to thank God when she prayed. Well, she could be thankful now, couldn't she?

"God, I'm not very good at praying yet . . . but I'm hoping it's all right to just speak to You like this. Thank You for taking care of me and bringing me to El Tovar. Thank You for introducing me to Mr. Harvey all those years ago. Without him, I wouldn't be here. I wouldn't have met Ruth, Frank, Ray, and all the girls."

As each face came to mind, she prayed for each of the Harvey Girls. Women she'd come to love and respect. Caroline's vibrant smile flashed across her mind. "Father, please heal her and help her to know she is forgiven. Please make a way for her younger brother to get the care that he needs." She let out another long breath as her thoughts went back to the man who'd captured her heart. "Thank You for giving me the chance to meet Ray."

As she thought about the man she'd come to care deeply for, her throat clogged. Neither one of them had the best examples growing up, but somehow, God's love had still shone through.

That was what it was all about, wasn't it? The love of God. It transcended time, social class, circumstances . . . all of it.

A smile grew on her chapped lips. Nothing else really mattered.

Soon she would be in her Savior's arms. And there couldn't be anything better than that.

"Emma Grace . . ." Someone was rubbing her hair back from her face. "Emma . . . please . . . it's me. Please wake up."

But the darkness pressed in. She didn't have the strength to open her eyes.

"Don't go back to sleep. We need you awake." The voice was soothing and made her feel warm inside. Who was that?

Sleep was the only thing she wanted right now. It was so comforting.

"Emma Grace." The man's voice was firmer now. "Don't you leave me. We have our whole lives ahead of us. This entire canyon to explore." He choked up.

His words tugged at her heart. She wanted to wake up. She did. But how?

Then there were warm lips on her forehead. "Please wake up."

She shivered and opened her eyes. A fuzzy outline appeared. Then her heart kicked into high gear as she recognized him, and her mind broke out of the fog. "Ray!"

The pathetic squeak of Emma Grace's voice was all he needed to spur him forward. She was alive. Alive! *Thank You, God.*

Her eyes fluttered and closed again as she went limp in his arms. Placing his cheek next to her chilled one, he whispered in her ear. "Stay with me. You're safe now. I . . . I love you."

Tears stung his eyes as his throat threatened to close on the last words. He loved this woman with all his heart, and he wasn't about to let her die here. Not like this. Not at the hands of his own father. He couldn't imagine what had made Dad do something so horrific.

Money. Always about the money. Dad had jumped at the chance for more . . . and it made Ray sick to his stomach. The only consolation he had was that the older man's mind was slipping, and he wasn't the man Ray had known anymore. But the sheriff and his men would have a doozy of a time rounding up all the men his father had hired. What else had he ordered them to do? Had Ray stopped the madness in time, so that no one else would be hurt?

"Ray!" More footsteps sounded behind him and the sheriff entered the cave out of breath. "You found her. She's alive?"

"Yes, but barely. She's chilled to the bone."

"Give him a blanket." The sheriff waved at one of his men. "I thought for sure we'd go tumbling down the side of the canyon at the pace you were going." The man sucked in great big gulps of air and relief filled his voice.

"Can't keep a man from the woman he loves." One of the sheriff's men handed over a blanket with a smile.

Ray worked at the knots in the rope around Emma Grace's hands. Her body was completely limp against his, and it broke his heart. How long had she been without food and water? She'd been missing for two whole days. Had Dad left her here this whole time?

He wrapped the blanket around her and lifted her up into his arms. Ray nodded at the men who'd come down with him.

The sheriff eyed him. "The trek back up is going to be grueling. Should I get one of my men to fetch a litter or pallet of some sort?"

Ray shook his head. "No. That's not necessary. I'll carry her."

No matter how long it took or how much his legs ached, he would never let her go. Ever again.

Epilogue

Emma Grace signed her name at the bottom of each page. Ray sat on one side of her in the fancy lawyer's vast office, while Mr. Scott sat on the other. "I think that's everything." She set the pen down. Her parents' estate was sold, and now the company was too. She was finally free of it all.

Mr. Wellington stood on the other side of the shiny mahogany table. "Thank you, Miss McMurray. I promise that I will do my very best to take care of your father's company."

She shook her head. "It's your company now. But thank you for doing the honorable thing." It still amazed her that the man hadn't demanded marriage, even though legally he could have. On top of that, he'd repaid all the other contracts in addition to buying everything from her. At first, it had seemed too good to be true, but Mr. Scott had convinced her that there truly were some good and decent men left in the world. A fact that she was coming to understand better and better each day.

She turned to Ray. "I don't know what I would have done without you. Thank you for coming to find me."

303

"You mean the first time I came into the El Tovar dining room? Or in the cave?"

"Both." She placed her hand on the side of his face. Who cared what anyone thought about the public display of affection. She loved this man.

The deep fondness in his eyes made her heart leap. Just like it had when he'd come to the cave and gently untied her hands, lifted her in his arms, and carried her to safety.

Ray Watkins was a good man.

"I hope you know by now that I will do anything for you. I love you." He leaned forward and squeezed her hand.

"I love you too." She stood and the men stood with her. With a nod to Wellington and then the other board members seated around the table, she lifted her chin. "Gentlemen, thank you for seeing this through for me. I know everything is in good hands. Now, if you'll excuse me, I'm anxious to get back home."

Mr. Rosewater—one of the longest-standing board members in her father's company—tucked his thumbs into the tiny pockets of his waistcoat. "You're returning to the Grand Canyon, then, I take it?"

She looked up into Ray's eyes. "Yes. The manager was gracious enough to give me a few weeks off to take care of things here, but I'm anxious to get back."

One of the other board members shook his head and chuckled. "It's hard to imagine a woman of your status as a Harvey Girl."

She tilted her head and raised an eyebrow at him. With a smile, she used the sweetest voice she had. "One of the best, I might add."

"I just might have to take a trip out to this Grand Canyon to see it for myself." The man smiled.

After a round of good-byes, Ray offered his arm, and they walked out of the building with Mr. Scott.

The older gentleman leaned on his cane at the top of the steps. "I guess now it is my turn to say good-bye, my dear."

Emma Grace stepped toward him and placed a kiss on his cheek. "Thank you. For everything."

"I hope you enjoy your life out west." The man nodded to Ray. "Take care of her, Mr. Watkins."

"Oh, I intend to."

She watched the man walk away and turned her eyes back to Ray. "I have an idea of what I'd like to do first."

"What is that?"

"Let's go see your father."

His eyebrows lifted.

"I'd like to see if he's lucid today . . . and if he is, I want to tell him that we are going to pay back all the men he owes. Everyone he swindled or stole from. Perhaps that will help his mind to heal." After the sheriff back in Williams had sorted through the facts surrounding her kidnapping and all the appropriate authorities were notified, Mr. Ray Watkins Senior had been escorted back to Boston to face the charge of murder of Emma Grace's father. It had been clear to the judge and jury that the man wasn't in his right mind but it had taken some work to get him moved out of the jail. On the days when he was lucid, he lived in guilt and shame. She wanted to give him some peace if she could.

Ray pulled her into his arms. "You have shown him so much mercy. You amaze me every day."

"Isn't that what Jesus did for us?" Content to stay in his arms, she allowed her thoughts to travel back to the first time they'd visited the senior Mr. Watkins in jail. He'd been convicted of murdering her father after his confession, but even so, she'd offered her forgiveness. For everything. The change that God had done in her was truly amazing. She didn't feel an ounce of anger toward Ray's dad. In fact, she loved him.

It had lifted her heart more than she'd ever thought possible. No longer did she feel weighed down. Soon after, she'd asked to have Ray's father moved to a mental hospital where, hopefully, he could get some help. When clarity of mind was his, he cried over what he'd asked his employees to do. He was horrified that he'd turned to hiring men who didn't mind stealing and breaking the law. Five of his men had been jailed over thefts across the country and eventually Emma Grace's kidnapping. The art and jewels had been returned—including the priceless Harvey collection—but so much damage had been done.

But then, he'd drift back into the place only dementia could take him, and a different sort of agony began. The man had been tortured by his own thoughts for too long. Perhaps that would change with their visit today. Whether he was lucid or not, Emma Grace was determined to share with Mr. Watkins about how Jesus changed her life. He bridged the deep divide and paid the price for anyone who believed. He did that for her. She wanted to tell that to everyone she met.

"And after we see Dad?" Ray's chest rumbled with his words.

The possibilities they'd discussed the past few weeks were almost endless. Both of them had the chance at a complete fresh start. And they'd chosen to do that back at the canyon. While Watkins Enterprises would be caught up in legalities for some time, Ray had already told her that he wanted to sell it and do philanthropic work. And perhaps learn how to properly weave a basket.

She lifted her head and looked deep into his eyes. "Let's go home. Mr. Owens has agreed to keep me on as a head waitress until we are married. After that, I can help out a couple of days a week, as needed. He's already sent in the request to Mr. Harvey's son to allow a married woman to work at a Harvey House."

"Married. I like the sound of that." He rubbed tiny circles on her back.

"Me too." The fire in his eyes warmed her all the way to her toes. "In the meantime, you can have fun learning all you can about photography from Emery and Ellsworth. Then we can discuss all the ways we want to help people. But first I want to help Caroline's brother get the surgery he needs. They've waited far too long."

"That's a wonderful idea."

"I'm glad you think so, Mr. Watkins."

"How soon can we get married?" The corners of his mouth hiked up in a mischievous grin.

Her heart threatened to beat out of her chest. "Hmmm, good question. How about as soon as we can get the minister to come to the El Tovar?"

"Perfect." He lowered his lips to hers and kissed her with such passion that her knees went weak.

Everything inside her came to life. She reached up and ran her hands through his hair.

A whistle from below reminded her they were in a very public place. As she pulled back, heat filled her cheeks, along with a smile she couldn't resist.

He released her and took her hand as they walked down the steps to the street below. "Shall I build you a house on the edge of the canyon, like the Kolbs'?"

"Maybe not *that* close. But one with a view would be nice."

Note from the Author

"You cannot see the Grand Canyon in one view, as if it were a changeless spectacle from which a curtain might be lifted, but to see it you have to toil from month to month through its labyrinths."—John Wesley Powell

You are precious to me.

Yes, you.

Reader.

Lover of story.

I've said it hundreds of times and will say it again, I couldn't do what I do without you. Thank you.

This story is my twenty-seventh release and my twenty-third fiction release. I thank God for His amazing grace to me and for the gift of story.

In *A Deep Divide*, we journeyed to the Grand Canyon, in a time when it was much less accessible than it is now. The El Tovar Hotel was—and still is—a glorious oasis on the edge of one of the most magnificent wonders of the world. The original layout had more rooms for guests and a great many *fewer* of the bathrooms that it boasts today. But the historic hotel is a sight to behold and a place you'll want to make reservations well in advance if you want to stay there. Sitting in the dining room, I could envision the Harvey Girls serving in that very space. Other than the tables being square now rather than round, there's not much visible difference in the main room, and it's easy to think back to the more than 115 years of history that have played out in there. If you get a chance to go, I highly recommend the beef stroganoff.

Even though I visited the hotel and did a good deal of research with a resident expert—Mr. Edward Small, who started working there back in 1973—we couldn't ascertain exactly where the Harvey Girls' quarters were in the first few years. I found some floor plans in a neat little booklet from a collection of the University of California Libraries. It was the reprint of an advertisement brochure called, *El Tovar—a new hotel at Grand Canyon of Arizona*. In it, it shows the original 103 rooms that Ed told me about. But the twenty that are shown in the south basement wing are much smaller than any rooms offered on the other floors, so I admit to taking some artistic license with my imagination about the Harvey Girls' quarters as I placed them there. The only other mention I found was in Michael Anderson's *Living at the Edge*, which states, "Although the single young women shared abysmal living conditions with other village residents during their first two decades . . ." but there was nothing to show where the Harvey Girls actually resided. And since Mr. Fred Harvey was always so good to his "Girls," I made the executive decision to put them in the basement. What I do know is that Colter Hall was constructed in 1937. It became the Harvey Girls' residence and eventually a female dormitory, of which it remains to this day.

Another fun historical fact is that I used the real Kolb brothers throughout the story. Their home/studio still sits on the very knife's-edge of the canyon and is a place I highly recommend visiting. While there was a great deal of conflict between the Kolb Brothers and the Harvey Company/AT&SF Railroad the first few years, I decided not to get into the particulars here. But Emery and Ellsworth Kolb were fascinating pioneers and explorers of their time, and you will see more from them in the rest of this series. To see a couple of their crazy and adventurous photos, just do a search on the Kolb brothers and their famous set of pictures titled *View Hunters*. Along with several other professional photos of the Grand Canyon and a few of my own, I actually have one of the *View Hunters* hanging in my office. For more information about them, you can visit truewestmagazine.com /knuckleheads/.

If you are interested in learning more about the canyon and the Harvey Girls, here's a list of further reading:

Fred Harvey Houses of the Southwest by Richard Melzer

The Harvey Girls: Women Who Opened the West by Lesley Poling-Kempes

Harvey Houses of Arizona by Rosa Walston Latimer

The Harvey House Cookbook by George H. Foster and Peter C. Weiglin

The Amazing Kolb Brothers of Grand Canyon by Roger Naylor

Living at the Edge by Michael F. Anderson

Appetite for America by Stephen Fried

Hopi House: Celebrating 100 Years by Christine Barnes

Fred Harvey: Creator of Western Hospitality by William Patrick Armstrong

Mary Colter: Builder Upon the Red Earth by Virginia L. Grattan

The Story of the Grand Canyon Railway: Cowboys, Miners, Presidents and Kings by Al Richmond

I can't wait to share with you the second book in the SECRETS OF THE CANYON series, coming October 2022.

Until then,

Enjoy the journey,

Kimberley Woodhouse

Acknowledgments

If you aren't aware, it takes a boatload of people to get this book into your hands. I'd like to thank a few of them here.

My amazing Crit group: Kayla Woodhouse Whitham, Darcie Gudger, Jana Riediger, and Becca Whitham. Where would I be without you? I love you all.

All the Bethany House team. You are amazing. Seriously. I adore each one of you and am beyond grateful: Jessica Sharpe, Jennifer Veilleux, Amy Lokkesmoe, Brooke Vikla, Rachael Wing, Noelle Chew, and the rest of the crew.

I also need to shout out to my advisory board for my writing ministry: Karen Ball, Sheryl Farnsworth, Jeni Koch, Jackie Hale, Christi Campbell, Amanda Schmitt, Martha Ilgenfritz, Kayla Whitham, and Tracie Peterson. Thank you for praying with me for this.

Becca "the short" and Kailey Bechtel need huge rounds of applause for being willing to read and read and read . . . (with very short deadlines, mind you). Thank you.

The amazing Jaime Jo Wright and my daughter, Kayla Whitham, helped to save the day in the final crunch of this story when I had too much going on and had to figure out a way to consolidate threads. I don't know what I would have done without you two. I love you both.

A huge thank you goes out to John J. Devinne Jr., reference librarian and government information research specialist at the Boston Public Library, for helping me to find the exact law about presumption of death back in 1905. It wasn't an easy time period as the law changed that year, but his research was exactly what I needed.

I had the privilege of meeting Grand Canyon historian Edward Small when I traveled to the El Tovar. Ed is a fascinating man who has put together tons of research in the almost fifty years that he has worked at the hotel and/or canyon. Thank you, Ed.

Thomas Ratz was also our server one evening in the spectacular El Tovar dining room. What a wonderful guy. He has worked at the restaurant for forty years. He was the best.

To my husband of thirty years this year: you get better and better at brainstorming, encouraging, and cheering me on. Thank you for all you do. You really are Superman. I love you.

My kids: Josh married to Ruth, and Kayla married to Steven. What an absolute hoot it is to be your mom. I love you all so very much. Thanks for all you do to keep me going in the right direction.

Special kudos to my first grandchild, who was born as I was working on the final page proofs of this book. It took me a little bit longer than usual, but I wouldn't trade baby snuggles with my little man for anything. Your editorial coos and comments were priceless and oh so helpful to Nana.

And to my Lord and Savior Jesus Christ: I am nothing without You. Thank You.

Kimberley Woodhouse is the best-selling author of more than twenty-five fiction and non-fiction books, which have earned her many accolades and awards including the Carol Award, the Holt Medallion, the Reader's Choice Award, and others. A lover of history and research, she often gets sucked into the past and her husband has to lure her out with chocolate. Married to her best friend and very own Superman for three decades, she lives and writes full-time in the Poconos.

Sign Up for Kimberley's Newsletter

Keep up to date with Kimberley's latest news on book releases and events by signing up for her email list at kimberleywoodhouse.com.

More from Kimberley Woodhouse

When her grandfather's health begins to decline, Havyn is determined to keep her family together. But everyone has secrets—including John, the hired stranger who recently arrived on their farm. To help out, Havyn starts singing at a local roadhouse, but dangerous eyes grow jealous as she and John grow closer. Will they realize the peril before it is too late?

Forever Hidden with Tracie Peterson • THE TREASURES OF NOME #1

You May Also Like . . .

When Madysen Powell's supposedly dead father shows up, her gift for forgiveness is tested and she's left searching for answers. Daniel Beaufort arrives in Nome and finds employment at the Powell dairy, longing to start fresh after the gold rush leaves him with only empty pockets. Will deceptions from the past tear apart their hopes for a better future?

Endless Mercy by Tracie Person & Kimberley Woodhouse
THE TREASURES OF NOME #2
traciepeterson.com; kimberleywoodhouse.com

Fleeing her past, naturalist Tayler Hale accepts a position at the popular Curry Hotel in Alaska. There, she must work with Thomas Smith, who calls the hotel home. As Thomas struggles to get used to the idea of a female naturalist, unexpected guests and trouble arrive at the Curry. They'll have to band together to face the danger that follows.

Under the Midnight Sun by Tracie Person & Kimberley Woodhouse
THE HEART OF ALASKA #3
traciepeterson.com; kimberleywoodhouse.com

After scarlet fever kills her mother and siblings, Gloriana Womack is dedicated to holding together what's left of her fractured family. Luke Carson arrives in Duluth to shepherd the construction of the railroad and reunite with his brother. When tragedy strikes and Gloriana and Luke must help each other through their grief, they find their lives inextricably linked.

Destined for You by Tracie Person
LADIES OF THE LAKE
traciepeterson.com

More from Bethany House

On assignment to help America win the War of 1812, Evan MacManus is taken prisoner by Brielle Durand—the key defender of her people's secret French settlement in the Canadian Rocky Mountains. But when his mission becomes at odds with his growing appreciation of Brielle and the villagers, does he dare take a risk on the path his heart tells him is right?

A Warrior's Heart by Misty M. Beller
BRIDES OF LAURENT #1
mistymbeller.com

Left to rue her mistake of falling in love with the wrong man, Maisie Kentworth keeps busy by exploring the idle mine nearby. While managing his mining company, Boone Bragg stumbles across Maisie and the crystal cavern she's discovered. He makes her a proposal that he hopes will solve all their problems, but instead it throws them into chaos.

Proposing Mischief by Regina Jennings
THE JOPLIN CHRONICLES #2
reginajennings.com

Assigned by the Pinkertons to spy on a suspicious ranch owner, Molly Garner hires on as his housekeeper, closely followed by Wyatt Hunt, who refuses to let her risk it alone. But when danger arises, Wyatt must band together with his problematic brothers to face all the troubles of life and love that suddenly surround them.

Love on the Range by Mary Connealy
BROTHERS IN ARMS #3
maryconnealy.com

◆ BETHANYHOUSE